so good in black

Also by Sunetra Gupta

Memories of Rain

The Glassblower's Breath

Moonlight into Marzipan

A Sin of Colour

so good in black

a novel by

sunetra gupta

First published in 2011 by

Clockroot Books
An imprint of Interlink Publishing Group, Inc.
46 Crosby Street, Northampton, Massachusetts 01060
www.clockrootbooks.com
www.interlinkbooks.com

Originally published in India in 2009 by Women Unlimited, an associate of Kali for Women

Library of Congress Cataloging-in-Publication Data

Gupta, Sunetra.
So good in black / by Sunetra Gupta. -- 1st American ed.
p. cm.
ISBN 978-1-56656-853-1 (pbk.)
1. Americans--India--Fiction. 2. Bengal (India)--Fiction. 3. Indic fiction (English) I. Title.
PR9499.3.G8957S6 2011
823'.914--dc22
2011004780

Front cover image: *Clockworks* copyright © Tracy Hebden|Dreamstime.com

Printed and bound in the United States of America

To Olivia

And he can't stand Beelzebub
'cos he looks so good in black, in black

—*Neil Finn*

so good in black

Child on the seashore, I loved your mother once. How unkindly these words pound through my blood as I walk down this dry path towards you, how cruelly they beat their rhythm within me, as though already relentlessly rehearsed.

I halt at the low iron gate that separates the garden from the beach, from here I have a good view of you, a slender young thing in a crimson frock, you stand with your feet planted slightly apart, turning your head slowly from side to side, methodically surveying the various life forms deposited about you by the retreating sea. Those that you wish to save, you seem to be trapping under glass jars, into each of which—when uprighted with the sea creature squirming within—you ladle a liquid from a bucket by your side, seawater perhaps, or some other kind of nourishing brine. A dog barks, causes you to look briefly over your shoulder, I catch a glimpse of your delicate features, your large quiet eyes, my head reels, again I feel a sickening familiarity with this precise moment, as if it might somehow already be embossed upon the meager felt of my imagination, a moment such as this.

Footsteps behind me, and then his voice:

Max, is it you? he asks.

Yes, Byron, it is, I reply softly.

How did you get here?

By car, with Piers.

Piers is here?

Yes, Piers is here.

I see, he says.

The afternoon sun sends forth a faintly acrid light, the waves spread and sink like the wings of birds leaving their skeletons ridged upon the thin sand. Byron takes his pipe out of his mouth and uses it to point to the girl.

Ela's daughter, he says, but perhaps you had already guessed that.

I thought she might be, I tell him.

He lights a match, and for an instant I am mesmerized as I have been so often before by the grandeur of his most ordinary movements, for a brief second I am set free from the circumstances of this visit, and then the flame sputters and dies, and with it the vision.

I think I know why you are here, says Byron.

I was afraid you would say that, I reply.

It's not what you think it is, Max, he says.

I haven't quite had the time to form an opinion yet about any of this, I confess to him miserably.

You were never a man for having opinions, were you? says Byron Mallick.

A courting couple comes suddenly into view, clearly having ventured a long way from the highly populated central beaches to find some solitude. The woman wears a garish yellow sari of some diaphanous synthetic material that flutters seawards like a streak of unpleasant mustard against the receding tide, and her lover is as anonymous as they come.

Byron surveys them coldly. Then, turning to me, he pronounces these terrible words:

A little chalk in milk will not kill anyone, Max.

Then it's true, I reply despairingly.

Byron Mallick sighs.

What is true is that some of the inferior batches were sent from my factory to Damini's refugee camp.

As part of your pledge to supply them with milk at cost price?

These were added free, says Byron.

Oh, marvelous.

Better surely for them to drink something resembling milk than no milk at all, he retorts.

Damini did not think so.

No, I gather she did not.

And you were trying to prevent her from sharing her views with the world.

That I was, Max, but only through pleading…

pleading with her to let an old man hang on to his reputation during his last few days upon this earth... surely you, of all people, can see that I would not use any other means...

It is hard for me, indeed, to imagine that you would.

I was hoping you would say so, says Byron quietly.

An unfortunate coincidence, then...

That she should have been found a week ago flung from her bicycle down a mountainside? I'll say it is, Max.

Just rotten bad luck.

You sound like you don't believe me, he says dryly.

I believe you, Byron, I'll keep on believing you until there is no room left for belief anymore, if it should ever come to that, but I'm still shocked about the chalk in the milk.

How can I make you understand, Max? These children are already on the brink of starvation—what harm can a little bit of chalk do them? Choices are more complex, Max, when most of your customers live below the poverty line—the market adjusts according to its own ethics, ethics that those of you who have enough to eat cannot dictate—we live by a sort of ethical imperialism these days, trying to tailor our rules to meet the standards that are acceptable to a fatter economy, and nobody gains, nobody.

Bespoke ethics, is that what you are offering? I ask.

You were always very clever with words, says Byron Mallick sadly.

The child hears our voices and turns around, fixes her unperturbed gaze upon me, my head reels, this is so far from what I had been prepared for when I emerged yesterday into the heat of a June afternoon in Calcutta with a crumpled black linen suit in my carry-on bag, ready to attend a funeral, be face to face again with a woman I once loved, and then move on, perhaps finally move on.

She tips the water out of her tin pail, carefully arranges her glass jars within it and starts to comes towards us, her red dress lopsided upon her shoulders, she seems small for her six years of age, and pale, ivory pale.

This is my friend, Max—says Byron to her, waving his pipe in my general direction.

Pleased to meet you, I tell her.

She nods and sets down her cargo, and fixes her large gaze upon me.

And what might your name be? I ask her.

She casts her eyes down, seems to be reluctant to answer.

We call her Riju, short for Adrija—Byron answers for her.

It is not a name that I have ever come across before and for this I am grateful, although why I cannot say. Grateful too for her silence, as velvet as her mother's had been, once, in the palm of my hand.

But then she suddenly breaks into speech, and it is as if a spell is broken for me, for her voice is shriller than I expected it to be and full of the kind of confidence that a tightrope walker might newly have gathered of his trade.

Have you seen my mother? she asks.

I saw her yesterday, I reply.

Where? she asks.

She came to the airport to meet me.

Have you come a long way? she asks.

From London.

Have you come for the funeral?

Yes, I have.

But that is not till Wednesday… her voice trails off as she notices her grandfather shuffling down the sandy steps with a mug of tea in his hands. Ela's father, Nikhilesh, how he has aged in the fifteen years since I last set eyes upon him. She darts away from us and runs up to meet him.

Be careful, he warns her, this tea is hot.

And then he sees me—

Max Gate? he asks.

Yes, I reply lamely.

He transfers his mug of tea to his other hand in order to shake mine.

I am glad you have come—Damini would have appreciated it, he says.

What the dead would have wanted. How hard we try to honor their desires after they are gone, what strange comfort we derive from pleasing them thus, submitting to their imagined feelings as we would never have done had they still been alive.

Damini… I start to say but choke on my words.

Nikhilesh places a quiet hand upon my shoulder. I swallow hard and fix my gaze upon the receding sea, the sand tight as oilskin from its touch.

I know how much you cared for her, says Nikhilesh.

And, as he says so, the smell of her returns to me, Damini, in that hot newspaper office filled with the smoke of those foul bidis that she purchased in bundles from the paan shops that sold them to the working classes, and favored apparently over conventional cigarettes not just for ideological reasons. How strikingly handsome she was then, with her long and lustrous hair and chiseled features. I remember the dense sheen of her beautiful dark skin, entirely unpampered by oils or potions, and those lips the color of scorched earth. Only her eyes perhaps were a trifle too large, and looked from some angles as if they had been plucked off the face of a traditionally stylized idol of Kali. She was surprisingly tall for a Bengali girl, and moved with an angular purpose that immediately fascinated me when Ela took me to meet her for the first time, her cousin Damini, dearer to her than any sister she might have had, she had told me. It was not exactly something I was looking forward to, I knew that Ela had been confiding in her about us, and anticipated some kind of stern appraisal, possibly even silent censure. I need not have worried, for Damini was on her way out when we reached her office and simply glanced over me quickly with the barest hint of a smile.

I was just about to leave, she said, I need to visit the family of a factory worker who has been found murdered this morning.

I noticed the dark circles of perspiration under the armholes of her sleeveless green blouse, and how one end of her green sari was tucked firmly into her waist. Upon an arched shoulder was a cloth bookbag, and several layers of tribal bangles decorated her arms.

Murdered? said Ela. How?

Stabbed, said Damini, body flung from a train, miles from anywhere.

Who does he leave behind? asked Ela.

No children, thank God. But a wife, yes, and parents and dependent siblings, of course.

How awful! I said.

Damini looked me straight in the eye.

You can both come with me, if you like, she said.

No, said Ela, before I could contrive an answer. No, I'd rather not.

Well, I have to go now, said Damini.

When will you be back? Ela asked.

Probably around three.

I'll be there at the station, said Ela.

I can look after myself, Damini replied.

I know, said Ela.

Damini disappeared down the dark stairwell, but we lingered, Ela and I, in the taper-lit aftermath of her dramatic exit. Ela pressed the button to summon the ancient elevator that had, only minutes ago, brought us to this floor.

Will you go? I asked her.

To the station? Yes, of course.

I'll come with you, I said.

I'd be glad if you did, she said.

And so it became a habit of ours, in the months that followed, to meet Damini as she returned from her various perilous missions, of which there were many, for she had a fire in her then born out of some primordial sense of injustice which led her easily into situations where most would fear even lightly to tread. Regularly, Ela would telephone me at work late in the afternoon to say that she was worried for her cousin, and I would pick her up from wherever she might be—whether a rehearsal nearby or at the university where she had just started her graduate studies in dance—and take her in my car to where we might wait for Damini, most often Howrah Station, looming before us in its kidney-bean colored sadness, while we inched towards it in the awful traffic, our hands aching to touch. Oh, I can still taste her anxiety, so easily did it bind and dignify our desire as we paced those sour stretches of concrete platform, commuters heaving around us, and the odd coalsome gust from afar of some last remaining steam locomotive as we waited, waited, until she would appear unharmed, at last, Damini.

—

The child whispers something to Nikhilesh in Bengali, and they begin to walk back together to the house. Byron and I follow them, girl and grandfather, up the sandy steps and along the rough path towards the house, so open and white, so embraceful of all human folly, a place where he has never before held me in his thrall, a house that holds no bookdust upon which to trace our histories—a neutral place, those in the professional business of reconciliation would call it.

For although I did spend a few weeks here not long after he first purchased it from an ailing Bengali industrialist fifteen years ago, very little of that time was with Byron Mallick. He had brought us here, my wife Barbara and I, to celebrate the New Year of 1989, but I had come down the very next day with a bad case of food poisoning and so she and I had stayed behind, intending to return as soon as I was well enough to bear the car journey. And then my brother-in-law Piers had turned up unexpectedly, and somehow the three of us had lulled each other into remaining here for much longer than we had imagined we might, in this house by the sea.

Piers O'Reilly had arrived in Calcutta having suddenly tired of teaching English to high-school students in Bangkok, expecting to surprise us, spend a few weeks in our care, and then head back home to London. When told by the caretaker that we were not there, he had then made his way to Byron's home, who had explained where we were and put him on the train to Kharagpur. Afterwards, there was a seventy-five-mile bus journey, followed by a long cycle rickshaw ride to Byron's villa, some distance from the main town, where I lay recovering from my illness while Barbara busied herself with seaside things as best she could when she was not looking after me.

He had found me, still feeble, in the garden—this garden—a trashy novel on my lap, he had picked it up and laughed, is this the kind of thing you're reading these days, Max? he inquired.

How the hell did you get here? I asked.

By means mysterious, he replied.

I had not the energy to parry with him, and so had simply closed my eyes.

So Bangkok did not work out, then? I said.

You could put it that way.

And at this point his sister had arrived, swinging some fresh fish, and he had been obliged to explain less elliptically how he had got here and why.

What an amazing place, eh? he pronounced upon finishing his own tale.

It's still a bit run down inside, Barbara warned.

You know I thrive on decay, Piers replied, eagerly eyeing an old cast-iron summerhouse standing in the corner of the garden in a state of marvelous desuetude. The rest of this garden was then in a fairly miserable state, the lawn as dry and prickly as an unshaven chin, the borders overtaken by scurvy grass, just a few stone urns here and there to indicate that someone had cared for it once. Byron has since effected a great transformation, I hardly recognize it as the same place where I had once nursed a fever and terrible indigestion, all compounded by heartache, or perhaps actually a distraction from it, who can remember, and what does it matter now?

It was a time in his life when he was more adrift than ever, Piers O'Reilly, heir to his ailing father's estate, but unable as yet to have charted out a sensible course for his own self, already in his mid-thirties, but having not moved much further than where he had been left with his Ivy League degree in art history, after four years of playing out the role of an Irish aristocrat with great relish but very little sense of where it might finally take him.

He and I had been undergraduates together at Princeton—he a foreigner of seemingly noble descent, and myself just a local boy from Fair Haven, New Jersey, bound at the time for medical school to follow in the footsteps of my gentle father, be a credit to my good mother and all of that. It was Piers O'Reilly who had whispered in my ear that I should forget all this and embark upon a very different course with my life.

You should be a writer, he had told me, after reading one of my essays that I had begged him to check for errors of grammar and style, you really should be a writer, he had said.

Really? I had replied, for it had never occurred to me to pursue such a career.

I never submitted to his request to join him in the various creative writing courses he took, but the idea that I might be a writer grew and consumed me, gained fuel from my attachment to his sister Barbara, for she was convinced that my prose was of no ordinary distinction, and her confidence in me swathed me for a decade or more, even after the possibility no longer seemed real that I would make my living in this manner.

Yet now it is a prophecy fulfilled, I have become—as Piers predicted of me almost thirty years ago—a writer. Not the sort of writer of fiction as I had hoped to be, but a travel writer, a leathern skin that becomes me more than any other, I am sure. For after Barbara left me I lingered in Calcutta for about a year, and then quite suddenly I resigned my job at the US Consulate and returned, for no obvious reason, to the apartment in London which

Barbara's mother had helped us purchase just after our marriage—which, due to certain financial adjustments, had become very much my own. I had planned to sell it, but did not. I had planned to sell it and move to New York and live the life that I had always hoped to live, as a struggling artist with no ties, no responsibilities, nothing to commend himself but the enormous capacity to take risks with his life, his emotions, and his prose. None of this, I did. What I did do is decorate and settle down in my London flat, allow Piers to flatter his friends enough to send me commissions for articles and semi-fictional short stories, chomping slowly through my savings until suddenly, just like that, I did not need to anymore, because the world—almost all of it that I cared about anyway—was happy to maintain me in the capacity of a travel writer, a responsibility that I have discharged effortlessly ever since.

We walk onto the gravel drive where the car that brought us here is still standing, recovering from its long and arduous journey. I follow Byron up the stairs onto the wide terrace where Piers is sitting upon the parapet, smoking a cigar.

Welcome back to Digha, says Byron to him pleasantly.

You have done a lot to the garden, says Piers, blowing foul smoke into the afternoon air.

Do you like it? asks Byron.

Not my style, replies Piers.

I, however, feel a curious attraction to what lies beyond the desiccated lawn—a wide border overgrown with oleanders and coastal rhododendrons, densely populated with Victorian statues that Byron must have lugged down from the warehouses in Calcutta to place in their straggly embrace, it resembles a cemetery more than a garden.

What can I get you boys to drink? asks Byron.

One of your clever cocktails would be most welcome, says Piers.

I check my watch, it is just past five-thirty.

I'd love a cup of tea if that's possible, I tell Byron.

Of course, says Byron, setting off towards the kitchen to relay this request to his staff.

A cup of tea? repeats Piers to me.

Why not?

I cannot think of any beverage less suited to this occasion, he replies.

—

It was he who had brought me news of Damini's death, Piers O'Reilly, already with half a bottle of whisky inside him, banging at my door, telling me to open up for god's sake, for god's sake, please be there, Max, he had implored. I opened the door and he stumbled in and cast himself upon my sofa and told me that Damini had been killed, a stupid cycling accident apparently, just a rock perhaps upon the dark path, but with disastrous consequences.

She's dead, Max—he said—she's dead.

I closed my eyes, for a moment it seemed that my own path to the end was etched upon me with an enormous and uplifting clarity, all the punctuation marks that my life had been begging suddenly fell into place, the rest will be easy, I told myself. The rest will be easy, a voice from somewhere else affirmed.

I am flying out to Calcutta tomorrow, said Piers.

I nodded, not sure of what to say.

Will you come with me, Max? he asked.

No, I will not come with you, I replied.

But she was such a close friend of yours...

Not recently, she was not.

Surely you hoped sometime to settle your differences?

What has that to do with it—she is dead now, she will not care.

You can be awfully cynical sometimes, Max, said Piers.

After he had gone, I dug out an old address book and found the telephone number of her relatives in Calcutta, in the house in Dhakuria where she had lived with her three uncles—younger brothers of her father—sharing with them a set of rooms around a courtyard with a tube-well, and a kitchen whose walls were so close to the railway line that the pots trembled upon the earthenware lips of their stove every time a train went by. Even here, Damini's eyes had seen beauty everywhere, taught me too how to find it in the sudden violent pink of the pond lilies creeping through green slime, the hands that swept through grains of rice picking out the debris, the shapes of the fruit that lay patiently waiting in their woven baskets to be washed and peeled and shared among many, and the children—the smiles of the children when she brought them some sweets or a new book to look at with pictures of lands far away. It was a place she had taken me to often, for after Barbara left me and Byron too seemed seldom in Calcutta anymore, it was Damini and her earnest circle of friends who provided some interest in my life outside the contemplation of my fruitless love and the havoc that it had caused. To the outskirts of the city we would venture, or into the wet fields beyond, to visit the victims of an economic system in the paroxysms of transition, either to inveigle them into providing yet another account of acute injustice or to simply sit in wonder at their ability to survive in their current conditions, of daring to dream of a life ahead or of a life long left behind, or lived entirely in the recesses of their intellect and imagination. Often we would travel in my car as that would reduce the time taken to reach our destination by a good many hours, and sometimes allow her to be back in time to make her newspaper deadline, or at least to give a lift into Calcutta to some critically ill child or long-suffering geriatric to be delivered into the jaws of a government hospital. In between these journeys she would stop the taxi and buy sweets for her cousins' children and stop at their home in Dhakuria for half an hour, without ever asking me whether this suited, and I would spend the time smiling furiously at the young women who brought me strong and excessively sweet tea and mountains upon mountains of savories, quickly whipped up in their various tiny kitchens, wives of all her cousins, attempting to cohabit, without friction, an unreasonably small house.

I telephoned there and spoke to one of Damini's

cousins, a college lecturer, who remembered me well.

My daughters still talk about you, he said.

They must be in their twenties now?

Yes, indeed, and both married. One of them is in fact in an advanced stage of pregnancy, so we are trying to keep this news from her.

He began to cry on the telephone.

I have no words for how I feel, I confessed to him.

Neither have we—any of us, he replied.

After this conversation, I wandered into the kitchen, desperately in need of a drink, and found to my irritation that all I had left was a bottle of reasonably good quality champagne, not even chilled. A less infelicitous opening of a bottle of bubbly there never was, but I needed sustenance there and then, and a trip to the off-license in my current state of mind was out of the question.

I poured myself a miserable mug of the sparkling stuff, eager to hide its distinction under sorry porcelain, drained it with speed while watching the dawn break, I noticed among the vehicles parked on the other side of the street a van bearing the words "Hope and Clay"—builders they declared themselves as—hope and clay, hope and clay.

I had drunk most of the bottle when my former mother-in-law, Mary O'Reilly, telephoned.

Max? she demanded.

Yes, Mary?

Could you possibly do me a favor? Could you meet Justin at Paddington station, and look after him for a while?

Justin is the eldest of my ex-wife Barbara's three sons, who has been boarding since the age of eight at various schools in and around Oxford. His brothers, who are much younger, have yet to be subjected to this fate, and still live with Barbara and Gerard—her second husband—in Kenya, where their father runs a very successful tourist resort.

I've been trying to find Piers to ask him, but he doesn't seem to be answering his telephone, said Mary.

I thought about explaining to her why, but could not quite find the words.

His train gets in at 11:57, she said. Give him something to eat, won't you, if he's hungry—I'll pick him up from your flat at 4 o'clock or thereabouts.

"Thereabouts" is a term that in Mary O'Reilly's usage has no recognizable boundaries, but it did not displease me as such to be burdened indefinitely with the boy, indeed I could not have wished for a better solution for what to do with myself just then.

Leave him with me as long as you like, I said to her.

I was on the platform when the train pulled in, and eventually located young Justin. Where's Granny? he asked.

Detained, as usual.

He chuckled, and I felt glad to have entertained him already with such small effort.

What would you like to do? I believe we have a few hours to kill, I said to him.

There's an exhibition on Calcutta that I'd quite like to see, he said.

I had forgotten that he was fourteen years old, and therefore by the standards of his school, an adult, or at least compelled to assume the preoccupations of one.

Fine, I said, after initially being taken aback.

Mother speaks so often of the years you spent there, he said wistfully, as if he was somehow aware that although Calcutta was still available to him, that particular phase in its history was long gone.

I didn't think your mother was happy there, I said to him.

I think it was you who was unhappy, not her.

I wished I could tell him this, but I did not, I wished I could tell him this: I think we were both unhappy but I have remained essentially within the contours of that unhappiness, whereas she has left it far behind.

Instead I said: I think you are right, Justin.

We took a bus to the exhibition.

Shall we have a sandwich at Fortnum's beforehand? I asked.

Oh, yes please, he said.

To see him eat filled me with pleasure since in consuming sandwiches and cakes he still exercised a boyish passion, and that was just as well for as soon as we entered the exhibition he gathered himself into a perfect caricature of erudition, spewing facts and dates at a most amusing rate, and the recent image of him stuffing his face with cream buns is all that kept me from reacting in what might have been a cruel manner.

We stopped before a lithograph of Warren Hastings.

He looks sad, I remarked.

At least he doesn't look like a girl in this one, said Justin.

I laughed, and Justin realized he had slipped a little.

The real question is—was he or was he not an honorable man? he said.

He was acquitted eventually, I reminded him.

But financially ruined, he parried.

True, I admitted.

Mother used to tell me stories about his ghost and the Baroness Imhoff, how you can still hear them in his garden house, said the boy.

Warren Hastings's Belvedere, now the National Library, how often we would find some excuse to go there, Barbara and I, wander in the peaceful gardens while the books that we had ordered made their way up from what had once been his wine vaults. Many of our friends and acquaintances lived in splendid houses nearby, and often before a lunch invitation, we would pass a few hours at the National Library, it was one of our greatest delights in our first few years in Calcutta. Here, the famous duel was fought between Warren Hastings and his disloyal legal officer, Philip Francis, who would later play a major role in his impeachment. Warren Hastings, the first Governor-General of India, whose seven-year impeachment became for Burke a pulpit and for Sheridan a proscenium, Warren Hastings, enshrined forever in their agitated eloquence, once head scholar at Westminster, fully conversant in Bengali and Urdu by the time he took on the role of Governor-General, could he really be the perpetrator of such black deeds? Did he not believe he was merely serving the East

India Company as best as he could? Victim or villain? Who was he, Warren Hastings, accused of exercising tyranny over the lord of the holy city of Banaras, and over the ladies of the princely house of Oude, while in his spare time writing a preface to Charles Wilkins's translation of the Bhagavadgita into English, a more intriguing personality hardly exists in the history of British India, lover of Philadelphia Austen and putative sire of Jane's cousin Eliza, who was he really, a common liar or a man ahead of his time?

I flicked through the exhibition brochure to see what they had made of this man and arrived inadvertently at the list of benefactors—and who should be first among them but Byron Mallick, who else but its most wealthy denizen would be sponsoring this exhibition of Calcutta. An inexplicable chill ran through me and I suddenly took Justin's hand in mine.

Are you okay? he asked.

Why do you ask?

You look a bit ill, he said.

I am still trying to recover from some very bad news, actually.

Oh, no. What?

An old friend has just been killed, I told him.

Oh, that's horrible, said the boy.

I think we had better go on back to my flat, I said to Justin.

But we haven't seen much of the exhibition, he protested.

I don't want to be late for your grandmother.

There's very little danger of ever being late for her! he exclaimed.

And, of course, he was right, for Mary O'Reilly did not show up until well after six o'clock, by which time Justin had eaten everything that was still edible in my refrigerator and store cupboard, and I had already consumed a bottle of red wine.

Why did you not tell me? she demanded of me accusingly when I opened the door for her.

About Damini?

I've never quite learned how to pronounce her name, said Mary O'Reilly.

Won't be necessary anymore, I said.

Your ugly cynicism simply makes me all the more determined to say it correctly—to honor her memory, Mary replied.

Did you actually ever meet her?

No, but we had a lot of contact by e-mail. I organized a number of charity events to raise money for her shelter—and it was my idea really to get the unfortunate women to produce merchandise that we could sell in this country.

Well, I knew her very well, I told Mary O'Reilly.

Are you going to the funeral? she asked me.

That I don't see the point of, I replied.

Piers has managed to get a flight out this evening, she said smugly.

For a week I did nothing but sit at home in a daze, canceling all my appointments, keeping myself alive on gin and lumpfish roe, and endlessly rereading Paul Auster's *The Invention of Solitude.* From time to time I would sit down in front of my computer with the intention of writing something about Damini, I knew that I owed it to her to bring her extraordinary life into some kind of brief focus now that she was gone.

Damini, how to cherish her? She who was formed so quickly in my mind upon a single encounter, and never untrue to such an original impression ever in our long companionship, and yet, bitter, so bitter that I had woven without her permission our many journeys together into the wilds of West Bengal into a book, a simple book, dedicated naturally to her, my entire advance for which I eventually donated to the shelter for battered Tibetan women that she was engaged in setting up at the time, just a book with perhaps some good consequences—for all.

I had no idea how deeply it would offend her, how she would make a great public outcry about how I had so easily pillaged those extraordinary encounters and precious truthfilled moments, exploited the dispossessed, the subjects of her own tireless investigations and incisional reporting, those for whom she had never been able to do much herself than lift their conditions into newsprint for impermanent scrutiny. That was five years ago, and the main price I paid for it was the loss of our friendship, for the censure that it received only augmented my book sales, set me up well enough anyway to live the life I live, and write some others.

Damini, how to speak of her in terms that would finally reconcile us, one dead and the other alive, a distinction so fine these days to me that I might as well be ringbound within a Gothic novel, why seek anyway to do her justice, what justice did she ever do me?

Obituaries appeared in the Calcutta newspapers, got forwarded to me by Piers, who was firmly there now, occupying his usual room in the beautifully decayed mansion where Ela lived with her husband and their six-year-old daughter, under what was still effectively her mother-in-law's roof. Obituaries, long and full, but contradicting one another in their basic facts—was it 1962 that she was born, or could it have been as early as 1959? Most of her childhood was spent in the south of India, but was it Kerala or Tamil Nadu? At the age of fourteen, she returned to Bengal with her parents and spent a couple of years in Durgapur where she attended the Carmel Convent School, or—according to another source—the Loreto College in Asansol. Her higher secondary and further education were conducted at Lady Brabourne College in Calcutta, regarding that all the newspapers were in agreement. And most conceded also that after graduating with honors in political science, she had become one of Calcutta's most promising investigative journalists, but had nobly given up this exciting career about five years ago to move to Darjeeling and set up a shelter for Tibetan women refugees.

Who cares, though, but for the skeleton of the truth, I thought, fingering the painted wooden egg that she had given me as a farewell present when I left Calcutta in 1991, an object that I had never removed from its place of honor on my desk, the last few years' events notwithstanding. Who cares but for some equivalent plotline, and somebody somewhere still to remember the finer details for a while.

Why are you leaving? she had asked me, standing there against my packed boxes, feet planted characteristically apart.

Why do you think? I responded, hoping that she might mention Ela, open up the opportunity for a final confessional, that gut-wrenchingly satisfying closure I so desperately sought.

But she only lit a cigarette—a conventional filter-tip for a change, inhaled and sighed—do you know what you want to do next? she asked.

And why would I want to know that? I found myself saying.

Come on, Max, we're not actors in a play anymore—she replied.

By which she was referring to a piece of street theater into which she had inducted me over the winter to play the role of the ghost of Lord Cornwallis, a few weeks of intense enjoyment that had brought me dangerously close to not submitting my resignation to the Consulate, but in the end had not quite been enough.

No, this is for real, I said to Damini.

I wonder if I will ever see you again, she said.

I'm sure our paths will cross.

Probably so, but meanwhile here's this for good luck—she said, handing me her farewell gift, a painted wooden egg, utterly unwrapped.

I had never seen anything quite like it, so much detail scrolled upon a dark and forgiving black, gold-veined leaves amid a sea of hieroglyphs, and amid them—dominantly—two crucifixes, narrow and grim but connected at the base by a generous shape resembling nothing so much as a leopard-skin brassiere.

I was prepared to believe that it was of some significance, or at least of unusual provenance, but she just shrugged her shoulders and said she had picked it up at the Cottage Industries store where she usually shopped for gifts for foreigners.

You'll write to me, won't you, I said as she was leaving.

That depends, she replied.

On what?

On whether you write to me.

Oh, I'll do that, I promised.

And, indeed, we did maintain a correspondence for a while—on my part, mainly postcards scribbled hastily from the many destinations to which my work took me, but from her always a fat envelope stuffed with newspaper cuttings of her recent articles, and a page of long flowing handwriting never containing in sufficient detail what I really wanted—which was news of Ela. I filed away her cuttings, though, and it was when I chanced upon them again while cleaning out my cabinets some years ago that I thought of making a book out of my experiences with Damini, a book that I felt would celebrate her, and our friendship. By then we were no longer regularly in touch, but when I was briefly in Delhi to promote the book in 1999, Damini did come all the way from Darjeeling to see me. I was a little shocked by her appearance, her hair was streaked with an abundance of gray, and her face and limbs showed signs of real emaciation rather than a sparse elegance of flesh.

She had given up journalism, she told me, she had given up journalism in favor of a more silent engagement with the purpose of delivering the world of oppression, of easing the unnecessary pain that she had become so acutely acquainted with in her years as a reporter. She had procured funds to set up a shelter in Darjeeling for battered Tibetan women and their children, why this cause rather than any other I did not think to ask. Byron Mallick, she told me, had been very helpful to her, had given generously towards the initial costs, and helped put in place a number of schemes that might lead to self-sufficiency, such as the manufacture of fruit preserves and handmade stationery, which he had arranged to market in European boutiques. He had also consented to supply, at cost price, the formula milk that his original pharmaceutical company in Bengal still manufactured, while agreeing with her that breastfeeding was to be encouraged as the best means of nourishing an infant.

He has been extremely supportive, she said.

This surprised me greatly, as Byron had never betrayed much affection for Damini. Indeed, he had complained several times to me about how his relationship with Ela, once of pure delight, had been irrevocably altered by her association with Damini.

So Byron has been helpful to you? I said to Damini.

Very helpful, she confessed.

I wonder why, I said.

Soothing a bad conscience perhaps, she suggested.

Quite probably, I said.

So you are not as enamored of him as before, then?

Our friendship has decayed a little, I admitted.

That does not surprise me, she said.

I offered her a cigarette but she refused it, she had given up smoking, had decided of late that it was a filthy expensive habit that she could do without. I smiled and lit one myself.

How is Ela? I finally dared to ask.

Trying to resurrect her career, she said. But equally, as engrossed in the decoration of her home and garden, she added rather disdainfully.

Nothing wrong with that, I said.

She has her little girl to look after, of course, added Damini, her tone changing to one of intense affection.

I took a sip of coffee, and stubbed my cigarette out in the saucer. I had wondered at times—although not as often as I might have expected myself to—what Ela had made of my sudden success as a writer. Did she abhor the ease with which I used the wretchedness of the lives that I had encountered to craft a new aesthetic? Or did she appreciate the honesty of my art, as others did, so many others—indeed the word "honest" was used so often in the reviews of my books that I had begun to wonder whether it was not the tone of honesty that I had perfected, rather than honesty itself.

I remember, said Damini, how hopelessly you were in love with her.

That was a long time ago, I said.

Why did you not pursue it? asked Damini.

She was already married, I reminded her.

You were always a coward, said Damini pleasantly.

And you have always been unnecessarily cruel to me, I replied.

She called for the waiter to bring us the bill. I fished my new book out of my bag—this is for you, I said.

She took it from my hands and smiled.

I don't know when I will have the time to read it, she said.

It is dedicated to you, I told her.

To me? she asked.

Yes, to you, I replied.

Then I shall have to read it, she had said with a laugh.

Damini, how to write of her, when I knew so little of the many textures of her life save from the intensity with which Ela had described their cousinly love, their time together as young girls in the leafy colony attached to a steel plant, a hundred miles or so to the northwest of Calcutta, where its executive staff resided. Damini's father, Shankar Kanjilal, had recently been appointed to a high-level management position there, having distinguished himself in his previous job in some remote corner of South India, transforming the economic prospects of an entire area, creating jobs, wealth, and opportunities for all, as his daughter would later mockingly say. A fine trajectory for a young man who had found himself penniless and in charge of four younger siblings and distraught mother in 1947 when the Partition of Bengal forced them to relinquish their modest home and flee to Calcutta. Distant relatives had grudgingly taken them in, but become fond of him principally for the academic promise he showed, and his fine singing voice, his wonderful sense of humor. He gained entry with ease in a few years time to Presidency College, where he became good friends with Byron Mallick and Nikhilesh Mukherjee, hostel dwellers, not inconvenienced like him by poverty but by distance from their families. They would pay for their coffee house snacks, theater tickets, and day trips to the seashore—while he was able to bring them to the small house in Dhakuria, where they were welcomed by his relatives, his clever and sophisticated companions, entreated to partake of their simple meals, made to feel at home. When Nikhilesh developed an interest in his sister Ruby, then only in her first year in college, it was seen as a good sign, and when he married her a few years later, it was a joyous occasion for all—all except Byron Mallick, who could never understand why his closest friend should seek to situate himself within a family of such limited refinement.

Shankar Kanjilal himself married the daughter of a wealthy businessman to whom he had been appointed as tutor, and removed himself rapidly from all potential frictions by accepting a job in a far away corner of south India, where they lived in happiness with their one daughter, Damini—born soon after their marriage—until he was wooed back to Bengal by the offer of a very plummy job in the steel belt. And with that move, Damini came to enter the life of her cousin Ela, who was by then in boarding school in Calcutta, her parents being in Africa, where

Nikhilesh for many years taught at a Ghanaian university, and he and Ruby enjoyed an existence not too dissimilar—I imagine—from what sustained her elder brother and his wife in their pleasant habitation near the hydroelectric plant in Tamil Nadu.

When time came for Damini to go to college in Calcutta, she elected worthily to stay with her relatives in Dhakuria, the very same house that her father and his three brothers and her aunt Ruby had arrived at in 1947 with their meager possessions and terminally ill mother, where they had been given temporary refuge but had then become gradually indispensable for the income they brought in and the care they offered and the very decent marriages they made. Those who had taken them in then were gone by now, having been tended in old age with loving care by Damini's uncles, and now the house was theirs for the same peppercorn rent still, but theirs alone, and they had brought in wives, produced infants, and now all had good jobs and incomes augmented always by Shankar Kanjilal's earnings, for he had never ceased to section part of his salary for them. With Damini choosing to stay there, rather than at her maternal grandparents' comfortable home on Rashbehari Avenue, Shankar Kanjilal greatly increased the amount that monthly flowed into the Dhakuria household—and to this Damini brought her own earnings when she joined the newspaper office after graduating from Lady Brabourne College, and swiftly rose there in ranks. At the time that I met her, she had secured for herself both a unique reputation as the most fearless of investigative journalists and a wonderfully reckless lifestyle to go along with it. Her parents were, as far as I knew, still in Durgapur—her father now close to retirement—but she had stayed on in Calcutta in her uncles' home, and then, about five years ago, moved to Darjeeling with her sickly lover, Dhritiman, to set up a shelter for battered Tibetan women—that was her life, as I knew it, Damini, but how to actually write of her—a challenge that my gin bottle and I were clearly not equal to, I feared.

I was struggling, late one night, with this task that I had set myself, my only way of mourning Damini I reckoned, when the telephone rang. I let the instrument chime its dreadful tune until the answering machine kicked in.

Max, it's me—I heard her say.

Ela? I asked, picking up the receiver with a trembling hand.

Max, will you to come to the funeral? she said.

For a few moments, I was simply silent. It had been seven years since I had last heard her voice. I let her words wash over me like absolution arrived far too late for a sinner.

Will you come, Max? she repeated.

Do you want me to? I asked, as gently and steadily as I could.

I think Damini would have wanted you to be there, she replied.

I'm not so sure of that, I said.

Well, I am sure of it, Max.

I will come, Ela, if you wish it.

I do wish it, I wish it very much.

I replaced the receiver, dizzy already at the thought of seeing her again, and yet some part of me plunged into a palpable guilt that I was using Damini once again to get something I wanted, something I had desired these last seven years, that might not have happened otherwise.

Less than an hour later the telephone rang again. This time it was Byron.

I am very glad to hear you are coming after all, Max, he said to me.

A hint in his voice that it was he who had suggested to Ela that she make the request, knowing it would then be impossible for me to deny.

I haven't decided yet that I will, I said.

No?

I was going to call my travel agent in the morning.

Look, Max, I can arrange a ticket for you, if you'll let me.

That's very kind, Byron, but I think I can handle this myself.

And you are welcome to stay at my flat, although I probably will not come up to Calcutta until the day of the funeral, he said.

He explained that he was calling from Digha, from his house by the sea where he had convinced Nikhilesh to withdraw with his granddaughter, so that she might be shielded from the many attitudes of grief that were likely to surround her in Calcutta, the raw and redflecked sympathy of strangers, the many awkward murmurings that were liable to destroy whatever precarious equilibrium her child-mind might have sought and achieved, for she had been very close to Damini, had just returned from spending a week with her in Darjeeling when the dreadful news had come that she was missing, and soon after the very much worse news that she had been found, dead.

We Bengalis are not particularly skilled in dealing with tragedy, he said to me.

I'm sure you are right to keep the child—and yourselves—as far away as possible from it all, I said to him, my voice grinding mechanically against my skull.

Yes, it is calmer here, and not as fearfully hot as in Calcutta, said Byron.

I can imagine.

I'd recommend that you come straight down here if the roads weren't so difficult, but you'll be cool enough in my flat.

I'd probably prefer to stay at a hotel, I told him.

Wherever you are more comfortable.

It would be odd to be in your flat without you there, I offered by way of apology.

No need to explain, I'm just glad you're coming, said Byron.

I don't know that *I* am glad to be coming, I said.

Look, Max, it is important that you make peace with her, he replied.

She is dead, Byron, all opportunities for peace to be made are gone.

You're wrong, Max, peace is one of the few things we can achieve with the dead, peace and very little beyond that, he said.

Whatever you say, Byron, I replied.

—

Seven years had passed since I had last seen her, and the thought that I would be setting eyes on her again filled me with no ordinary anticipation as I sat, obscenely eating oysters at Heathrow Airport and filling myself with very reasonable Muscadet, for my flight had been delayed for a good hour and a half.

Six of the little beasts I was brought by a genial Brazilian waiter who complimented me on my choice of accompanying beverage, and all were fine except one, all fine Irish rock oysters, stately plump but one, this one pale and brown-frilled as a Lippi madonna, and I gazed upon it but could not bring myself to raise it to my lips. I concealed it in my napkin and disposed of it afterwards in a trash can.

Here I was on my way to a funeral, the greater part of my mind given to the fear that she, whom I loved as no other, might shrink back from me, a man now almost in his fiftieth year, my face bearing every trace of years of hard drinking and too much travel, the blue of my eyes threatened already by the incursions of a subtle and yet utterly permanent gray. Or would none of this matter to her, she who had once—somewhat irresponsibly—claimed that my name would forever be engraved upon her heart? That she may not have altered much in appearance I knew from a leaflet that someone—I suspect Byron—had put in the mail to me last year, advertising a series of dance recitals she was to give in Paris. So tantalizingly close: Paris. And although I had allowed myself at the time to briefly surrender to the image of her waiting for me in that city somewhere with a glass of wine or a coffee at her elbow, although I could not help entertaining for a moment the notion that she might wish me to be there in the audience, I had not in the end tried to see her on a stage in Paris, or track her down within its unquiet streets.

I was not sure, however, whether she would still be waiting, Ela, when my plane landed the following day in Calcutta for we were several hours late, besides which she knew it would not be difficult for me to make my own way to the Grand Hotel, where I was booked to stay for the next few days. I knew not what to expect as I rescued my bag from the overhead locker and waited patiently in line to be disgorged once again into the pungent heat-twisted winds of the city where my devastating obsession with her had once, long ago, found its perfect camouflage.

I only had hand luggage, and so was among the first of the passengers to emerge, and there she was, waiting, her arms crossed upon the sweaty rail, there were the same eyes, as yet unlined, simply more mature in their tilt, the gentle curves of her cheeks and lips endowed now with a more angular grace. I looked upon her helplessly, no words of greeting suggesting themselves to me as suitable for this occasion.

I was worried that you wouldn't come after all, she said.

Her long fingers, refined by the repeated mystery of gesture, twisted into each other as she spoke.

Well, I have, I said.

How swiftly and easily did the dams break again, and what came flooding in was deeper and wider than ever, promising not to be contained while desire might still feed upon memory, and perhaps even afterwards. Looking at her, and wanting so desperately to draw her near, I was suddenly grateful that my life has passed without any denial of it having been completely hollowed out by her. I beheld her, there in the dusty light, the crowds swilling around us, I met her eyes and realized that so much of me was made up of her absence that to apologize for it, even to myself, would be madness.

We walked across the hot tarmac towards her car, and slid gratefully into its chill interior.

Will you drop him off at the Grand Hotel and then come back here? she said in Bengali to the driver.

Are you not coming with me? I asked, half pleased at being able to decipher her command, yet in despair of what it meant.

I have to wait for Damini's aunt, she's old, she's flying in from Bombay.

When will I see you again?

I'll try and come this evening, but it may be late.

Will you please be sure to come? I pleaded.

How can I promise anything at a time like this, Max? she answered.

I'm sorry, I said, I'm just overwhelmed by seeing you again.

At this she shut her eyes as if unwilling to allow herself to travel down the same ungraveled track, and then simply said, I'll try and come tonight.

She climbed out of the car and shut the door with an apologetic smile.

Grand Hotel, sir? asked the driver in English, perhaps slightly confused by our interchange.

Yes, the Grand Hotel, I reaffirmed.

The Grand Hotel, I wondered how it might have changed in the fifteen years since I had left Calcutta. Countless receptions we had attended there, my wife Barbara and I, when I had worked at the US Consulate, but I had never before been a guest at the hotel.

Before we set off the driver got out and extracted from the trunk a large white coolbox which he placed on the seat beside me—refreshments, he explained. I prized open the lid, it was packed with soft drinks and mineral water and bottles of beer.

Thank you, I said to him.

You are welcome, sir, he replied.

The car traveled slowly through ruined and unfamiliar stretches of the city. I opened a bottle of beer, drank it with my eyes shut like an infant seeking sleep, I could feel the streets leak past me while I sat sunken in the seat leather, insulated from the terrible heat without. Sometimes I would open my eyes a little and let the colors in, the smells were blocked by the sealed windows, as was the noise, the incessant noise.

Eventually, we arrived at the Grand, the car halted under the portico, white-gloved fingers opened the door, I shook myself out of my torpor and stepped out, was immediately obliged to surrender my one small case to a porter who followed me with it to the reception desk. I was only halfway through the paperwork when I received a tap on my shoulder, it was Piers.

So you came in the end, Max, he said to me.

Yes, I came, I replied.

—

Adrija reappears, at her heels a strange-looking puppy, it runs towards Byron, who is returning from the kitchen, jumps up at him and looks adoringly up into his eyes.

Come here, Kimbhut, the girl says sternly.

Why don't you take him for a walk? suggests Byron.

Will you come with us? she asks.

I can't just now, but Vargas will if you like, says Byron, gesturing to his manservant, who is walking towards us with a tray of tea and biscuits and something that looks like a plain gin and tonic for Piers.

What kind of dog is that? asks Piers, once servant and child have left.

Byron explains it is a cross between a caravan hound and an Irish setter—part of an unexpected litter that a dog-breeder friend of his was seeking to give away. I remember that Byron had been a member of the Kennel Club of Calcutta and had often dragged Barbara off to its various shows, for she had a great affection for canines.

A good idea, a dog, under the circumstances, I tell him.

Always a good idea—a dog, he replies.

He throws a fig roll to a seabird that has suddenly swooped down onto the dry grass.

I presume you chaps are planning to stay the night, he says.

That may not be necessary, says Piers.

Byron nods.

But you'll have dinner with us, won't you? he asks brightly.

When is Ela arriving? asks Piers.

Not until after dinner, I shouldn't think, says Byron.

Well, then, we'll stay to dinner, says Piers.

I watch him against the softening sky, Piers O'Reilly, taking a great gulp of gin and tonic and wiping his lips. He holds the glass against each eye in turn to cool them, and then sets it down and lights another cigar. How untroubled he seems, how determined, whereas I am all despair and confusion, protected by nothing other than the dignity of my own disbelief.

He had come knocking on my hotel door earlier this afternoon, Piers O'Reilly, his mouth set in an uncharacteristic solid line, his eyes fixed as if upon some distant point in neither of our horizons. Get up, Max, he had said, we are going to Digha.

I looked at my watch, it was just past twelve-thirty, I had had about two hours sleep since I landed in Calcutta the previous day.

No, Piers, I am not going to Digha, I said wearily.

I need you to come with me, Max, he said, throwing a shirt from my open suitcase in my direction.

Whatever for? I asked, pulling a pillow over my face.

For reasons that you will never believe, said Piers.

I sat up and rubbed my eyes, then padded into the bathroom to splash water on my face, came back and put on the shirt that Piers had cast in my direction, pulled on my jeans—the whole thing was oddly reminiscent of our undergraduate days, when Piers would regularly interrupt my slumber with some urgent scheme that he wished me to participate in—like driving for hours to rescue a friend who had been left without clothes in a cornfield in Ohio by some pranksters, or simply to head to New York in the middle of the night because he so felt like it.

So we are going to Digha, I said, why?

I'll explain to you in the car, said Piers.

What car?

Arjun's driver will take us there, he replied.

This is getting more and more mysterious.

This is much worse than mysterious, said Piers O'Reilly.

Come up to the library, says Byron, there's something I'd like both you boys to see.

I set my empty teacup down and follow him up the open stairs to the second story. We start to walk down the length of the balcony towards the library—a long room at its end extending over the terrace, affording it the best views to the sea and also creating a covered area below, perfect for dining in the evenings, fitted as it is with its own rustling chandelier, and small ceiling fans to supplement the sea breeze. Piers comes up behind, tinkling the ice in his glass, a sound so light and yet so portentous as to make me want to break down and cry, but the reins must be held tight for the moment, I know, I know, and I do as the circumstances bid, for once, that is what I do.

We enter, and my eyes fall immediately upon an elaborate

contraption on the desk at the other end of the room, consisting of a telescope and other odd bits.

What is all this in aid of? asks Piers.

The transit of Venus, Byron answers.

Which you intend to observe?

I made a promise many years ago to someone that I would, someone who is no longer alive.

And it is not like you to break your promises, is it now?

I like to try and keep my promises, says Byron.

Especially to the deceased, says Piers O'Reilly.

I walk over to the desk in its brightly lit bay, and inspect the complex arrangement of lenses and filters, they seem to gaze back at me with some degree of embarrassment, as if recruited against their will for the purpose of recording the celestial event.

It has been exactly a hundred and twenty-two years since it last happened, says Byron.

And so? says Piers.

Captain Cook traveled halfway around the world for it, says Byron, pressing his case.

Why?

Their plan was to calculate the distance of the earth from the sun.

Celestial triangulation?

It is interesting, is it not, says Byron, how the distance between two things becomes obvious when something is placed between.

Provided you have more than one point of view, says Piers O'Reilly.

I hear the child's voice, the puppy cavorting, and the sound of plants being watered. They have clearly returned from their walk. I look out through the window and see Vargas, hose in hand, attending to a dry rosebed—an unusual task for him—the dog periodically jumping up at him and being admonished every time by both him and the girl. And there, beyond all of this, the sea, the sea, in deep retreat.

Here, at this very desk, I had sat once and made a final attempt to write a novel and failed, fifteen years ago, the views to infinity mocking me as I sat slave to a tyrannical first sentence, enduring the many possibilities of my narrative and never gathering the conviction to be faithful to any one of them. Here I had sat, pen in hand, playing with a single sentence until it had become as bitter as overstewed tea upon my tongue. While Barbara and Piers took long walks, and read and listened to music and amused each other otherwise, I had shut myself up in this room, with something that felt like a novel inside me, but really was only masquerading as one.

Why I had chosen to try and write again I do not know, except in some feeble effort to avert the impending crisis in our marriage that would cause Barbara to leave me in less than a month, why did I think that to commit some of my distress to paper might lead me to a route out of it, why indeed? For the first five years of our marriage, I had struggled with the notion of being a writer and she had graciously put up with it, perhaps because Piers was so convinced that I had it in me to be one and there was nobody she trusted more than her brother then. Their mother, Mary O'Reilly, had helped us buy a one-bedroom flat in Notting Hill Gate, never imagining what an astonishingly good investment it would be for all of us. We worked as freelance journalists, surviving on the O'Reilly's connections, and I tried to produce the novel that everyone by now, even my family in distant Fair Haven, New Jersey, was certain would shoot me to fame. But writing a novel, or even a few short stories, as Piers in desperation finally suggested, seemed firmly to elude me, no matter how much I dedicated myself to the process. Finally, I decided that I had not seen enough of the world or known enough of life to be able to do this, and found myself applying to the US diplomatic service. Barbara, like any excellent wife, was very enthusiastic, saw it as a wonderful way for us to be truly together, a foreign environment serving both to insulate us and possibly throw some surreal grist into the mill of our marriage. My first posting was to Monrovia, Liberia, a few peculiar months when we often seriously wondered whether we had made a terrible mistake, but the scent of political unrest had Mary O'Reilly soon pulling strings to get us out of there, so not long after we found ourselves in Nairobi and the four years we spent there were the best in my life, unmarred as they were by either pain or ecstasy. And then Calcutta, and all that we had put together over these years being suddenly pulled apart by my disastrous inability to shake off such a thing as a simple obsession.

Byron picks up an orange from a fruit bowl on a nearby table and proceeds to elegantly peel it and then divide it into its constituent parts.

Scurvy, he says suddenly, was another of Cook's concerns—he put his hundred men on a diet of malt and pickled cabbage and made them bathe and shake out their bedding daily in the hope of avoiding it.

Scurvy, yes, from the simple lack of vitamins, the dreadful disease that bruised the sailors' skin to black ink, caused their gums to rot and drop their teeth, and eventually led to a hideous state of hypersensitivity, so that such a thing as the smell of fresh rain on the decks might cause a victim to weep in agony, while a man in his last stages of scurvy could be killed, like a rabbit, just by the sound of a gunshot.

They staved off scurvy all right, says Byron, but then died, half of them, on their way back from Tahiti by picking up malaria—a disease which has no respect, as you know, for either diet or hygiene.

We have not come down for a history lesson, says Piers.

I am well aware of that, says Byron Mallick.

I think I'll go and play with Adrija for a bit, says Piers.

Have a fruit first, says Byron, it's good for you.

I sit down on a nearby armchair, I am tired beyond any definition of fatigue that I have known before, I have hardly slept in the last forty-eight hours. Here, in this chair, fifteen years ago, I had courted inspiration, fickle maid that she was to me, no not even that, just smilingly absent while I sat and waited and the sea foamed dully outside, and my wife and her brother played endless games of Scrabble and cards, and Byron's trusted servants made sure that our every need was met.

You are falling asleep, Max, says Byron.

I open my eyes. I am sorry, I tell him.

Nothing to apologize for, he says.

I try and stand up but am overtaken by spell of dizziness, and sit back down suddenly.

Are you all right, Max? Byron asks.

I feel as if I am rising and falling, as though a great heart were beating underneath me.

Just slightly carsick still, I reply.

It's a long journey to Digha, says Byron.

I sink my head into my hands.

Have a rest, Max, says Byron, it may fall better into place for you when you are less tired.

So it might, I concede.

He explains that the car that we have just heard drive in belongs to one of his neighbors—an elderly gentleman by the name of Chaudhuri—perhaps I remember him from fifteen years ago when he was already resident in Digha?

Vaguely, yes, I say to him, for want of a better reply.

Come down when you are feeling better, he says.

I lean back in my chair, and when I close my eyes, they are not the branches of my perplexity that stand out against the starkness of my inner solitude, but images of him, Byron Mallick, on that winter evening in Calcutta when we first met. I can still trace in my mind the shadows that were cast upon his noble face by the hurricane lamp, we were in the middle of a power cut and for some reason the generators at the Alliance Française were not working that day, a few battery-powered lights had been scattered inside the building and many lamps were lit outside, the traffic roared away in the darkness outside, it was like being on a ship tossed upon a dark but friendly ocean. I watched Byron as he lit his pipe, the smell of sweet tobacco filled the air, I began to cough, he patted me on my back, and from nowhere great holes suddenly began to appear in the solid conviction that I had thus far successfully charted for myself the best course for my life.

Nothing like the excitement of a new friendship, said Barbara a little sardonically, a few days later, as I rearranged the furniture and the objects in the living room in preparation for his first visit, fussed over what wines we had to offer, and jotted down questions in my notepad that I would like to ask him. He appeared to have an extraordinary knowledge of the history of Calcutta, he had all but finished a doctoral thesis on Orientalism and Warren Hastings when he suddenly determined that his future lay in business rather than academia, and persuaded his father to send him to London to study accountancy. This had clearly not been an unwise decision, for he was now an extremely wealthy man and lived in tasteful splendor in a marvelous mansion block flat in a very fashionable part of Calcutta, and commanded huge respect in several circles as a patron of the arts and a benefactor to society, as well as a man of enormous individuality and depth.

I cannot believe you have not yet met Byron Mallick—he is quite an extraordinary person, the French

Vice-Consul had said to me, steering me through the crowd towards him.

And then he had left me there, face to face with an alarmingly handsome man almost half a head taller than myself, whom I guessed to be in his mid-fifties, probably on account of the pipe that he held with such elegant ease in the bowl of his right hand, but in fact was slightly younger, it turned out.

Max Gate? he repeated when I told him my name.

Thomas Maximilian Gate, I said, as if prompted to offer it in full.

Byron is only a nickname, he told me in return.

I thought it might be, I said.

I was struck immediately by something in his manner, a sort of effortless charm, he stood out so completely from the crowd of desperately refined people that I had to endure daily. I found myself in his wonderful flat the very next day, crowded with books and works of art and objects of great curiosity from many parts of the world, I had meant only to have a quick drink but ended up phoning Barbara and asking permission to stay to dinner. This she very happily granted, perhaps our relationship was already starting to fissure, but I would never have suspected at that moment that what I was setting in train was a series of events that would lead in less than two years to the end of our marriage. I left Byron's flat that evening with an extraordinary sense of thrill, even risked—without checking first with Barbara—inviting him to dinner in a couple of days. I felt that I was embarking on a grand and fantastic voyage, that a great wind had risen that would finally take me out of the doldrums of my early thirties. Was there no trace of doubt within me that Barbara would be coming along? or at least steering a similar course on a friendly vessel, was there no hint at all that she might not?

We had arrived in Calcutta just six months earlier, in the autumn of 1986, expecting that life would here would contain much the same proportions of excitement and banality as we had found convenient in my two previous postings. We had been so happy in Kenya, life had seemed so perfectly arranged, it never really gnawed at me that I was not writing, indeed I wondered whether I would ever really try and steer that narrow course again. Calcutta was never quite as cozy, it had a different richness to it, a faded damask quality that both of us relished. Surely, Byron Mallick could only add to our experiences of this marvelous and ruined city? Such were my thoughts when I opened the door to him that February evening in 1987. He entered, smiling, wonderfully handsome in his discreetly embroidered kurta and dark linen trousers. He had brought for me a book to borrow: *Calcutta, Past and Present*, by K. Blechynden, and for Barbara a bouquet of tuberoses which he gave her as soon as she appeared, wiping her hands on her apron.

You have a curious name, she said upon being introduced.

It is not my real name, he replied.

No more was said of this until we sat down to our meal when, as she placed a plate of tomato jelly in fennel salad in front of him, she suddenly asked with uncharacteristic directness—well Byron, are you going to tell us what your real name is?

For a moment Byron looked as if he might ask her, like Rumpelstiltskin, to guess. Then, digging his spoon into the wobbly red substance, he said—Bankim, my real name is Bankim.

Why Byron then? Barbara persisted.

It's a long story, and not a happy one, sighed Byron Mallick.

It was his father, he told us, who had given him the nickname "Lord Byron," but this was in direct and painful mockery of his mother's efforts to force him at a very young age to make poetry the greater part of his life, encouraging him to memorize long pieces of verse and compose his own.

I would often overhear my father warning her that it was unhealthy for me to spend so much time among books at my age, hear her sobbing quietly later in the sitting room as she sat alone and sewed, said Byron.

You see, he continued, she had had very different expectations of life, she came from a wealthy and progressive household in Calcutta, had shown much talent for creative writing and music as a young girl, but suddenly—and quite inexplicably—been exiled by her marriage to a small village before she could finish her degree in English literature.

We learned that it was in the astringent wake of this great disappointment that Byron had spent his childhood, drinking daily with her of the bitterness she felt at having been suddenly told she was to be married within a month to a civil servant currently posted to a far corner of North Bengal. She was his only real companion, his mother, for he had been forbidden to play with the village children and did not go to school until after his seventh birthday, the village *pathshala* having been deemed entirely unsuitable, and his mother firmly against his making the hour's journey by bullock cart every morning to the nearest town until he was older. She was perfectly capable of teaching him at home until then, she had argued, and for once her husband had allowed her to have her way, perhaps he too was worried about subjecting his pale son to such a cruel routine at such an early age.

Yet, when the time came for me to go to school, said Byron, to rise at dawn and scrub myself clean, put on my overstarched uniform, my socks and shoes, check that all my books were in my khaki satchel, allow my mother to run a comb through my hair and stand by the door with her waiting for the bullock cart to take me into town, when the time came for this, we were both ready—my mother and I. The excitement that it brought into my life seemed to give her a certain sense of purpose, she hummed with a new energy as she made the arrangements for this new venture, woke up at some unearthly hour to personally prepare my tiffin, pack it into the shiny metal carrier, shine my shoes and press and re-press my shirt collar and cuffs, and the handkerchief that she pinned onto my pocket—I was glad for her to be able to live through me in this way, it was from my mother that I learned the true role of ornament and detail in the establishment of human dignity, said Byron Mallick.

It sounds as though you were very close to her, said Barbara.

We were, said Byron, until I abandoned my university career for commerce, she never forgave me for that.

Never? asked Barbara, almost challengingly.

Never, Byron confirmed, but my father was on my side for he maintained that trade was in our blood—my ancestors, you see, had once been cashiers to Lord Clive and Warren Hastings.

Cashiers? she asked.

Native commissioners, he explained. "Responsible for the disbursement of restitution money, collection of godown rent, and the supply and transit of the Company's goods," he quoted dreamily, wiping his lips with our wedding linen.

How interesting! said Barbara.

It is possible that it was one of my forefathers who advised Job Charnock to move his factory to the left bank of the river, he said.

And if he had not? asked Barbara.

Calcutta would never have existed, said Byron Mallick.

—

How rapidly he had once drawn me into a world that I had never believed I would wish to know, enticing me to spend most of my evenings at his curious flat in Calcutta, under the slow arc of the polished fans that hung from the tall ceilings, between piles of books that he had never read and in the company of a piano that he had never really learned to play, he kept me in his thrall until the early hours of the day, and then would walk me home in the sticky sweet dawn just as the first trams were beginning to creak awake. And easing myself cautiously under the mosquito net to lie beside Barbara, trembling from the exhaustion of a long night's entertainment, I would begin to wonder if some part of my fascination with Byron was not somehow physical, for his large gaze would so often follow me through the day, causing me to pause and reflect upon my every action and decide whether it was worthy of repeating to him. And Barbara, constantly questioning with her eyes my strange fascination for this man, led me to wonder even more—without any anxiety—whether there was some latitude in my sexuality. I did not fear such a revelation for I was certain I could accommodate such emotions without causing anybody any distress, no more at least than I was already causing Barbara by submitting to my need to know this man, to commit to him so much of my precious time.

I laugh now, or should I say snigger, to think of myself dutifully analyzing my emotions, broadening the margins just slightly to allow the intrusion of Byron Mallick and his fascination with eighteenth-century Bengal into my existence without upsetting the overall balance of our lives. For none of this would prepare me, not even slightly, for what was about to happen about a year later when, one afternoon, at the Calcutta Club, a young man who had been playing cricket on the lawn, would ask if he might join us for tea. His name was Arjun Mitra, and he was the eldest son of a High Court Judge with whom Byron had had a long and mutually beneficial acquaintance, and who, he assured me later, came from one of the oldest and most established families in Calcutta, the kind who could let their mansion crumble without any obvious consequences for their status. Arjun, despite having established himself as the fearless editor of a radical political journal, had never been able to unshackle himself physically from his privileged past, he continued to inhabit his parents' grand and gently rotting home, and occasionally even consented to play cricket for one of their clubs—which is why he happened to be there, then, looking impossibly handsome in his white cricket clothes, the cable-knit jumper with its maroon V-neck stripe, he flopped down beside us, peeled off his batting gloves and waved to a boy to bring him some refreshment.

Uncle Byron, he said, how are you these days?

We don't see you here very often, Arjun.

No reason why you should, I'm not a member myself.

No, it wouldn't do to be a member of this institution in your current position, would it? said Byron Mallick, taking a puff from his pipe.

You talk of my political inclinations as if they were some sort of transient addiction!

Are they not? I hadn't noticed. Anyway, is your lovely wife here?

She is, indeed.

Do call her over, said Byron Mallick, I'd like to introduce you both to my friend, Max.

I pushed my chair back and stood up as she approached, she tucked a stray strand of hair behind an ear before offering me her hand to shake, a shadow of turmeric upon her nails, eyes darting suddenly from very far away to meet mine. I stooped to shake her hand, my eyes fixed upon the sparsely decorated border of her beautiful sari and many mysterious folds that it created around her naked ankles, and then I set my thoughts aside with a sense of acute reverence, as if I were about to enter a religious building that I knew, once inside, would take my breath away.

I am Max Gate, I remember telling her hurriedly, anxious that we should return to the territory of our normal lives, for already I had been transformed by her, and the struggle to escape had already begun.

Ela is performing tomorrow at the Academy of Fine Arts, perhaps I can tempt you to come, Max? said Byron Mallick, also raising himself from his seat.

Yes, of course.

And Barbara?

I'm sure she would be delighted to accompany us.

I am very proud of this girl, he said, his hand moving to rest lightly on Ela's head. I sensed a warning in his voice, and smiled weakly.

Ela pulled at Arjun's sleeve—you should change, she said, we are late enough as it is.

That we are, her husband acknowledged.

After they had drifted away, Byron Mallick said to me: I love her like a daughter, Max.

I knew he had been her local guardian for several years while she boarded at a nearby girls' school, where her parents had left her when she was eleven years old in the hope that she might acquire some Bengali roots.

I still wonder, said Byron, why Nikhilesh chose me

to be her guardian rather than one of their many relatives. Perhaps it was the memories of our childhood, where the rescue and tending of doomed animals played an enormous part, that tipped the balance in my favor, the canings that I bore regularly for sheltering a condemned goat under my bed or feeding the last of the milk to a mangy cat...

And how would that have persuaded him to entrust you with the welfare of his child?

Perhaps—said Byron Mallick, emitting a short laugh—perhaps Nikhilesh continued to believe, as I myself did at the time, that these actions were rooted in compassion rather than defiance.

For six years she had been in his care, growing from a slip of girl into a graceful maiden with a great talent for dance. It was he who had encouraged her to make a career of it despite her parents' wishes. They had reacted by removing her to a Sixth Form College in England, after which she had dutifully gone to University College in London to acquire a degree. But then she had returned, Byron told me triumphantly, returned and married her childhood sweetheart, who worked at an international bank in Delhi. About six months ago, however, he had given up this job to become the deputy editor of an overtly left-wing journal in Calcutta, much to Byron's dismay.

From the corner of my eye, I saw her return to the table at the far end of the long veranda where her mother-in-law was still finishing her lunch, she bent down to recover something she had clearly left behind, and before she left, she looked once in my direction, and I turned to look at her, and in that brief moment a part of me that had floated free all my life sank lovingly inwards, like an ivory shipwreck, never never to rise again.

We did not go to that performance, for Barbara was unwell, but the following week Byron sent tickets for a solo recital that she was giving at a nearby hall, he hoped we would join them for dinner afterwards, he wrote in the accompanying note. I allowed Barbara to decide whether we should go or not, and when she said she thought we should, phoned Byron to say so. I had done nothing but think of Ela since our brief introduction, and spent the next few days almost in awe of seeing her again so soon.

Will I ever forget first watching her dance, grateful, oh so grateful, to be at the end of the row so that at least some part of me might find relief in contact with nothingness, while Barbara sat beside, clearly enchanted, and Byron to her left, radiating a very paternal pride. And yet afterwards, while we dined—just the four of us—at his favorite restaurant, he had taken her performance apart, piece by piece, almost intoxicated by his own detachment, while she simply sat and smiled, as if very far away. Barbara was clearly disturbed by his behavior—how could he do that to her, she exclaimed several times on the way home.

She didn't seem to care at all, I pointed out.

Perhaps it's his way of telling her he is taking her seriously, surmised Barbara.

Perhaps, I agreed.

I thought she was stunning, said Barbara.

Yes, I said, and then looked at her apologetically, for

both of us were taken aback by the misery in my voice.

I have a fearful headache, I lied.

I took myself off to bed but hardly slept that night, for a pain was knotting itself around me whose dynamic I found myself observing almost with curiosity, so unfamiliar and intensely physical was its character.

At five o'clock my alarm went off, for Byron had convinced me to accompany him regularly on his extended early morning walks around the lake in South Calcutta, and quarter past five was the hour that he had appointed for me to be ready and waiting for him downstairs in my tennis shoes. I stifled the alarm clock to prevent it waking Barbara, got up and brushed my teeth and dragged on my clothes, drank a few glasses of ice cold water, and came down just as he was pulling into the portico in his ungainly Ambassador, for this was before he acquired his Maruti Jeep. He had told me that he preferred to drive himself at this time of the morning so as not to have to wake the driver, and I had been touched by the consideration he appeared to show for all those who served him.

You are strangely quiet today, he remarked, as we drove through the empty streets.

Still recovering from last night's performance, I said truthfully.

Quite mesmerizing, is she not? said Byron, smiling.

Indeed, I replied.

We parked at the Rowing Club, and commenced our circuit of the lake in the oily morning haze, our necks already pricked as we emerged from the car by the sharp rays of the sun. It was on these long walks that he spoke with most candor of his past and his future, particularly in the near anonymity of the winter smog. He would speak of himself as he might have to a mirror rather than to my person, and this I found strangely intoxicating, especially since when we met later in the day, after each of us had concluded our particular business, his tone was quite different, less lyrical and more consciously entertaining. I felt it was a rare privilege to have access to both his morning and evening selves, and when I told him so, he laughed and replied: It is not surprising that we should change as the day wears on, as do our ragas, losing the languid semi-tones and acquiring first a sort of clarity, and then a harder mystery as we step into the evening and from there towards the depths of night.

After we had made a full circuit of the lake, we would return for coffee to the Rowing Club, the spell would be broken as we entered the clubhouse, and we would resume our more normal modes of conversation. He would ask one of the waiters to pack something nice for Barbara's breakfast and I would bring it to her later on a tray, for she was usually still in bed when I returned to our flat.

And so I did on that day, arranging the small croissants that the club had provided on a plate and placing a steaming mug of coffee beside it. She was sitting up in bed when I entered, her chin on her knees.

You don't have to do this every day, you know, she said to me.

But I like to, my darling, I replied.

And then feeling a sob rising within me, I excused myself and went to have a shower. It was cold for late

February, cold enough to bathe in warm water, and this gave me some paltry relief.

Morning passed in a daze at work, and at lunchtime I found myself heading towards Byron's flat. I had convinced myself that I needed to drop off a borrowed book, it was not unusual for me to stop by like this on my lunch break, he would always invite me to join him at the table, and often I would, for this untroubled hour, bounded on either side by duty, was one in which our conversation had a different discrete energy which I particularly enjoyed.

But that was not what I had come to seek on that day, and as if in fulfillment of some unformed prayer, it was Ela who answered the door.

Is Byron in? I asked.

He asked me to meet him here about half an hour ago, so I'm sure he will be back soon, she answered.

I'll come back another time, I said.

Or you could wait, she suggested.

And so I took off my shoes and followed her across the cold pitted marble floor to the sitting room, where she lowered herself casually into Byron's leather armchair, and gracefully crossed her ankles under the fine folds of her sari. I sat down across from her, feeling oddly ill at ease in my socks.

We thought you were wonderful last night, I said.

I am glad you enjoyed it, she replied.

A servant brought me a glass of fresh lime soda. I took a few sips and placed it upon a side table. The coaster nearest to me had upon it a black and white photograph of Marilyn Monroe and it was upon this image that I placed my sweating tumbler. I remembered how she had been described—I could not think who it was by—as a glass of milk with lipstick around its rim, and for no clear reason my eyes filled with tears. I took out my pocket handkerchief and dabbed them away.

The dust, I explained to Ela, the dust here does funny things to my eyes.

I am not surprised, she said calmly.

When I was seventeen, I had unexpectedly realized that my father had for quite some time, had an attachment with another woman, nothing that interfered with our robust family life, but suddenly palpable to me as we made our way, my father and I, and she and her son—who was a school friend of mine—through an exhibition of pop art at the Met. And, in the rawness of my pain, I discovered within the images an emotional intensity that I had never imagined them to contain, found myself unexpectedly moved when I had come solely with the expectation of being intellectually entertained. Lifting my glass of lime soda once again to my lips and staring at Marilyn Monroe, I felt perhaps that my tears had come in the same slate-veined acknowledgement of the ruthlessness of human love, my father's infidelity prefiguring my own descent into the same abyss.

She checked her watch. I have to go now, she said.

Can I give you a lift anywhere? I asked hopefully.

Oh no, it's too far, she said, I am going to visit my old dance master in Tollygunj.

I know Tollygunj, I said, we swim quite often at the Tolly Club.

But it is quite a distance.

I would be happy to take you there and bring you back, I really have nothing else to do in the next few hours.

Alright then, she said.

I had no sense then of how she saw me, nor can I imagine now what she made of me at the time, a gaunt thirty-five-year-old American, hair already starting to gray, did the blue of my eyes that others described as intense seem weak to her by comparison with the other dark eyes that had looked her way, did my freckled sunburned hands appear alien as they rested beside her on the sweaty seat of the Ambassador, as we sat at a polite distance from each other in the back while my driver took us through the narrow streets to her dance master, did she perceive me at all then as someone within her life or simply as a presence without, merging with the fantastic tapestry of Byron Mallick's existence that had at one time enveloped and protected her. At length we reached her master's home—I will not be long, she said quietly—and I realized then how focused she had been on this journey together, this last visit she would make to her dying mentor, and I was glad that the space that might have been filled by our conversation had been consecrated to this rather than anything else. I waited inside the car and smoked a cigarette while she went inside to see him, I watched the children playing cricket in the late morning heat, fishing the ball out of the open drains where it often fell, and wondered what a different life this was to the many to which she was already accustomed, and the many that might follow, in none of which—at the time—I seemed to have any place.

She did not stay long, returned with tears in her beautiful eyes, he can hardly speak anymore, she told me, her hands still trembling from having touched in farewell those feet that had once given magical instruction to her own.

For a while we sat silently together in the back of my car, the stillness of her seeping into me as my driver took us back into the center of town, we could have simply held that silence, but some guilty part of me wanted to break it so I asked her when she had started to dance, and she told me how even in the depths of Africa, her parents had found for her a teacher of Bharat Natyam, the South Indian style of temple dancing that her mother so adored. In Calcutta, Byron had found a teacher for her who had trained her in Odissi style, it was he whom she had just visited, he was dying now of throat cancer, in its last stages, she said. Under this man, her talent had burgeoned beyond all ordinary expectation and by the time she was in her mid-teens, she was already performing on stage. It was precisely at this time that her parents suddenly came to the decision that she needed to finish her education in England. They, who had sent her to be assimilated into their own culture, had now begun to fear that she might become trapped within it, and also that what she achieved in dance might be at the expense of her academic progress. But she had come back, picked up where she had left off five years earlier, and with Byron's help reestablished herself as a dancer of promise.

And so I learned a little of her history in that time, although not so much about herself, for to each of my questions she responded slowly and factually, as if trying to slide her answers on to a piece of paper under the ponderous weight of my obvious physical attraction to her.

The traffic was bad on the way back, and we were stuck for a while upon Dhakuria Bridge behind a bus bulging with passengers and belching huge clouds of exhaust that swirled around the car, almost magically enclosing us in its air-conditioned interior for a few moments. How I longed to be alone with her, anywhere, nowhere, somewhere that my desire for her could either soar or settle—if need be—like a dying bird into my palm, rather than fluttering in anguish in the air between us, unready for anything.

Where would you like me to drop you? I asked her.

If it is not too much out of your way, my in-laws' house in Gurusaday Road would suit me best, she replied.

Isn't that where you live as well?

I have not been married long enough to call it my own home, she replied.

Later she explained to me that women of her generation in Calcutta were inclined to treat their parents' homes and their in-laws' homes as two alternative residences, and refer to them as such. It was not so bad, she assured me, to feel like a guest in both, not so bad at this stage in life to be mistress of neither.

This I did not know, however, when I requested my driver to drop the memsahib off at Gurusaday Road, and was consumed the rest of the way by a deep and absurd desire to provide her with a cottage with hollyhocks in the garden, or a glass-faced New York apartment, just for the two of us, that she could call her own.

Eventually we drew up under the portico of the stately but somewhat decrepit old house where she and Arjun lived with his parents. I had feared that she might be glad to escape from me, and that this would leak towards me in whatever words of gratitude she was about to offer, but instead we looked at each other, tried to smile and could not, and perhaps in that precise moment, became intensely and irrevocably bound to one another.

It was in Byron's flat that we began afterwards to meet regularly, not by strict design, but because both of us were drawn there, knowing that it was the place where we might find each other. I—in my long lunch breaks—would wander over and linger in his drawing room even if he happened to be out, for the servants had been instructed to always allow me to wait for him to return, and she, too, would often drop by at this hour, to refresh herself between rehearsals and meetings, and whatever else took up her time in those days. For a long time we conversed as strangers, exchanging details of our lives with no particular purpose, but as our afternoons together lengthened to fulfill a raging urge I had never felt before to be in another's presence, our words and actions came to be shaped by that need into intricate messages of love. I did not dare touch her, of course, at first, but one afternoon—after I had wholly abandoned the idea of returning to work that day and telephoned the office to say that I was unwell—I found that this insignificant deceit had unleashed between us a set of different possibilities, and closing the drawing room door to the eyes of the servants, I took her in my arms and kissed her, not on her lips but on her neck and upon her shoulder, burying my eyes in her long dark hair.

She submitted briefly to this but then pulled herself away and walked over to the tall window, and stood shaking, with her hands upon the peeling sill.

I'm sorry, I said to her, I should not have done that.

You can see my old school from this window, she said.

I came and stood by her, inhaling the perfume from the pale streaks of sandalwood paste that clung to the hollow of her neck, and feathered a few strands of her hair, while she tried to guide my eye towards the stately buildings in the distance where she mastered trigonometry and algebra, learned the lengths of the world's rivers. She pointed out to me the oddly bloated roof of the swimming pool where she had perfected her breaststroke, the window of the sick room where she had spent many hours alone battling with tropical germs.

I knew that she had despised the lack of privacy in this life, the row of beds in the long dormitory with only the little white cabinet beside to cling to as her own territory. Even her wardrobe had to be shared with two other girls, an Anglo-Indian girl called Cecily Haliburton whose father sent her clothes from abroad, and a jolly little Assamese child who could never keep her things straight. She had very little in common with any of the boarders but had good friends among the day scholars, wished always that her parents would return to Calcutta, and that she could have a normal existence such as theirs. She kept a diary that she filled with imaginary letters from her father saying that they were coming back or moving to some other part of the world and had decided that she need not remain in boarding school any longer. She looked forward to the weekends when Byron Mallick would bring her to his home, here she had a room that she felt was her own, and the sounds and smells of the booklined rooms and corridors soon became dearer to her than the disinfected stretches of her parents' home in West Africa. She came to treasure the Sundays that she spent within the heavy walls of his mansion block flat, lying upon her bed with her wet hair spread out to dry under the ceiling fan, reading books that she had found on his shelves, some with beautiful incomprehensible names, *Eyeless in Gaza*, in a mill with slaves. Sometimes she would fall asleep, wake with the sad taste of the afternoon upon her lips, and instead of hauling herself out of the strange liquid gray that edged every such awakening, she would let herself remain in its grip, for soon she would have to return to her boarding house, the clatter of forlorn heels as the girls came down to supper, always boiled chicken on Sunday evenings, followed by tinned peaches and evaporated milk.

And where was I at that time but wrenching myself free from my parents' expectations while she tried desperately on a different continent to conform to hers, where was I but being led away from the clear course in life that they had set out for me by an Irishman named Piers O'Reilly, my first roommate at Princeton, later to become my brother-in-law and always to remain my friend. He and I had arrived there by very different routes—I having strenuously distinguished myself from the hordes of applicants from the state of New Jersey, by spectacular test scores and a number of victories at national chess championships—while, he, oh he, Piers O'Reilly—this is more what I imagine than what I know to be the circumstances that led him there—I see him stumbling into one of his mother's luncheons in their home in Holland Park, being led by the arm by one of her American friends into the conservatory, asked by her if he did not want to attend a small party they were having for young people who might consider Princeton as an alternative to a university on the British Isles, I see him at first almost made indignant by this suggestion and then suddenly thinking what a hoot it might be, I see his head reeling with the possibilities of reinventing himself and yet remaining true to who he really was, I see him being sucked mildly and easily towards that green space where he and I would meet and forever be entwined by love and death and marriage, the dissolutions and resurrections of all of these, not to mention our abiding trivial pursuits.

For me—Fair Haven, New Jersey, and for her, a decade later, a university town in West Africa, what could be more separated in space and time than for each of us to have spent our first tender years than this. And yet the dark that gathered outside my window was not so different to hers as we lay in our beds drawing our small selves about us, knowing that all this pleasantness—our loving parents, their delightful friends, our adventures with other children, heels pricked by dry grass, barbecued food awaiting us and bottles upon bottles of soda—knowing that this, *this* could never be all.

And here we were now, looking into each other's eyes,

knowing that this, *this* that we had achieved since, was also not enough, could we have chosen otherwise in that moment than to kiss each other, fully and deeply, on our mouths, that August afternoon in the year 1988, could we not simply have touched each other upon the cheek and tenderly smiled upon what might have been if the time was right, and just let go?

We kissed each other for the first time and then she left, no more words were exchanged, and I lingered in Byron's flat, unsure of how to return home. Eventually I decided to walk, and walk I did, the rest of the afternoon. I could not tell you where I went but I think I must have headed north, sought comfort there among the dark and patient alleys, the old houses, dense with decay, I walked and walked and then when I could walk no more hailed a taxi to take me back home.

I entered cautiously, found Barbara sitting in an armchair reading. She appeared to be waiting for me.

I have some news, she told me, I have found myself a job.

A job? I said, my head still packed with the scents and sounds of another woman.

A job, she affirmed, at the British Council library.

Why? I asked. Are you bored?

Not bored exactly, she replied.

What then?

Just stung with torpor, she said and walked quickly away.

And I, of course, hung back. I, who should have followed her to where she had begun to pour herself a whisky, taken her by the shoulders and asked her for a better explanation, I hung back and rejoiced at being enclosed within my afternoon's memories. Memories too young to really deserve such a name, fresh and slippery, of the taste of her skin, the smell of her hair, of what was said and not said, the precious moments of exquisite honesty amid painful dissimulation.

I looked up at Barbara, standing by the tall window with her drink in one hand, watching people going about their business in the street below, I saw her elegant shadow framed between the splendid shutters and I realized that there was no point trying to pretend anymore that this would pass, or even if it did that it would not scar us for the rest of our lives.

I half expected her to turn around there and then and confront me with this truth, so palpable in the space between us, girded by crowcall and the hurrying sound of tired feet as office-goers trooped towards their bus stops. So stern was her figure against the harsh white afternoon that I could only bury my head in my hands and sit in expectation of her demanding that we face the reality of our situation. But instead, she turned brightly towards me, tossed back her drink and said, why don't we go for a swim at the club? It was as if she had caught a glimpse of what her life would be like without me and humbly retreated.

There is a knock on the door and Byron enters, with him is the girl. I look at my watch, it is just past seven, it seems that I had, leaden with remembrances of my own and others, plunged for a while into some kind of sleep, a dreamless void in which I had found no more peace than in wakefulness.

Vargas is summoning us to dinner, says Byron.

I stand up, still swaying slightly, how can this night pass? I hear myself asking, dinner yes, first, but what will follow?

Are you feeling any better? Byron asks.

A little, I reply.

Some food and wine will help, he says.

No doubt, I say in hapless assent.

I pick up a piece of paper that has been lying upon a table beside me, held down by an inkwell in the shape of a squat bull.

Is this one of your drawings? I ask Adrija.

She nods.

I think it is very good, I say.

She puts out her hand to take it from me.

Can I keep it? I ask her.

She shakes her head, and I am of course relieved, for what would I do with such a thing as this?

It is for my mother, she says firmly.

Byron takes her by the hand and starts to lead her out of the room.

We are eating on the terrace, he says to me.

I'll join you in a minute, I promise him.

I walk out onto the balcony and reach into my pocket to extract what I deeply require—a cigarette.

Barbara and I used to smoke all the time, lighting cigarettes for each other was part of the rhythm of our marriage—when she suddenly gave it up after a few weeks in her job at the British Council, yet another ritual that held us together disappeared, and even though I received this with the fatalistic ease of a man desperately in love with another woman, I could not but ask her why.

Going for long hours without smoking has made me realize how little I actually miss it, she replied.

Eventually she would come to the same conclusion about me, but this still seemed a remote possibility then.

For a very long time she had tried to pretend it was not there, dear Barbara, or that what had lodged itself between ourselves would pass—which of course it would have, if she had waited long enough. She had thrown herself with great energy into her new job at the British Council library, it was a lifeline that she felt she could first use to deflect herself from my painful state, and in due course throw in my direction so that I too might extricate myself. She would regularly bring me books to read and I would read them, but never with the enthusiasm that she hoped to rekindle within me for such things.

One afternoon, as she was busily cataloguing a pile of books that had just arrived, she fell into conversation with a young man called Arunavo, a student of physics at Presidency College, who was looking for a book on quantum mechanics. He was a frequent visitor to the library and the next time she bumped into him, she invited him into her office for tea. He told her he was new to the city, his family lived in Bihar, that he had been forced to lodge in a dark and dingy room in a boarding house mainly occupied by tired professionals rather than young students—having left it too late, expecting that one of their many relatives in Calcutta would offer to house him, which none of them had done. Their friendship grew, and soon they were regularly going to films and exhibitions together, attending public lectures, and having long and animated conversations over lunch. She brought him home several times, the bright young man whom she had befriended, delighted in feeding him cakes and pastries that I often picked up for her on my way home, or bits and pieces of exotic food that her mother regularly sent us, blood orange marmalade, dried figs, canned venison paté. I found myself a grateful spectator to their games, and now when I come to think of it, my feelings towards the boy were not dissimilar to those I bear these days towards her sons. They would spend hours at the dining table together carefully looking through our piles of *Sight and Sound*, or with him drawing endless diagrams to explain some fundamental problems in physics which he felt sure she would be able to understand. As always, I was amazed at the breadth of her intellectual curiosity and imagination, as I had been when I first met her, and yet this no longer awakened within me that tremendous desire I had once felt to be with her, to touch her and smell her, and hear her voice.

Winter came and Arunavo went home for his vacation, a long six weeks, and they seemed unduly unbearable to both of us, the chilly evenings when we both sat by the small radiator in the living room and drank whisky and read in silence, the tedious Christmas parties that we attended out of a sense of having nothing better to do, the dazzle of winter sunlight on the cheap decorations in Park Street, the pernicious smog that snargled our throats and noses—in all of this, just one bright memory, of New Year's Eve at Byron Mallick's new beach house. He had been away much of that winter attending to his rapidly expanding interests in Bombay and Bangalore, but had come back to finalize the purchase of his new villa in the seaside town of Digha, and had decided on the spur of the moment to combine a housewarming party with the grand and frivolous act of ushering in a new year, the last of that decade. He took us down that morning in his new Maruti Jeep, his other guests were arriving later—some by car, some by train, but for a few hours we had the house to ourselves.

They have cleaned it up as best as they could, he warned us, but I'm not sure we have running water in all the bathrooms.

Byron, we are used to this, said Barbara, don't forget that we lived in the bush for several years.

A most salubrious bush by all accounts, joked Byron Mallick.

Don't worry about us, said Barbara.

Words that fell harshly upon my ears, for worrying about us was all I had been doing for the past few months. I stood upon the great white balcony and drank in the sea air and wished so very acutely that I might have been there with Ela, just the two of us in that marvelous house, wished that I might have been waiting there upon the balcony with my hands upon the chalk-stained parapet, waiting for her to emerge from within. I stood there, rooted in this reverie, nodded vaguely as Barbara passed by in a scarf and sunglasses announcing that she was going for a walk, stood there staring out at the endless sand, until Byron Mallick appeared by my side.

What do you think? he said presently.

It's lovely, I said.

The Brighton of the East he called it, Warren Hastings, in a letter to his wife, said Byron Mallick.

That long ago, I murmured.

That long ago, 1780, to be precise.

They had been married three years by then, Warren Hastings and his beloved Marian, but had been lovers for many years before that, for he had met her on the Indiaman in 1769 when she had with her a husband, a Baron

Imhoff, soldier and miniaturist, good-natured enough, it seems, to eventually trade her for some stability in his finances and assurances of security for the two sons she had borne him. Hastings had lost his first wife in 1759, and a daughter as well that year, and sent his only other child—a son—back to England, where he thought he might be safe. The child was looked after by Jane Austen's parents in their vicarage in Steventon but succumbed within six months to diphtheria. The connection to the Austen family was through Jane's aunt, Philadelphia, the wife of Warren Hastings's surgeon, and another woman he had loved, and of whose only daughter, Eliza, he may well have been father as well as godfather, all such interlinkings now deliciously adrift in the murk of time, yet his love for Marian somehow different, somehow able to shine above the turbulence, making him an object of my envy two hundred years later, as I stood and gazed upon the same sand, and the same sea, with a pain he no longer had to bear.

It is very beautiful, I told Byron.

It was always a dream of mine to own a house by the sea, he said to me.

You are a very lucky man, Byron.

And you, Max. Lucky to have Barbara—the kind of luck I have never had.

And for the first time I began to wonder why he had not married, Byron Mallick, with his splendid good looks and regal bearing, I had seen him very much at ease in the company of women, mostly other men's wives, but seen him also subtly shake them off like gauzy insects that one might let rest, out of a certain fascination, on one's clothes, but only for a while.

In due course, several such women appeared for the party, with and without their husbands, and other persons who had acquired what was seen now as the very rare privilege of being among Byron Mallick's inner circle of friends. They seemed this time to be more of a mixed crowd, a few of them rather coarse, clearly his business contacts, he had even invited one or two prominent politicians, none of whom I knew to be individuals for whom he had much respect. A great bonfire was lit in the front garden, trays of delicious food circulated constantly, and a variety of drinks was to be found upon a table at one end of the long ground-floor veranda. There, under a fine starry sky, we raised our glasses at midnight and sang Auld Lang Syne, first in the original and then—not by Barbara and myself of course—to the words that Tagore had set to the same tune, which Byron assured me had the same, if not more intense, poignancy.

The following morning I woke up with what I thought must be a terrible hangover, but rapidly turned into a raging fever. Byron apologized that he could not stay, he had a flight to catch that evening, so Barbara was left to nurse me alone while I shivered and moaned, and called frequently for my vomit pail. The servants were exceedingly helpful, the cook made me papaya stew to soothe my insides, and lying listless in bed I consoled myself that it was better to have passed my illness here than in our high-ceilinged Calcutta flat, thick with winter damp, with totally unreliable servants and nowhere really for Barbara to escape to when she needed, whereas here she could take herself—

as she frequently did—to the shore, and return with a variety of crustaceans that she kept in glass jars for amusement. Three days later, I was well enough to sit in the garden and read one of the few books I had found in the house—a cheap romance that must have belonged to the previous owner—which I found curiously engaging.

It is all I can possibly absorb in my current condition, I justified to Barbara, who quickly walked away as if not wishing to receive any further evidence of how puerile and underdeveloped my taste in literature actually was. I saw her heading in the direction of the beach, singing to herself. I read a few more pages and then dozed off. When I awoke, the sun was overhead, I turned onto my side and watched for a while a dark dung beetle laboring up the garden path with its large load, but then sat up as I heard the bell of a rickshaw outside the gate. It was Piers—Are you better?—he shouted to me as he counted the money for the rickshaw puller.

What are you doing here? I asked.

I decided to surprise you, he said.

Barbara appeared with some fresh fish she had purchased from a man on the seashore. Piers, she exclaimed, how on earth did you get here!

I decided to cut short my time in Bangkok, he said. I arrived in Calcutta and you were not there, so I went to see Byron and he put me on the train to Kharagpur.

And so we came to spend a good ten days here in this unlikely house by the sea, the three of us, Barbara, Piers and I, with the year 1990 just begun, the long tide leaving us spent of all but the most private of anguish. It was not an option that I had considered even in the depths of my despair that Barbara and I might be apart. Instead I sought to embalm some of my suffering in prose, perhaps I was finally capable of writing a novel, I thought to myself, finally perhaps. I sent another telegram to my office to say that I had worsened, and I shut myself in the library with some paper and a nice fountain pen, but nothing came of it. What Piers and Barbara did in this time I do not know, except that they took long walks and she sometimes played the harp that oddly resided in the drawing room, barely tunable—and therefore a pleasing challenge to Barbara, who would wring wonderful music from it after hours of strenuously adjusting the strings.

Eventually we returned to Calcutta. Piers stayed on for another two weeks, but he had already visited us once on his way to Thailand so there was nothing much left to show him, and besides I had to put in my time at work to compensate for my extended absence. Still, I tried to get away whenever I could to enjoy his company, he had a great fondness for the College Street Coffee House and would often spend the afternoon there, reading, and I would try and join him as soon as I was reasonably able to leave the Consulate. One afternoon, having found a comfortable excuse to leave just after lunch, I found myself in the Coffee House before Piers had arrived, instead came upon Ela and Arjun sharing an oily omelette together before he caught the train to some distant corner of Bihar where he had been granted an exclusive interview with the manager of a factory that—in his opinion—survived by exploiting the local tribal community.

Do join us, said Arjun.

I reluctantly complied, and was relieved when Piers came in almost immediately after, placed a pile of second-hand books, newspaper-wrapped, upon the table and allowed me to make introductions. I could see that he was immediately fascinated first by Arjun, and then after he had left, by Ela, whose near silent presence I had been enjoying while her husband held Piers's attention. After Arjun grabbed his briefcase and dashed off Piers turned to Ela—that was not a very emotional farewell, he said.

We are accustomed to parting, she replied.

From that inauspicious start their conversation unfolded, layer by layer, while I watched helpless, as an extraordinary affinity revealed itself. She had just been lecturing across the road at Presidency College on the history of dance and had her slides with her, which Piers insisted on examining. What he said of each pose that he squinted at made her laugh, and also argue. I had never seen her so at ease with anyone, I felt a little confused, and sensed that somehow she enjoyed my confusion.

Over the next week or so Piers saw her daily, while I stamped visa applications in my office and stared out of my window at the winter murk. Piers journeyed with her hither and thither but mostly sat in restaurants and cafés, or in some sedate corner of her own home, enjoying her company when I could not.

I understand you have been spending a vast amount of time with my goddaughter, Byron joked to Piers, the evening before he was to return to London. He often called Ela his goddaughter when speaking to foreigners.

I have indeed, Piers replied.

Don't forget that she is married, said Byron.

Sir, I am avowedly asexual—Piers reassured him.

Just as well, for I'm sure Arjun would arrange for you to be neutered otherwise, said Byron, enjoying my obvious discomfort.

There, Max, said Piers—there's a plot for you to pursue.

Plot means very little to Max, Barbara said, tired by then of my literary exertions.

Byron looked me straight in the eye and said almost accusingly—I did not know that you wrote.

It is hardly of any consequence, I replied.

What do you mean?

I don't think I will ever write again.

Why not?

Because, contrary to what Piers thinks, I do not actually write very well. In fact, I can hardly write at all—believe me, I know, I have one single sentence in my head and every now and then I think it might lead me somewhere, but it never does.

Is this fiction we are talking about?

Yes, why?

Because if I were you, I would try my hand at something that is not fiction.

Like?

Like travel writing, for instance.

Travel writing?

You do keep a journal, don't you?

Intermittently.

Well, you have certainly gathered plenty of material over the last few years.

That I have.

Well, I would try and write something around that.

I'll have a go.

I did not give it a try, however, until I returned to London a year and a half later for what I had thought would be a few months at most to sort out my finances, before I took up residence in New York somewhere, somehow, and tried to finish my novel. They were simply little incidents that I had attempted strenuously to turn into short stories, and had resisted all but the slightest of embroidery. But I found it therapeutic, both in terms of dealing with immediate events, and also preparing myself for a different future. I showed them to Piers and before I knew it they had appeared in print and dragged along a number of commissions. Thus almost effortlessly was I assimilated into this life, and soon abandoned all thought of moving back to my homeland, where Teddy Ginsberg and his cronies had been waiting to welcome me back into their fold. Instead I slipped into the role that I had both courted and resisted for such a long while, of an American writer abroad with a wealth of knowledge and a storehouse of cynicism to equip him for a long career as a commentator on almost anything of any interest—and indeed I have written on the astonishing grace of the gardens of Pompeii with as much ease as I have recounted an encounter with a Bengali intellectual incarcerated in a village telling me how his rabbit suffered a heart attack upon eating too many marigolds.

This I know, though—that I would never have turned

to travel writing if Byron Mallick had not fixed his penetrating gaze upon me that evening in Calcutta and said to me—Fiction is not your natural home, Max.

How do you know? I asked him.

You hardly read any fiction, he pointed out.

This was true, but I had never associated the reading of novels with the writing of them.

I read a lot in Digha, I said nonetheless in my defense.

All trashy novels left behind by the previous owner, said Barbara, suddenly on Byron's side. And I who should have found her defection a relief, was plunged instead into a greater misery.

I am sure you are all correct, I said bitterly.

Might be interesting to try writing nonfiction, said Piers.

You, even you, I thought.

Byron Mallick tapped his pipe upon the table.

You are no storyteller, Max, he said.

Piers went back to London, taking with him our last trickle of hope, and the dreaded evenings began to enclose us in ever firmer folds of flat gray. A few days later Barbara's young friend Arunavo came back from his winter vacation, which he had been forced to prolong on account of his sister's wedding. He came to see Barbara straight away, and the two of them walked the entire distance from the British Council to his hostel in College Street, where he had left behind by mistake the gift he had brought her from his hometown. He talked excitedly about some experiments he had set up in his room at home, but her brain was as cottonwool packed heavily between her ears, she was glad he did not notice her inattention or her despair, his eyes danced brightly in his face as he continued to describe his feats. As they entered the courtyard of his hostel, the smell of moss and old urine hit her with the pungency of lust, and she felt a slight discomfort as Arunavo innocently mentioned that the one advantage of living in a hostel for professionals was that the level of surveillance was low and you could bring whomever you liked to your room. He unlatched the door and moved aside to let her in, welcome to my humble home, he said.

It was a narrow room with a desk overflowing with books, a rickety chair and a bed neatly made, a mosquito net carefully rolled up into one corner.

I wouldn't trust the chair, said Arunavo, it's better if you sit on the bed.

He offered to make her tea and reaching under the bed retrieved a newspaper parcel—Happy New Year, he said, thrusting it into her hands.

She unwrapped it slowly, it was a bamboo vase, she stared at it in confusion, it is for dried flowers, he explained.

For dried flowers, she repeated.

I'll go and get some hot water from the kitchen, he said.

She sat alone, staring out of the high window at a patch of pale winter sky, when suddenly she felt a cold wet nudge upon one of her ankles, she gave a low shriek and pulled her legs up onto the bed. It was a dog, a ragged mongrel, who fled as soon as she cried out.

Don't mind him, said Arunavo, returning with a steaming kettle, he's quite harmless, he sneaks in whenever he can, keeps me company when I study, he sits quietly under my chair, I usually save some bones for him, not that the food we get here is even fit for a stray dog, he said laughing.

The dog wandered back in. I call him Amadeus, said Arunavo fondly.

It was a vision of grace, and it told her as sharply as no words ever could that she owed it to herself to leave me, to leave me straight away, and when Arunavo came looking for her a few days later at the library, she was gone.

—

Places have been set for us around the circular teak table in the sheltered area of the terrace, the electric chandelier has been switched on and hurricane lamps placed upon the parapet in case the power should suddenly fail.

I apologize for keeping them waiting, then sit down next to Adrija and pour myself a glass of red wine from the bottle that Nikhilesh immediately passes me.

Where is Piers? I ask.

He went for a walk and has not yet returned, Nikhilesh explains.

We'll have to start without him, says Byron.

Vargas brings in a tureen full of steaming rice. He leaves it on the table for us to serve ourselves and picks up from the sideboard a silver platter bearing slices of fried eggplant, which he dispenses with a large pair of tongs.

Vargas, how are you these days? I ask him as he neatly lowers the food onto my plate.

I am very well, sir.

He had been a clerk in one of Byron's companies before being singled out for the position that he now occupies—not quite Jeeves, but as close to that ideal as Byron felt he could achieve when he approached the light-skinned and fairly well-dressed man whom he had been watching for some time, with a view to asking him if he might be willing to consider such a proposal. Vargas, it turned out, was not as young as he looked and was actually in his forty-fifth year in 1976, he had no family save an ailing mother who was installed in an old people's home on Lower Circular Road, conveniently close to Byron Mallick's flat. Yes, of course, sir, was all he said when Byron explained to him what he had in mind, as if he had no choice in the matter.

Tenderly he spoons some rice onto the child's plate, he knows her heart well for she has regularly been entrusted to his care, he has sung her lullabies learned from his Portuguese grandmother, he has taught her how to fold a sheet of paper into the shapes of boats and birds that flap their wings, he has taught her how to mix batter for fairy cakes and let her eat them later on the carpet while watching television, picked up each crumb as it has fallen from her lips so as not to anger his master.

Look, a butterfly! the child exclaims, as a beautiful Blue Tiger drifts in and settles upon the tablecloth beside her plate.

Byron reaches over with his empty water glass and traps it. The child runs off and returns after a few minutes solemnly balancing a small empty aquarium in her arms. Into this Byron tips the stunned insect, which falls to the floor with a soft thud, but then quickly recovers and begins to flap around. The floor of the aquarium is covered with dry leaves, and a few carcasses of other insects that she has clearly attempted to keep in it.

I used to have Black Mollies in there, she says to me, noticing my curiosity.

No one had had the heart to deny her the request to take them with her to Digha, but they had not survived the journey, for somehow the fish tank had overturned in the trunk of the car and the water had drained out, and they had found the fish lying inert under a pile of colored gravel. Vargas is still trying to get the smell out of the suitcases that were supposed to have protected them from such a fate.

Interesting creatures, Black Mollies, says Byron, they live in rivers but occasionally journey to the sea to let the salt water kill their parasites, and then return again to their freshwater homes.

Kotha akuler khola hawa, dibey shobo jwala juraaye—quotes Nikhilesh with a mixture of wit and weariness.

Should I translate for you? asks Byron cautiously. As if my Bengali was ever good enough to make sense of such an utterance.

Eto din tori bahilam, she shudur patho bahiya, says Nikhilesh, clearly liberated by the two glasses of Cabernet Shiraz that he had rather rapidly already consumed, *shoto baar tori dubu dubu kori, e pathey bharasha nahi aar.*

Long have I steered this course, translates Byron, almost in harmony, but now my boat threatens to sink, I have no faith any more in my route.

Kotha akuler khola hawa, dibey shobo jwala juraaye—Nikhilesh repeats.

I long for the open sea wind to wash me of my pain, comes the echo from Byron.

Enough, says Nikhilesh, enough.

I had first met Nikhilesh at a screening of *Ivan the Terrible* that Byron had asked me to come to at the Gorky Sadan. The film was due to start at 6pm so I did not have time to go home first. I got there early, not realizing how close it was to my place of work, and stood waiting somewhat nervously outside. They arrived together, Byron and his friend, a short wiry man with a shock of gray hair who looked many years older than Byron himself, this was Nikhilesh, Byron's oldest friend, recently returned from Africa, where for many years he had been a university lecturer. He seemed a little exhausted, although by what but the burden of his self-imposed early retirement I cannot guess. I caught him napping several times during the screening, his head bowed, hair falling over his face.

I knew that Byron and he had been friends since childhood, ever since that magical morning when the bullock cart that took him to school had pulled up to the gates of Byron's house, and he had been amazed to find perched upon it another boy of his age, introduced to him as the son of the new doctor, who would be traveling with him from now on to town and back, every day. Byron's time at school had passed so far without event, he had been easily accepted by his peers but had made no close friends, he still took care at tiffin time to eat slowly enough that he might not be left sitting unengaged afterwards, so he was delighted to have a companion from the same village and someone also to break the tedium of the journey, an hour each way, jolting along the high track, his senses too rattled even to think clearly, let alone to read. Better still, on weekends, he was allowed to wander out with Nikhilesh on his own, explore the terrain that previously he had only been able to look upon from the upstairs windows of their house, or from the shoulders of a servant carrying him to market as a special treat.

I sat between them in the clammy dark watching *Ivan the Terrible*, with Nikhilesh frequently jerking himself awake as his slumbering chin hit his chest, and Byron on my other side perfectly composed but in fact utterly elsewhere in his thoughts, there was not much of their past that I had knowledge of then, and yet somehow I felt already accommodated within it like a prodigal younger brother, yes, something like that. After the film ended we stepped out into the evening, Nikhilesh and I lit cigarettes and Byron his pipe, and I boldly asked if they might wish to return with me to my flat where we could content ourselves with the ample leftovers from the previous night, and some whisky.

Barbara was not entirely displeased to see us, she fell straightaway into a conversation with Nikhilesh on the book she was reading, which he himself had apparently recently finished.

I busied myself with reheating the lasagna while Byron attended to our drinks.

He is married to the most dreadful woman, he said to me suddenly.

You don't like each other?

Ruby Kanjilal, she was in college with us, I never knew what he saw in her.

Do they have children?

Oh yes, said Byron, a beautiful daughter—married and living in Delhi.

Ela, Ela, that first mention of you, why did it not strike like a gong against my heart? Why did the fork with which I was mixing salad dressing not slip at that moment unexpectedly from my hands—are time and space really so separated here upon this earth as to not allow such a thing?

She is a dancer, said Byron.

Oh yes? I said.

A very good dancer, he insisted.

I'm sure she is, I told him, raking the rest of the garlic out of the press before tossing the instrument into the kitchen sink.

Perhaps, if you are lucky, you will see her on stage someday.

I'd like that, I said to Byron Mallick.

They spoke easily, as we ate, of their life together as undergraduates in Calcutta in the 1950s when they had shared a hostel room, Byron and Nikhilesh, how cheerfully they had struggled to be assimilated into their new urban surrounds, what vast promises the city held for two young men such as themselves, not just within itself but as a gateway to the world beyond. Both had distinguished themselves academically and were well into their doctorates in history when Byron had suddenly determined that academia was not for him. He had by then already gained something of a professional reputation, published a number of important papers in historical journals and written extensively for some of the more erudite little magazines. Despite this, it was Nikhilesh who had been appointed to the post of junior lecturer when it had unexpectedly fallen vacant the previous year. It was explained to Byron that his work, although original and exciting, was seen by some as lacking in scholastic depth, while Nikhilesh—they felt—was less concerned with dazzling his audience than producing something of true worth.

Perhaps it was just jealousy, he admitted to us with great candor as he helped himself to some more of the reheated okra and eggplant lasagna, perhaps it was just petty jealousy, but it did make me realize I was better off outside academia.

You are incapable of jealousy, Nikhilesh said.

How do you know? Byron asked, raising his fine eyebrows and smiling.

I know, his friend replied confidently.

Vargas brings us our main course, lamb and lentil curry, just as his mother would have made it, this Goan specialty and the Brazilian fejoada having no doubt descended from some common Portuguese one-pot ancestor.

The dog Kimbhut has been waiting by the child's feet and now eagerly attacks the portion of dhansak that is ladled into his bowl.

Quite a pampered pet, I comment as Vargas finally begins to serve us humans.

Horace Walpole served his cat oysters, says Byron.

No, that was Dr. Johnson, Nikhilesh corrects him.

Yes, of course, says Byron, I am definitely losing my memory.

I notice that the child is sculpting the rice into some sort of troglodytic landscape rather than eating it. Vargas brings her a small bowl of lentils, which she pours happily onto her plate to create a lake in one of the hollows.

Eat your food, Byron says to her firmly.

The girl makes a boat out of a small lettuce leaf to sail on her lake of daal. Byron reaches over and removes it and tosses it into the garden.

Vegetables are for eating, not for playing with, he says.

Do not be harsh on the girl, says Nikhilesh.

Once he had had the upper hand, Nikhilesh, in the days of their childhood when they had roamed the red fields before the rains, sheltered in abandoned shacks during the first storms of June, read to each other upon the muddy veranda when it was too wet to wander out and in the winter sat wrapped in shawls in the syrupy sunlight, doing crosswords and playing chess. Under the clay-colored skies their friendship had grown from plain companionship to something of a substance so rare and hard that it had easily survived their diverging interests and moralities these many years.

On the day the results of their school-leaving exams were announced, Byron Mallick lay ill in bed with typhoid, and as Nikhilesh walked to his home with news of their overwhelming success, he had had to fight hard against the presentiment that when he arrived, his friend would be no more. One of his sandals tore upon a jagged rock in the road, consolidating his apprehensions, and he walked the rest of the way barefoot expecting the worst. The door to the courtyard was slightly ajar and Nikhilesh could hear his friend's mother quietly crying inside. He coughed and entered, and there lying pale upon a bamboo mat was Byron, not dead but utterly exhausted, his fever in remission. Nikhilesh clasped his outstretched hand and without any words conveyed to him what they had both hoped for—that both were bound for college in Calcutta—they had done it—they had made that first most difficult leap. And indeed nothing in the cascade of successes that became their lives tasted as sweet as this first victory. For Nikhilesh, recognition came almost too cheaply after that, and before he was thirty he was already established as one of the most promising academics of his generation. And perhaps he found this too confining, for before long he packed his bags and took his wife and young daughter to live in Africa, preferring a junior post at a foreign university to the tired sequence of honors that he knew awaited him in his own land. As for Byron, he made a fortune in pharmaceuticals, which was not quite as effortless but easier than he might have thought on that memorable train ride in the third-class compartment of the Tufan Express, sitting wedged together with their knees knocking against their metal trunks, packed with starched clothes and the few books that they saw fit to take with them to Calcutta. There was a particular moment on that fateful journey when he had leaned out of the window to hail a tea vendor and spied a couple of youths of much greater means boarding the train, their wristwatches flashing as they raised their arms to beckon their coolie, that for the first time in his life Byron Mallick realized, to his astonishment, that part of his ambition was to be rich.

Byron turns his bright eyes towards me.

Tell me, Max, how is life treating you these days, anyway? he asks.

Fairly well, I reply.

Have you been back to India much, he asks, a hint of accusation in his voice.

Only once, I confess.

But still feel qualified to write about it?

My experiences from the time I spent here are inexhaustible, I assure him.

—

In Calcutta they shared a hostel room which Byron attempted vainly to keep in order, for Nikhilesh could not care less about its condition. Nor was he as excited as Byron about being finally in a metropolis, teeming with life and ideas, and corners that when turned could take your breath away. While Byron ranged further and further into the life of the city, Nikhilesh curled his unwashed self into a tight ball and read and read.

And for the first time they found themselves in the company of women, women who were their intellectual equals, if not better, some of them beautiful, a few quite ravishing, and all but one or two very dignified and remote in their manner. Conversation with them was an exhilarating game in which they both became more and more skilled, vying happily with each other for lines most loaded with innuendo, and later speculating on how the female mind worked as they lay in their bunk beds in the dark.

And then the day came when Nikhilesh fell in love with their friend Shankar Kanjilal's sister. She offered great resistance to his attentions at first, and Byron found himself in the quite unfamiliar role of comforting an oft-distressed Nikhilesh. This he found hard for he could neither fathom his friend's obsession with her, nor understand why he should seek to be permanently associated with a family of such little sophistication as theirs—for Nikhilesh had made up his mind to marry Ruby Kanjilal, which he did in the course of time.

Byron Mallick has few memories of their wedding except that it was raucous, the bride—although already on the heavy side—was borne easily upon a plinth by her five brothers and made to circle Nikhilesh seven times in this condition, to bind and tighten in a circle of seven nooses what they were about to undertake, as he gazed skeptically upon the scene, cozily fingering the letter in his breast pocket that granted him admission to an accountancy course in London, for he had determined by then that academia was not for him.

Soon after he departed for England, and by the time he returned, Nikhilesh had already left with his wife and baby to take up a lecturer's post in Ghana, and the two did not see each other again until 1973. By then she was eight years old, little Ela, permanently clad in a red and white poncho. On the chilly sunless day that they first met, the garment kept getting caught on the various large screws and other extrusions on the building site where they had gathered to review progress on the house that Byron had persuaded Nikhilesh to build as a retirement home in Calcutta. He could see that Nikhilesh was keen to return and reestablish himself in Calcutta, desperately worried that his daughter would not identify with their culture if she did not grow up in Bengal. His wife, however, was clearly determined to remain in West Africa for much longer, she told him proudly that she had learned to drive, and how easy and wonderful life was for them out there within their cosmopolitan university community, how pleasant it was for the child to grow up in such an intellectually stimulating and yet peaceful environment. Byron watched the little girl as she picked her way through the maze of concrete trying to define and imagine the outlines of what would later be her parent's home, he watched her as she skipped from brick to brick, immersed in her own game, and his heart filled with an unexpectedly tender awareness of her uncertain plight.

As they were leaving the site, she caught his arm and

boldly said—look, Byron, look—drawing his attention to another building in a slightly more advanced stage of construction where a homeless family was making use of an apartment, perfectly formed except for its exterior walls, they were going about their business pretty much as they would had the walls been in place, some were sitting in a circle upon the floor to eat the food that was being prepared on a makeshift earthenware stove in the space that would one day become a kitchen, some were sleeping on charpoys in the bedroom, one was washing himself with a bucket in the bathroom, which clearly had a drain, even if it had no other plumbing or an external wall. Look, Byron, look, she said, as if only he—and not her parents—would be able to comprehend the absurdity of the scene.

Three years later they would return, this time with the intention of leaving her in boarding school with him as her guardian, a responsibility that had excited him then more than he might have imagined, he who was resolutely determined not to have children, or even—having just turned forty—to ever marry.

And indeed, how blissful it had all been until the intrusion of Damini, that vacation with them from which Ela returned, so impossibly transformed, and began taping Pablo Neruda poems on the walls of her room that she had copied herself onto pages torn out of her exercise books, and started using terms like "comprador bourgeoisie" in her conversation like exotic flavorings.

It was not until Ela was in her third year of boarding school that Shankar Kanjilal had taken a new job in the steel belt of Bengal, about a hundred miles out of Calcutta, and Byron had put Ela on a train to Durgapur to spend her Christmas vacation with her uncle and his wife and their fifteen-year-old daughter, Damini. Shankar Kanjilal had always struck him as an unimaginative, although exceedingly well-meaning, sort of chap—and his wife, a rather reserved and quite unattractive woman. Byron did not expect that Ela would have much of a good time there, he imagined a dumpy daughter reading Mills & Boon romances and trying out different shades of toenail varnish to fill her dreary afternoons, not a person with whom she was likely to have anything in common.

Yet, in the New Year when she returned to Calcutta and resumed the routine to which they had both now become thoroughly accustomed, Byron found Ela to be subtly changed. In the summer vacation she always went back to her parents in Africa, and other times to various relatives for some of her holidays, but the room in his flat that she slept in was now as much a home as any to her, and suddenly for the first time she began to fill it with pieces of her own self. Their conversations became less easy, for she no longer seemed to hold in the highest regard every word that dropped from his lips, instead she appeared to question his every motive, and at the same time question her own. Byron Mallick found this crisis of confidence within her rather tedious, and was glad that at this time his flourishing business obliged him to travel more than ever.

She spent hours in her room writing long letters to her cousin, her new soulmate, Damini. She was restless to return to her uncle's home, and when he finally came and took her away to spend a long weekend with them, she contrived not to return for a whole week by complaining of a recurring bad headache. It was clear to Byron that it was to them she wanted to return for Easter, and also for a large chunk of the following summer as her parents were coming to India on home leave that year, and this suited her very well.

At least she was still out of his sight then, Damini, as she had a year of school left to finish, and exams to sit for at the end of it. The situation worsened when Damini moved to Calcutta to attend college, and piously insisted that she stay with their relatives in their cramped lodgings in Dhakuria rather than at her maternal grandparents' meticulous apartment in Ballygunge. And so in the years that followed there was no real relief from Damini's presence—even when she was not there, Ela spoke as if with her voice, spouting opinions that could have no foundation in her own experiences and knowledge, challenging Byron on his attitudes towards human rights without a clue as to how to defend her position, all of which he found tedious and distressing. So many times he would return from a business trip with the expectation of quietly spending the afternoon with Ela and instead, be met at the door by Vargas, who would warn him that they had a guest, aware of how much Byron detested her presence, and he would walk into the dining room to find them quietly studying together or worse still, engaged in some tiresome jejune debate. They always made an effort to include him in some way—once Damini even asked his help with a problem in coordinate geometry, and seemed horribly smug when he failed to provide a satisfactory answer. Byron Mallick had never had a woman doubt his intelligence before, and realized with some disappointment that he found this to be far more intolerable than being challenged by a man.

One evening, after a particularly pointless argument between the three of them about protectionism, from which Ela emerged in tears, hastily packed her things and strode off to her boarding house without saying goodbye, he wrote a long letter to Nikhilesh warning him of the influence that Damini was exerting over his only daughter. Although they had both been staunchly Marxist in their youth, Byron felt it appropriate to alert Nikhilesh to the fact that Damini was dragging Ela into the company of some very dodgy characters whom he suspected to be card-carrying members of leftist student federations. Ela did not find out about this until many years later, and when she asked her father if it had influenced his decision to remove her from Calcutta at such a critical juncture in her dancing career, he strongly denied it.

Nikhilesh's reaction had been to send her to a Sixth Form College in Warwickshire, as he had planned to do anyway for fear that her addiction to dance might distract her from fulfilling her academic potential. Byron's plan had backfired, but he consoled himself that at least she was out of range of Damini's immediate influence. In fact, nothing had been able to destroy the bond between the two cousins, neither time nor distance, nor the very different courses their lives took. For years they wrote long letters to each other in a potent mixture of Bengali and English, and then as their letter-writing habits withered, would speak on the phone at regular intervals.

For a decade or so their lives overlapped again in Calcutta, but then Damini removed herself to Darjeeling with her lover Dhritiman, and thrown herself into her new cause. Ela and Arjun had come to stay with her often in the small white flat that she rented in the heart of the township, it pleased them to have little Adrija spend time at the shelter in the company of the less fortunate—the women with their patient weatherbeaten faces and the round-cheeked children, so cheerfully enduring their many infestations and so marvelously accommodating of their mothers' despair—queuing with them for porridge, and playing afterwards in the small room packed with donated toys and picture books with titles like *A Pipkin of Pepper* from lands far away. Both her parents were keen for her to be weaned from the life of privilege into which she had been born—their grand mansion on Gurusaday Road, the broad and well-watered lawn where she skipped in her white school clothes surrounded by a multitude of roses, each individually tended by the gardener. Indeed, it had been planned that she would spend some of her Puja holidays in Darjeeling this year while Ela went on tour, but that of course was not to be.

Since Damini had moved to Darjeeling, the cousins had kept in regular contact mainly through electronic mail, for Byron had very generously paid for internet access to be available at the shelter. It was crucial, he said, that Damini be able to communicate directly with those who were purchasing the fruit preserves and handmade stationery that were produced there. People liked to know whom they were helping by buying these items—perhaps links could be established between the producer and consumer, not an economic link to cut out the middleman but an emotional link which left the middleman intact. Yesterday, Damini's effects had arrived in Calcutta, carefully packed, including the small personal computer on which she often wrote her e-mail messages in the evening and brought in to send from the shelter during the day. It was while scanning the crammed folder of "Sent Items" on this machine yesterday afternoon that Arjun Mitra had fished out the message that caused him to race up to Darjeeling, a message that Damini had boldly dispatched to Byron Mallick on the fourteenth of May, 2004, expressing concern that much of the formula that he was supplying to the shelter was actually ground chalk.

Someone is coming up the garden path whistling, it has to be Piers, indeed it is Piers, he claps his shoes together to rid them of sand, and then comes to join us at the table.

Where have you been? asks Adrija.

Just walking and thinking, he says.

Thinking about what? she asks.

Thinking about a solution to a problem, he says, helping himself to some slices of eggplant, now lying cold to one side.

And have you found one? asks Byron.

Oh, yes, says Piers, sitting down across from him.

A solution to what? demands Nikhilesh tipsily.

A problem, his granddaughter reminds him solemnly.

And you have found a solution? Nikhilesh asks of Piers.

I have, he answers.

Vargas offers us sliced mango with saffron pistachio ice cream for dessert.

A marvelous combination, declares Nikhilesh.

I made the ice cream myself, sir, says Vargas proudly.

Vargas has a great fondness for kitchen gadgets, says Byron.

So do I, I tell Vargas, who is plunged into embarrassment by such an admission on my part.

For I was the sort of child who would take a toaster apart and put it back together again—much to the delight of my father, who imagined that one day I would follow in his footsteps and apply such skills to the patching up of human beings—little did either of us imagine that my life would take such a strange course as this which finds me sitting here, under a saltworn chandelier, eating saffron pistachio ice cream churned up in Vargas's new Magimix's 2200 Gelato Chef.

But it is Piers here who is the food critic, says Byron to his servant.

Yes, sir, I have read a few of his excellent columns, says Vargas.

That's very kind of you, Vargas, says Piers.

Max is more fond of gadgets than of cooking, I fear, says Byron.

It had never occurred to me, either, when I was a little boy in Fair Haven, New Jersey, that I might do anything other than go to medical school, and when I was miraculously accepted by Princeton I felt as if I had already come most of the way in achieving this goal. My parents and sister drove me there on a beautiful September day, I was to be in Princeton Inn College—once an inn as its name suggested—in a room overlooking the golf course, and with a distant view of the dreamlike spires of the graduate college beyond. I had been told that I would be sharing with someone by the name of Piers O'Reilly—a young man with a London address, a very swanky London address my father confirmed, who knew about such things.

And there he was, Piers O'Reilly, in his crimson waistcoat and wintergreen corduroy bellbottoms, my mother regarded him with deep suspicion, but my father instantly engaged him in a perfectly pleasant conversation about London and his own time there during the War.

That he would lead me so consummately astray they did not know then, not even the empty bottle of vodka that he adroitly kicked under the bed as we came in would give them a clue about how far he would pull me away from what they saw as a fairly secure future for their only, and exceedingly mild-mannered, son.

They were aghast when, four years later, I broke the news to them that I would not after all be going to medical school, had instead decided to get a research degree in biochemistry from Oxford University. Secretly I hoped that this would leave me enough room to pursue what by then I had begun to see as my real calling—to be a writer—and also to engage fully in the kind of life that being Piers's friend and Barbara's boyfriend opened up for me. My parents made clear that they would withdraw all financial support if I embarked upon this other and utterly unfamiliar course, but this did nothing to deter me, I had funding to meet my basic needs for the next three years, and the O'Reillys to support me in my more expensive habits.

My father had not dismissed my intentions instantly, as I had expected him to do, but instead launched into an elliptical discourse quite uncharacteristic of him, weaving about me a web of allusions that he hoped would trap me into a different decision. When this did not happen, he reverted to threat, for me a more familiar territory, at which point I walked out and took the train to Manhattan, spent the night at a friend's apartment from where I telephoned Barbara, and explained what had happened.

Oh Max, she said, how awful for you.

I know I will be able to survive in Oxford, I told her, but I have to figure out what to do for the summer.

Can you hold on a minute? she asked.

I'd rather you called me back, I said.

Which she did, to say this: Mummy thinks you should just come here, we have plenty of room.

I'll do that, Barbara, on one condition.

What is that?

That you promise to marry me.

As if you needed to ask me that, she said.

That summer, all my moments of youthful perfection contained within the life that streamed constantly in and out of the O'Reilly's London townhouse, the beautiful self-assured daughters, their lovers and friends, Piers and his varied circle of acquaintances—how happy I was to stand apart from them and yet be at the heart of it, this life, the champagne and the oysters flowing late into the night, waking early to breakfast with Barbara's aging father while the rest of the household slept or wandered in to rehydrate themselves or place a bag of ice upon their heads before stumbling back into bed, my Barbara among them, always glad when I brought her a large mug of tea or a Bloody Mary, whichever I judged more appropriate, towards noon, and then climbed into bed to make silent love to her, deliciously cocooned by the eternally hungover world outside.

And then there were those occasions when we would jump into the car well after midnight to head to Paris, or Edinburgh, or just down to Dorset to watch the dawn break over the chalk cliffs, and eat hardboiled quail's eggs and cold cocktail sausages upon the dawnwet grass.

All this behind us, like beautifully aging wallpaper—not enough, it turned out for me, to frame a whole lifetime, but enough to dignify an awkward corner of it.

With what wonder I had once watched her go about her various tasks, my Barbara—digging the garden, mending a broken chair, sailing a boat, riding a horse, making notes in the margins of the clever books she read, the pile that lay always by her side of the bed, Nabokov's *Lectures on Literature*, Barthes' *Michelet*, *Suicide and Despair in the Jacobean Drama*, books that would never have held my attention beyond the first few pages, how I marveled at the rate she consumed them and yet found time to maintain her teaching job, keep our home in order and cook delicious meals. Had I not loved her once? Deeply, indeed, and yet not in any way that challenged any fiber of my being, for it was tarred right from the start by the ordinary sweetness of human interaction instead of by the nectar of the gods.

Dearly beloved Barbara, even in leaving me, she took pains for it be swift and utterly lacking in confrontation. I had come home for lunch, as I often did for it was only a short walk from the Consulate. She was not there so I had eaten alone, was washing my hands when I heard the door open, and knew immediately—as one does—that something was not quite as it had been before. Her face was pale and she carried a small bamboo vase in her hand, she did not speak to me but walked into the bedroom and sat down upon the bed.

I've got to get back to the office, I said.

She did not reply.

What is it? I asked.

I'm sorry, Max, she said, I think I have reached the absolute end of the line.

That was all. I picked up my briefcase, kissed her quickly on the forehead and rushed away. When I returned from work, she was waiting with her packed bags beside her.

Are you really leaving me? I asked.

What does it look like? she said.

Can't we talk about it later? I said.

No, she said, I have a train to catch in forty-five minutes.

We looked at each other sadly. I am sorry, Barbara, I said.

I know, Max.

The servants had started taking her bags down, and we followed them with a few of her smaller things. The little girl from upstairs skipped by us, smiling and waving, still in her school uniform. I remember thinking to myself that having children was something we might have done well together, and in the same instant being horrified that I might have consigned her to a life without children by my ridiculous inability to adapt to my fate.

Afterwards, I lived for a few weeks as if no substantial change had occurred in my life, I woke and ate breakfast, went to work, lunched often with Byron either at his home or at one of the clubs, played a lot of golf and tennis, met up again with Byron in the evenings, or—as was becoming more regular—with Damini and her radical friends. I hardly saw Ela, for never more than at that time did I want to worship her from afar. I knew she would be perplexed by my avoidance of her and some part of me also took a perverse pleasure in this, even though an other part of me hoped that she would see it as necessary after the fate that had befallen me—of being deserted without any real cause by my closest companion of fifteen years, no cause that would stand up in court at least. And then one day I bumped into her, just as the sun was setting in the February sky, we were both browsing at the same stall at the Calcutta Book Fair, I saw her and she saw me, and I came over to her—are you on your own? I asked.

She said she had indeed come alone, having time to kill between a rehearsal and an appointment with an old school friend at the Park Hotel.

Do you have time for a coffee? I asked her.

No, I'm walking there, so I should get going, she replied.

I'll walk with you then, I told her.

I'd like that, she replied.

And so we set off down the dusty avenue, the traffic noises insulating our scant conversation, she did not mention Barbara, and neither did I, what would I have said and what could she have said, knowing herself to be so central to the event and yet also so much outside? We spoke with the awkwardness of lovers meeting after many years rather than just a few weeks, but as we parted at the intersection of Park Street and Chowringhee, a wind rose, dull and red, seemingly sweeping us towards each other.

I love you, I said to her—words that had never before seemed necessary.

She smiled and bravely touched my cheek and then was gone, and in that moment a strange abyss opened in front of me into which I gladly fell, and there remained in an utterly piteous state, oscillating between deep remorse and futile desire until Byron, who could not bear to see me thus, whisked me off to Khajuraho for a few days in the hope that this might somehow settle me. He had arranged for a special pass so that we could enter the temple compound after dark, wander among the extraordinary stone carvings by moonlight, take refuge from our own enigmatic sins in their excruciating mystery. I will not forget Khajuraho, and how it honed the yearning in me to fine jade, the moonlight shining deep into the orifices of the temples, the glistening lizard coiled around a stone breast, and Byron Mallick singing over and over again a line from a Tagore song that he translated as: *sweet has become the anguish of separation on this beautiful night, the moonlight fills me with the music of unquenchable desire, and tender are the mirages that float upon my lids.* It was a curious magic, as intoxicating and unfulfilling as the charm of a midsummer night.

I came back from Khajuraho rejoicing in my solitude, for only in my solitude could I truly savor the precious architecture of my own obsession. I no longer awoke to the awful truth that I had caused Barbara so much pain, that we had not been able to weather such a period in my life as others surely did, many others who had agreed to set up a life together once. I consoled myself that if we had reached such an unspoken agreement, I would have been obliged to try and exorcise myself as rapidly as possible, and that was the last thing I wanted at the time.

Even now, as I recall the excruciating bliss of living each moment in the service of such a passion, my heart fills with a certain envy, as well as some pity for my condition. Ela's eyes followed me everywhere, her fingers were forever upon my arms and on my face, I filled my evenings with the poetry that we had shared within the hallowed walls of Byron Mallick's flat, I listened over and over again to the music that she had danced to, the dance dramas that she had brought to life, for me and countless others, none of whom could worship her as I did—in collusion with herself. I spent my time immersed in the possibilities of having her quietly observing me in my simplest tasks, like shaving or making coffee, of walking endlessly with her through ancient narrow streets, unfettered to our destinies, free to hold each other and to kiss with mature abandon in corridors and archways and under the open sky and finally return to our quiet hotel room to make love. How relieved I was to be able to indulge in such dreams without having to circumnavigate her angular despair when she finally packed her bags and departed, dear Barbara, and yet how I sternly I chose to ignore the fact that this was permanent, that she would never come back.

What none of us knew then was just how well she would do without me, that during a long trip to Kenya visiting friends to help get over the ruin of our marriage, she would meet the owner of a lakeside resort on Naivasha and spend the rest of her life with him, raising three boys, and sending me endless postcards full of genuine sympathy for the hash that I had made of my life.

As for her mother, Mary O'Reilly, she would never really let me exit her life—I was part of her brood, she never saw me any other way. After I returned to London, she would often show up at my cocktail parties in order to mingle with my motley collection of guests, for my life as a travel writer had quickly become cluttered with the sorts of people an existence of that kind naturally accrues, and she felt more at home among them than I. On one of these occasions, she met Byron Mallick, who by then had gained a firm enough foothold in international finance to regularly put up at a Mayfair hotel on his various trips to London. Usually, that sort of involution in my fate would have amused me, for I was still deep in the period of extended desolation that followed my return from Calcutta, when all irony was to be seized at like straws to a drowning man, and yet this did not please me, did not please me at all. I looked upon the regal shadows of Byron Mallick and the beautifully withered Mrs. Mary O'Reilly of County Cork and a shiver ran up my alcohol macerated spine. Their friendship had grown, thickened slowly and surely like some intricate rock formation that from certain angles was magnificent, yet from others faintly grotesque. And so he had become a regular visitor to her various homes, her house in Holland Park, the farmhouse in the Dordogne, the crumbling abbey she had purchased in a virtually unknown region of Italy, and most especially to her home in Cork, where she likes to spend her summers and also have her family congregate for Christmas. That she is currently heavily in debt to him is known to most of her friends and family, many of whom regard it as a perfectly reasonable arrangement.

—

Adrija sets down her ice cream spoon and yawns.

Let me take you to bed, suggests Piers.

Will you read to me? she asks him.

Of course I will, he replies.

The child takes a few sips from her glass of water, says good night to the rest of us, then walks away hand in hand with Piers, the dog Kimbhut tottering unsteadily behind after his absurdly privileged meal.

Nikhilesh and I are of an age where to go for a short walk after dinner greatly assists our digestion—you are welcome to join us, says Byron.

That's very kind, Byron, but I think I'll just stay here, I tell them.

When they have gone, I pour the remains of the Cabernet Shiraz into my glass and walk out onto the terrace, sit down upon a teak recliner and close my eyes in the hope that some kind of formless dark might enclose me for a while—until the child is asleep, and her grandfather and his friend have returned from their walk—when the real business of this evening might begin. But instead, like a shaft of music, there comes a memory of a winter afternoon in a crumbling schoolhouse somewhere near Howrah where Ela and I had sat and waited for a precious few hours while Damini judged an elocution contest, pressing the cold of a cracked inkwell to my fingers as we sat at separate desks, gazed at each other, and talked. We had been together, the three of us, to the Botanical Gardens, an arrangement that had been made the previous evening when Damini announced to us that she had to make the arduous journey to the other side of the river to judge the school contest, and I had gallantly offered to drive her there.

Why not combine it with a trip to the Botanical Gardens? Damini suggested.

Will you come? I asked Ela.

I will come, she replied.

And so we had set off after an early lunch, the three of us, with my driver, myself in the front seat and the two women in the back, the rearview mirror irritatingly tilted to occlude Ela from my view, so that each time she spoke upon our slow journey, her disembodied voice was all the more excruciating in its nearness. The Botanical Gardens were disappointing, overcrowded and littered, the grass dead and flat beneath our feet as we walked and walked, the two of us mainly in silence, while Damini spoke of this and that, her conversation encasing us like thin eggshell. We sat under a tree and ate some sweetmeats that Ela's mother-in-law had prepared for us, and then washed our sticky fingers with bottled water, I dried mine with a handkerchief but the women used the loose ends of their cotton saris, and then we walked back to the car, instructed the driver to take us to the school where Damini had agreed, as a noted journalist, to judge the contest. She told us to go, that she would be able to make her own way back, but I said we would wait, for nothing seemed more inviting than the somewhat sinister interior of the high-ceilinged classroom where I thought Ela and I could sit for a while. And so we waited, the cold creeping in around our ankles as the afternoon deepened, seated sideways at two sloping wooden desks, knees not quite touching, not daring to hold hands or kiss as we did so often by then in my own apartment, for Barbara had been gone now for a few months.

There in the gathering gloom, yellow-beaked mynahs flitting in and out between the tall bars of the windows, I asked her what I had never dared ask her before, although I already knew the answer. I told her I had decided to cut short my contract and leave Calcutta, move to New York and try again to be a writer. Would she come with me? I asked her.

I can't, she said.

I had always expected this moment to be perforated with anguish, and yet there was only an extreme tenderness, and a certain sense of liberty that we were not to be tethered forever to our passion, or to have to make excuses for its absence after it had faded.

She lifted open the lid of her desk and extracted from it a frail book—some sort of Victorian primer. She opened it to a page and read—*Curlylocks, curlylocks, wilt thou be mine. Thou shalt not wash dishes, nor feed the swine. But sit on a cushion and sew a fine seam. And feed upon strawberries, sugar and cream.*

Is that how you would like to keep me? she asked.

Yes, upon a velvet cushion, I said smiling. Upon a velvet cushion, for all my life.

And then we sat in sublime silence, each quite separately absorbed in the tragic grace of our situation, but closer to the other in those moments than we would ever be thereafter.

Damini returned and we drove back to central Calcutta, to Byron's flat, where he was hosting a cocktail party in honor of a friend's son who had just opened his first art exhibition at the Academy of Fine Arts. On previous occasions such as this, I had—naturally—quite studiously avoided Ela, but after what had just passed between us I felt no hesitation anymore in staying very close to her, which I did all the while, emboldened by the impermanence of our attachment. I spent the evening staring into her eyes. Presently Arjun arrived, clearly exhausted, and she drew away from me to join him and some of their other friends. I continued to watch her from afar, wondering what it was within ourselves that entwined us so completely that the prospect of hacking free was as desirable as being engulfed within the tendrils of our passion. Soon they wandered off, brilliant and self-possessed, a group of men and women on the threshold of their thirties or just having toed across, they drifted laughing into the night, Arjun clearly having been revived by his two whiskeys, they went forward into the raucous city just as the last birds came to roost upon the tired neon-scarred trees.

A few weeks later, I kissed her goodbye between packed boxes piled high in the living room of my flat in Calcutta, the cardboard jungle offering us more anonymity than anywhere we had found ourselves before, that and the knowledge that we were unlikely to meet again. I could not stop kissing her, nor she prevent herself from returning my kisses. Finally we had found a way to segregate our desire from our past and our future but we did not make love, perhaps because we played by a different set of rules then, or perhaps because of the everlong aftertaste of ecstasy already upon our lips. All that was left to do was to kiss and kiss and rejoice in the salt of each others' tears.

I left for London, and two years passed without any communication between us. And then one day, Byron rang with this request:

Ela will be in London next week to give a few performances. Can I trust you to look after her while she is there?

I stayed silent, my heart pounding in the most conventional way possible.

I know how you feel about her, Max, so don't use that as an excuse, said Byron.

I closed my eyes, the precious pain more stark within me than ever.

Byron, I would do anything to see her again, I told him.

Well you shall, it seems, without very much effort on your part, responded Byron Mallick.

And so a few days later, I had found myself navigating my way with some difficulty towards the hall in North London where she was performing, arrived nonetheless in good time and had not been able to resist seeing her straight away.

Max, is it you? she asked, as I pushed open the door of the dressing room where she sat masked in paint, holding in her hand Byron's note explaining why I instead of him would be there.

Could you not have waited until after the performance? she said.

I needed to know that you knew I was there in the audience, I replied.

Oh, Max, you are always there in the audience for me, she said.

You will ruin your makeup, I warned her.

Just one tear, Max.

I wiped it carefully off her cheek with a tissue. I wish I could kiss you now, I said.

You can kiss me later, she said.

And so I did when I dropped her off at her hotel after the performance, I kissed her then, but my lips were still too stiff with longing for such an act to grant us any ease, I kissed her nonetheless and then drove back home, with another few moments to fold and let flutter down into the cavern of her absence in my life.

I had persuaded her to let me drive her to her uncle's house in Birmingham the following day, instead of simply putting her on a train as Byron had suggested. I telephoned from the lobby of the hotel and she asked me to come up to her room, which was not what I expected, indeed I knew not what else to expect as I walked down the padded corridor like a man about to reenter one of his own discarded dreams. I realized that Byron had arranged for her to occupy his usual suite, and so there we were once again upon his territory, prepared to take further risks with our lives and ourselves.

Do not think I woo thee, angel! Should I do so, you would not be moved, so full of conflict is my cry. Against such utter counter force you cannot prevail. My call is like an open hand thrust out to seize, to defend, to warn off—while you, unattainable, recede far beyond its grasp.

On the dressing table stood an open bottle of champagne in its nest of ice, two glasses beside it, only one of them upturned—Piers was here earlier, she explained.

It's how he likes to start the day, I agreed.

I have not had any yet, she confessed.

Well, let us have some now, I suggested.

So that you can take advantage of me afterwards?

Precisely that, I said, feeling the gravel of my voice sinking deep into her.

And what was the quality of her surrender? Not to me but to the inevitability of our flesh coming together as this, where before the twistings of hot wind between us had been enough, what was the quality of her surrender but an utter sweetness, leaving me each time with the feeling of tipping the water out of a vessel of great simplicity just so that I may have the pleasure of filling it over and over again. And afterwards, it was as if we had been gifted with the ability to add substance to each other by mere touch, palms no longer pressing against each other like glass to glass, I took a sequence of small country roads to Birmingham just so that I might let my hand rest against her when I pleased, we stopped at Coughton Court where she wanted to see the roses. Tell me you belong to me, I entreated her. That I cannot do, Max, she replied.

For the next three years she managed to be in London quite regularly, every four or five months or so, and I cluttered my life between her visits with anything that might distract me from her absence, traveling more and more to replenish my barrel of experiences lest I scrape it too low, filling my evenings with friends, mainly friends, and those few women whom I felt obliged to please after having invested in the motions of courtship as a possible antidote to my pain, my enduring pain—that cylinder of black stone in which I was encased, which I learned eventually to treat with the same respect as it, in fact, accorded me.

The first few times it was in the anonymity of the hotel rooms that Byron had secured for her that we would make love, but as our physical relationship became more dense, we found it easier to be in my apartment, where our ordinary movements could frame our desire. I wondered sometimes why it did not trouble her at all to be there within the very same walls where Barbara and I had once shared a kind of bliss, taking turns to prepare the hot chocolate with peppermint schnapps when one or the other of us had to stay up to finish an assignment. We both worked in freelance journalism then, although my heart was in writing a novel, as was hers in my writing it—sweet devoted Barbara who searched long within every string of words I put together for some evidence of a voice. All this of course was resolutely in the past, it did not even carry any meaning for Barbara when she visited me from time to time with little Justin, for in those days she frequently returned with him from Kenya to stay with her mother in Holland Park. Another man's son, Justin, cruising unsteadily between pieces of furniture that we had collected together, Barbara and I, spilling apple juice from his toddler cup upon the rug where she and I had once frequently made love, how little it mattered to either of us. Still, I had thought that Ela might feel uncomfortable here, be reluctant to let me give pleasure to her upon the bed that Barbara's grandmother had given us as a wedding present, for fear that this might scatter harsh breadcrumbs into the conviction that our love was permanent in our hearts. That mere death would never undo it we knew even then, but much else might—this also we knew, and were consumed, each of us in our own way, by this fear. And what can I say of this fear except that it became an old friend, so similar was it in substance to the anxieties of childhood, so lean and pure in muscle, so desirous of being cast in ordinary terms of victory and defeat and yet unable to anchor itself anywhere. To protect our love from it became my main concern, and the lengths to which I went to do this surprised me, and in the end, probably did us more harm than I could ever have imagined. There were times when I would choose not to meet her, send Piers instead of myself to take her to a party, or come to a performance and leave without seeing her afterwards, all bewildering to her. She bore all of this with infinite patience, but it must have eroded, very gently but inexorably, the core of her faith in me. I was lulled into believing otherwise by the increasing intensity of our lovemaking, not realizing that what was feeding it was panic rather than lust. The last time she looked into my eyes, I saw despair, but I chose to let it merge with her need to draw me within her, imagined that the tears upon her cheeks afterwards were of relief rather than farewell.

What are you thinking, my lovely? I asked her later, finding her standing half-dressed near my bedroom window.

I am thinking, she said slowly, that I have never been so happy as in knowing that you desire me.

And less so in its fulfillment, perhaps? I asked her, gently moving her hair away from her eyes.

Oh, Max… she said.

I'm sorry, I said, I'm just not sure what I am supposed to do with such a thought.

I do not care what you do with it with regard to me, she said, but I hope you will use it well for yourself, she said.

I will, my love, I will, I said, kissing her upon her neck, never knowing that these would be the last words she would hear from my lips for the next seven years.

It was Byron Mallick, who relished my heartache with almost the same intensity as I suffered it, it was Byron Mallick who first brought me the news that she was expecting a child. It was not something he welcomed particularly himself, for he was unsure of how it would affect her dancing career, the pinnacle of which she had—according to him—yet to reach.

But a woman's call to motherhood is fierce, Max, he said to me. That is why I never wanted any part of it, he added.

I thought then that I would never see her again, that it would be wrong for me to even desire it, thought also that perhaps this was the time to finally go back to New York. But I never did, maybe it was just that I could not bear to put another ocean between us, maybe it was that life in London had arranged itself around me comfortably enough by then, cradling my nervous energy as easily as my need for peace, maybe it was just that. And then with my next book, I appeared suddenly to cross some sort of threshold of recognition and was able to expunge from my life all but the most meaningful encounters, the truly rewarding journeys, and so felt in some ways more complete and fulfilled than before. Eventually, I even fancied I had completely rid myself of the chalky sludge of her absence, purged myself of the continuous feeling that she was not there to reach for and touch, to share my thoughts with, to advise me on the most trivial of matters, I felt myself growing more and more accustomed to the realization that she would never be where I had hoped to place her, somehow, once, although—even then, even before the child—it would have shattered her life to achieve this.

And yet I still wandered through spaces unknown to either of us, relying on my imagination to find some way of accommodating her there—once, after a reading at a small campus university in the southwest of England, I walked for hours among the houses imagining her to be somehow ensconced there, no husband, only a child, a small sloping garden, glittery pink hairbands and miniature dolls' clothes scattered among the many precious objects that traced their history upon the broad sill, I looked through such a window and felt neither like an intruder nor a welcome guest, and regretted afterwards having subjected myself to such a blankness.

—

I drain my glass and inhale the sharp salt of the coastal breeze that blows towards the house, soon a dense darkness will fall and the sea will melt into the sky, as all things will, given time, our past and our future, the real and the unreal, what matters and what does not matter, those whom we loved and those whom we did not love, the flower that bloomed and filled our garden with its perfume and the flower that fell with the storm and was crushed into the mud.

In the distance are the two figures of Byron Mallick and Nikhilesh returning from their short postprandial sojourn. Nikhilesh stumbles and Byron reaches out to steady him. Once they had walked through fields and fields of rice paddy in the noonday sun, Nikhilesh was the stronger of them then, hardy from his outdoor existence, while Byron was pale and thin and prone to all manner of afflictions. How terrified he was of the cuts and bruises he would inevitably acquire from the most ordinary thorns and nettles, the insect bites that accumulated on his fair elbows and ankles, but Nikhilesh was always patient, always able to suggest a remedy—like rubbing the juice of one plant to neutralize the poison of another, or pinching his big toe to rid himself of pins and needles after they had crouched for hours under a tree to avoid a rainstorm.

They come towards me across the shadowy lawn, walking very slowly and talking softly to each other in Bengali. I wonder what Byron can be saying to Nikhilesh and as they draw near, I judge from its cadence that it is poetry, something no doubt that meant much to them in their youth, pulled out and laundered by Byron Mallick to sheath him in his new state of sorrow, the words clink together like soft bones in my head as they approach.

Not too hot an evening, eh, Max? says Byron, halting by the terrace steps.

No, not too hot.

He breaks off a few leaves of a plant that seems to be growing in abundance along the terrace wall, and gives it to me to smell.

Salicornia, he says, supposed to be good to eat.

I think it's what we called pickleweed, I tell him.

How well I remember tramping around saltmarshes on school trips, crushing the stuff underfoot.

We irrigate it with seawater, says Byron.

I believe the British call it glasswort or samphire, says Nikhilesh.

It has many names, those who regard it as a culinary delicacy call it sea asparagus, but I have an entirely different interest in it, says Byron.

And what would that be? I dutifully ask.

The future of this region lies in salicornia, says Byron.

Really?

The seeds yield high quality edible oil, it can be used as raw material in paper and factories, and the dry remains can be crushed to make fuel briquettes.

I have eaten pickleweed, but I had no idea that it was so versatile in its uses, I tell him.

I intend to invest heavily in the large-scale cultivation of salicornia in this area over the next few years, he says.

Pickleweed farms?

Soon the whole world will be cooking with pickleweed oil, he says with the grainless conviction of a man for whom no market is too hard a conquest.

You never cease to amaze me, I tell Byron.

Is that true, he asks?

Yes, it's true, I tell him.

From upstairs, Piers's voice floats down, he is reading to Adrija—*he got an atlas of the moon for Christmas and he read it like a storybook*—I know the book, I have read it to Barbara's sons with tears in my eyes, its connection to my own experience of the moonlanding too intimate for me to bear quietly—*and then I think of those two astronauts and how the prints that they made with their big boots will still be there tonight, tomorrow night and every night for millions of years to come*—I shudder at the proximity of these precious words.

Byron excuses himself and disappears indoors but Nikhilesh lingers upon the veranda. Vargas brings him a hot drink of which he takes a sip and sighs.

Hot milk and brandy, he says, nothing better to soothe the soul.

Two years ago he had lost his wife to cancer, and now this—her beloved niece Damini found smashed upon a hillside.

Life is so painfully odd, Max, he says to me.

Never odder than at this moment, I reply.

He looks at me, his eyes sunk deep into his sallow face.

The rest is analgesia—for me anyway, he says with some kind of a laugh.

I cannot think of what to say in return, and am relieved when Vargas appears and suggests that he escort him to bed.

Goodnight, I say to Nikhilesh.

This will not be a good night, he slurringly pronounces. I wonder what sedatives Vargas might have dissolved in his potion, and pray that they will keep him in their tight embrace for a long while.

And as he is led off, I am suddenly abrim with those memories of hers that his daughter had thought fit to share with me of their life in Africa, of adventuring on hot tricycles with a gang of other five-year-olds upon sandy roads fringed with elephant grass, the Easter egg hunt that the Baptist Mission had organized where colored stones had replaced eggs, the bird that she had tried to revive which had died in her hands, how the tenderness of these lost experiences had infused our passion, once.

Nikhilesh halts halfway up the stairs, and looks back in my direction.

This will not be a good night, he warns me once again.

Byron returns to the terrace, looking calm and refreshed, having quickly bathed and changed into informal Bengali garb, there he is with a glass of iced water and his pipe in one hand and a book in his other.

Have you ever come across this painting of Omai? he asks me.

I take the book from him and survey the color reproduction—it depicts the Tahitian, unturbanned, gazing disdainfully in our direction while the eminent eighteenth-century naturalist Joseph Banks points a finger so close that he might as well be poking him, and another eminent naturalist, Daniel Solander, takes notes. The two of them had been on Cook's first voyage as part of the Royal Society contingent traveling to observe the transit of Venus. They had failed then to return with a native, but had had their request satisfied in due course when Cook came back from his second voyage with Omai. As it turned out, Omai in no time transformed himself from just another ethnographic specimen into an elegant and enchanting gentleman much sought after by London's high society, became an object of curiosity to the intellectuals and wits of the time—Johnson, Walpole, Hester Thrale, Fanny Burney—this I remember well, for who would not?

It is rather more interesting than the portrait by Reynolds, is it not? says Byron.

Of which I remember that Byron had a reproduction hanging in his flat in Calcutta, I ask him if it is still there.

Yes, it is still there, he tells me.

I hand him back the book.

Take it to bed with you, Byron urges, it is an interesting read.

I was not planning on retiring just yet, I confess.

You aren't going to stay up for her, are you, Max?

I am slightly taken aback by his directness.

I think we are both planning to stay up for her, says Piers, joining us from within.

Very well then, I shall arrange for some more sustenance, says Byron, beckoning to Vargas, who is coming down the stairs with a pile of sheets, presumably with the intention of making beds for us somewhere downstairs.

He gives instructions to Vargas, and then pulls up another recliner for himself to sit down upon, places his glass of water upon one broad arm and proceeds to fill his pipe.

Do sit down, he says to Piers.

I'm happier standing, says Piers.

Suit yourself, says Byron.

I certainly shall, says Piers.

Suddenly, the lights flicker and dim, and our ears are filled almost unnaturally by the sound of the sea.

Low tide, says Byron Mallick.

The voltage returns to normal, revealing Vargas to be waiting with a tray of fruit and chocolates. He leaves it on the parapet while he fetches two low tables—one for it and another for the selection of drinks he is about to bring.

I study the book that is still in my hands, it appears to be on the voyages of Captain Cook, although you could not really have guessed so from its title.

You should read it, says Byron, picking out a pomegranate from the pile of fruit in front of him.

I'll make sure to get it when I'm back in England, I tell him.

It's really rather fascinating, says Byron, did you know, for instance that James Burney, Fanny Burney's brother, that is, was 2nd Lieutenant on the ship that brought Omai to Britain?

No, I did not know that, I reply.

No wonder then that the Tahitian was a regular visitor to the Burneys' home, along with Johnson and Burke and Garrick and the rest of that crowd, all wedged for me into a hazy meniscus between British, Indian, and American histories, for I had never done my homework on the latter half of the eighteenth century as well as Byron's various acolytes—indeed, the first few times I was present at his salon I had been impressed by the ease with which they spoke of these fantastic figures in another country's past, as if they might recently have encountered them at a dinner party. Eventually I realized that they were the same anecdotes that circulated endlessly among them—over and over again I would hear how Johnson had been so poor at Oxford that someone had once left a pair of shoes outside his door, how Burke had once drawn a dagger and plunged in into a lectern at the climax of one of his passionate speeches before the House of Commons, after which Sheridan had said, "The honorable gentleman has brought his knife with him, but where is his fork?!," and how all of them had thought *Evelina* was written by a man, all except Joshua Reynolds, who said he would give fifty pounds to sleep with the author, who turned out of course to be Fanny Burney, assistant keeper of the robes to the queen and chief chronicler of the trial of Warren Hastings, a "*miscellaneous hearer*" she had called herself—able only to grasp Edmund Burke's clever allusions "*as far as they were English and within my reach*," phrases I still remember, perhaps because they were so often repeated to me then by Byron, like lines of a poem in which he was constantly immersed.

There was a half-sister, you know, who was also an authoress, says Byron.

No, I didn't know that, I reply.

Sarah Harriet was her name, says Byron, James Burney had a love affair with her, lived with her in very miserable circumstances for five years before returning—on her insistence—to his own wife and children. All this while the Burneys pretended that separation between James and his wife was amicable, and that Sarah Harriet was simply living with him to keep house.

Always the easiest thing to cover up—incest, says Piers.

Sarah Harriet wrote five novels, says Byron, supported herself that way—even paid her medical bills from her royalties, tried to live in Italy for a while but could not afford it—ended up spending her last years in a boarding house in Cheltenham.

Carry on, says Piers, this is mesmerizing.

Jane Austen loved her works well, says Byron, yet no title for her of "the mother of English fiction" as Virginia Woolf would accord over a century later to her half-sister, Fanny—no, not for Sarah Harriet, just an unmarked grave in a Cheltenham cemetery and a liaison with her half-brother, the dashing Captain James Burney, to—only barely—keep her name alive.

There is a great industry now, is there not, in these side chains of literary phylogenies? says Piers.

Is there anything in this world, Piers, that you have not learned to dismiss? asks Byron.

Yes, there is, Byron, there is—gross moral turpitude, for example—says Piers.

I wonder what you can mean, says Byron, I do wonder what you can mean.

The lights blink out again and the night fills with the roar of the waves, becoming ever distant as the sea retreats—it will be almost dawn before the tide turns and the waters come rushing back in great fury, slapping against the sea wall that they have built in the town center and fanning in a wide arc upon the semiprivate beach beyond the garden wall.

Vargas reappears with a jug of cold water on a silver tray, a linen napkin neatly folded over it.

Can I get you anything, else, sir? asks Vargas.

I'm sure these boys would like some of that nice brandy that Monsieur B. sent us, says Byron.

The electrical power returns to normal as Vargas comes back with an outrageously expensive bottle of brandy and some glasses and yet another low table to place them upon.

I'll be in the kitchen for another hour or so, sir, if you need anything else, he tells us.

Thank you, Vargas, says Byron.

Piers picks up the bottle of brandy and examines it with a smile.

Are you trying to bribe us, Byron? he asks.

Worse than that, says Byron, I'm trying to make you like me again.

I've never liked you, says Piers.

Are you certain about that? asks Byron.

As sure as sure can be, says Piers.

Byron picks up a pebble that has been lying on a card table beside him and holds it like an egg in his hands.

Do you really believe any of this, Max? he asks me suddenly.

Something in his tone strikes me as vaguely pleading, this is almost as unendurable to me as his previous defiance, and for some reason I pray that in the moment of his inevitable disgrace he keeps his composure, as I prayed many years ago visiting him in a smart Calcutta clinic after a minor operation on his knee, I stood outside the door of his sickroom with the basket of fruit that Barbara had given me to take to him, praying that I would not have to see him in a state of any weakness for I was not sure how our friendship would accommodate it. But, in fact, he was as regal as ever in his invalid state, giving orders to the clinic staff with an easy grace. Indeed there was something remarkably cozy about the situation, Byron sitting up in bed in his silk dressing gown, peeling tangerines to share with me, and myself upon a chair at the other end of the small room, the two of us engaged in delightful conversation, and some part of me wishes that no less a plush incarceration await him now rather than the stark jail cell I am beginning to see in my mind, harsh lights fouling the burnished silver of his bent head.

My voice shakes as I reply—I really do not know, Byron.

Always the path of least resistance for you, Max, is it not, always the coward's way, to believe or not to believe, to love or not love, eh, Max? says Byron Mallick.

Was it cowardice, then? Was it cowardice that allowed me one day to rise and shake off all thoughts of her, unchoke my veins of that immemorial sap before life became something devoid of all sensation but the need to be with her? Was it cowardice, then, that took me to Hyde Park that morning in my running shoes to leave my hollow footprints upon the frosty grass, suck in the bitter cold, and run and run, until I arrived spent at the statue of Prince Albert, and there, as if supplicating to some deity, sacrificed my passion for her so that I might live again?

Piers O'Reilly folds his arms and looks straight into Byron Mallick's eyes.

You do not seem to be aware of the extent of evidence against you, he says.

What evidence? asks Byron.

I believe they are mainly in the shape of tape-recorded conversations…

Which are inadmissible in court, says Byron.

But very interesting to the newspapers, particularly the ones that you do not own, says Piers.

They have been manufactured, you must know that, says Byron.

Soon all the world will know that the roses that you smell are actually made of cellophane, says Piers O'Reilly.

"I looked up at the orator in a reverie of wonder, and during that space I actually felt myself the most culpable man on earth," quotes Byron.

What was that? asks Piers.

Just something Warren Hastings said of Burke, replies Byron.

You flatter me, says Piers.

I know, says Byron Mallick.

Can this be the man whom I once held so dear? whose first phone call from his hotel room in London would be to me? and first evening invariably spent over a bottle or two of wine in my living room crowded with the masks and figurines that Barbara and I had acquired in our happy years in Kenya, none of which she had ever wanted back.

Maps were my other passion, and my walls were thick with these—it was exactly as you might want a travel writer's den to look, much to the delight of those who were eager to shoehorn me into this role, and maps were what Byron brought me as gifts, maps that increased each time in rarity and value, so much so that eventually I became uncomfortable with the whole ritual. These should really be in a museum, I told him of the last lot of exquisite hand-painted relief maps of Sikkim that he offered me.

You think so? he said.

I think so.

And what about this one? he asked, gesturing towards a particular favorite of mine, from Gujarat in the nineteenth century, showing in fair and accurate detail the nearby lay of the land, but representing Europe as three circular entities comprising England, France, and "other hat-wearing countries."

Yes, that as well, I tell him reluctantly.

Why, Max, why?

It is just the responsibility of having these in my personal possession—an enormous responsibility, don't you think?

Very well, then, he said, folding up his gift and putting it away in his large Gladstone bag.

It was a turning point, from that moment on the magic of our friendship began slowly to dissolve. In time, we both became reconciled to the fact that things would never be the same again between us, but this—who could possibly have foreseen that it would come to this?

Byron pours himself a glass of water from the jug that Vargas had brought out to me hours ago, which still rests tepid but linen-lipped upon the parapet, he takes a small sip and then tips the rest into a potted camelia.

I assume that it is Arjun Mitra who is at the bottom of this? he asks.

He is making his way back from Darjeeling as we speak, says Piers.

With the evidence?

With the evidence, Piers reassures him.

Byron Mallick places his empty glass on the broad arm of his chair.

Am I to be given the chance to defend myself? he asks.

Probably not, says Piers.

And why?

Because you have a strange habit of wriggling out of difficult situations, Piers replies.

Well then, you tell me, what would satisfy you boys? he asks.

His tone is no different than that he had used many years ago to ask us where we would like to go when I first brought Piers to meet him in his flat in Calcutta. Piers was on his way to Bangkok, to teach English, having rather belatedly joined the "Princeton in Asia" program, for his social life in London had begun to pall a little with many of his friends marrying and moving to the country, and seriously engrossing themselves in producing and raising children. Bangkok seemed a worthy excuse to abandon all of those endless luncheons with talk of colic and teething, and the right instruments with which to puree carrots to their infants' liking, the relative merits of the preparatory schools that they had been put down for, how wonderful Bangkok with its perfect cuisine and its ladyboys and women blowing darts out of their vaginas had seemed at that juncture to Piers O'Reilly.

Also it meant that he could stop and see us on his way out, it was Piers's first visit to Calcutta, and he was suitably excited. For me this was a relief, as I had begun to be somewhat weary of Barbara's rather sour attitude towards the new interest in the city and its rich past that Byron had recently instilled within me. I looked forward to sharing some of my enthusiasm with Piers, but felt that Byron—only Byron—could be our rightful guide. Barbara had feigned a headache when we told her that we were invited to lunch with Byron and then to spend the afternoon with him touring Calcutta, and so we had left her at home with a pack of ice upon her brow and an easy novel to read.

I had thought we might go first to the Marble Palace but Byron suggested the Calcutta Museum, and there amid the heavy dignity of neglect, I observed a new dimension to his erudition unfold. He spoke with a gentle and calm authority in a manner that almost excluded me from his refined intercourse with Piers, and I had the distinct sense that he considered him more of an intellectual equal than I, who had studied such a prosaic subject as chemistry at university and perhaps even more than this, that it was from the New World that I hailed rather than the Old. I felt most miserable by the end of the afternoon, but my equilibrium was restored somewhat by Byron confessing to me later, over a gin and tonic at the Calcutta Club, that he had been a little surprised at how many obvious gaps there were in Piers's knowledge of art history. Piers had gone for a quick swim in the pool and when he returned, his dark hair clinging wet against his pale forehead, I felt reassured that although he was better placed to be a captive audience to Byron Mallick, I was still the one who could fulfill that role to his satisfaction.

And now here we are, in a different century, the tables in some measure turned, myself in the shadows struggling to absorb this, and Piers holding Byron in his slate gaze as he crushes his cigar on the parapet.

So I am not to be given the chance to defend myself? repeats Byron.

Most definitely not, replies Piers this time.

Byron Mallick's beautifully sculpted lips curl into a smile.

Just imagine, he says, just imagine what havoc this might create if you were to air your suspicions in public. Just imagine the distress to the family, the further trauma to the child…

There is a price for every truth—but this is not the one we intend to pay, says Piers.

So what is your solution then? asks Byron.

I think your best option is to quietly disappear, says Piers with a charming grin.

I have not "quietly" done anything for a very long time, Byron replies in a voice that is almost dreamy.

Well, here's your chance, says Piers.

You are no doubt just as familiar as myself with the

possibilities around here, Piers, what would you recommend? asks Byron Mallick.

Well, said Piers, it's a warm night—I thought we might go for a long walk on the beach.

So you want to drown me? asks Byron congenially.

I thought you might prefer to drown yourself, says Piers.

Byron Mallick gets up and walks over to an ornate Victorian mirror on the wall and straightens it.

Do you know how much money your mother owes me, Piers? Byron asks.

Oh, loads and loads, Piers replies.

And who will continue to pay her debts if I am gone?

Who will indeed, I wonder?

You do not care about your mother, do you? says Byron.

Who does? asks Piers O'Reilly.

Between Mary and Piers O'Reilly I have watched that gap yawn very suddenly, like the closed lips of a wound mischievously pulled apart, that sudden distance between mother and son. When I met him as an undergraduate, he would break off whatever he was doing every evening at six to telephone her, his mother—Hullo, Mary, he would say, kicking his young heels like a colt—and then some inane conversation would follow from which he would clearly draw sustenance, that was how it was then. And now, almost thirty years later, now it is I who will phone her to remind her that it is his birthday, and that she might remember to find some gap in her turgid social calendar in which to telephone him to wish him well. Mothers—never do I regret that I have been spared this transformation in mine, who keeled over at the age of sixty at a pacifist rally, still full of love for me. In those that survive longer, it is as if those seeds that were half sown, half a century ago, suddenly wake and rage, obliterate all but what they might have been when they had instead submitted to this other life. And so it is with Mary O'Reilly, who feeds her insomnia with oysters and champagne and the company of wanderers, so it is with Mary O'Reilly, that her duty to her son is now a stain of dried mercury, once bold and consuming, now a mere scar.

What you face is the death penalty, Piers says to Byron, lighting another slim cigar.

The death penalty, eh?

Not to mention the disgrace.

I have faced worse, says Byron Mallick.

For yes, he has, arrested in 1967 for shoplifting in Holloway, an act of which he was at the time wholly incapable. Facing the alternatives of simple suicide or dreary defense, he had chosen and succeeded in the latter. Many years later, he and I had gone there together, found the responsible employee and ensured that he went home that evening without a job to return to the following day, a man now in his late fifties, fully signed up to multiculturalism and all of that, his grandchildren cappuccino-colored, but himself still with a past, a past that included Byron Mallick sitting in his boarding house and contemplating ending his life. I was not sorry to see that revenge as a dish eaten cold, even though the change in the man's personal attitudes might not have quite justified it.

You have faced worse? mocks Piers.

Very much worse, Byron confirms.

In what way? Piers challenges him.

It was I who thought to take my own life then, says Byron.

In 1967, sitting in his dimly lit rented room, still in the overcoat within which he had supposedly concealed a plastic-wrapped pork pie before inconveniently dropping it while exiting the shop, it was he whom the security guard had detained rather than the young woman in a short yellow raincoat scuttling away with her arms crossed over her chest, it was he who had been searched rather than the sour-smelling pensioner who had emerged exactly at the same time with him from the shop, and on the side of the door that the pork pie had fallen, in 1967. Byron Mallick had seriously considered taking his own life, so much simpler a solution than battling for his reputation against such odds, and then his eye had fallen upon a letter left by his landlady on his desk, he had recognized Nikhilesh's handwriting and opened it, pulled out first a photograph, the first that he had been sent of Ela, hardly two years old, pouting at him, and holding it in his hands Byron had wept, wept, and wept in his cold English room until the cabbage frowst had condensed in whorls upon its glossy surface. Someday she will need me, he had thought, someday she will need me, and if I do not fight my case, I will not be there.

So, best then if I disappear? asks Byron.

Best indeed, says Piers, the rogue tide…

But who will clear my name if I am not alive? asks Byron.

We will see to it that your name is never sullied, promises Piers.

And I am to trust you on that?

You speak as if you have a choice, says Piers O'Reilly.

Choice, yes, it was choice that had suddenly made itself clear that November evening in 1967, and eagerly he had grabbed it then, how boldly he had ventured into the magistrate's court and shredded the arguments against him, how profusely they had apologized afterwards as if to a foreign dignitary whom they had mistakenly offended, how delightfully hardened he had felt afterwards, as if his insides had been sprayed with steel, he had walked into a jewelry store and purchased an antique brooch and sent it by secure airmail to his mother.

No one will know, tempts Piers, not a soul.

That I have been carried away on the neck of a graceless wave? says Byron.

You shall be remembered as one who possessed beauty without vanity, strength without insolence, courage without ferocity, and all the virtues of man without his vices, promises Piers.

Enough of this nonsense, says Byron Mallick, I have a very early appointment at a nearby factory, he explains.

Formula milk, perchance? asks Piers.

Actually, yes.

No chalk?

No chalk this time, this is for export, he replies without batting an eyelid.

More bespoke ethics, eh? I find myself saying.

Better than flatpack, replies Byron Mallick.

—

We remain, after he has gone, upon the terrace, Piers and I, waiting for Ela to arrive. I know that it is Piers's intention to leave straightaway when she does, bundle the sleeping child in the car and drive off. I suppose we will also wake Nikhilesh and offer him the choice of coming with us. Arjun's driver is sleeping on a charpoy in the garage, Piers has already warned him that he may be woken up any time and asked to take us back to Calcutta.

More brandy? Piers asks.

Why not, I say, holding my glass out to him.

He takes it from me and clumsily fills it, sucks the splashes off his fingers as he hands it back.

Where the hell is Ela? he says, examining his wristwatch.

She had set herself a difficult task today, I remind him.

What do you mean?

I was under the impression she was intending to visit a number of people to invite to the funeral whom she had no means of contacting any other way.

And how did you come to be under this "impression"? asks Piers.

I saw her last night.

When?

She turned up after you left to meet your film director.

You didn't tell me, says Piers.

I didn't see any reason to—until now.

No, of course not, he agrees.

For she had indeed come, Ela, late last night, after I had dined with Piers and retired to my hotel room, giving up hope of seeing her until the morrow, or perhaps the day after, or perhaps not at all until the funeral on Wednesday. Piers had gone off to meet some young filmmaker whose acquaintance he had made on one of his several recent visits to Calcutta. I had just mixed myself another rum and coke from the ample supplies of the mini-bar when I received a call from the lobby to say that she was there.

I'll come down, I told them.

And yet I did not rush, for some reason I did not rush. I downed my rum and coke, but not in a single gulp, put on my sandals, then took them off again, put some socks on and then put on my sandals again, and finally ventured out of my room to go downstairs and meet her.

She was sitting in the lobby, her hands folded in the lap of her crumpled white sari, she looked flushed and tired, she had clearly had a very long day.

It is very good of you to come, Ela, I said to her.

She stood up and looked full into my eyes.

I said I would, did I not?

I reached out to take her hand.

You do not have to keep all your promises to me, I told her.

We had first retreated to the hotel bar, had a few drinks sitting on stiff tartan-clad chairs, our knees at a polite distance from each other. She explained that her father and daughter were in Digha, where Byron had thought it best for them to be at this time, and that her husband was in Darjeeling still, trying to close the police case on this matter.

Surely there is nothing to investigate here? I said.

Suddenly, she began to sob, great soft sobs that I longed, as they emerged, to roll upon my tongue.

Let's go to my room, I said to her, let's please go to my room, where I can at least hold you.

I signed for our drinks and then we left the bar, took

the elevator to my floor. Finding ourselves alone in it, I told her:

You realize, do you not, that my life has been robbed of all meaning for not being with you?

Not quite as much as mine, she answered.

More meaning there to be robbed, I conceded.

We walked down the corridor to my suite, knowing that once we were inside we would fall towards each other. I shut the door and locked it, then drew her to me and kissed her on her forehead, I could feel her thoughts dodging each other like blocks of old ice, I kissed her eyes and then her lips, kissed her and kissed her, as if drinking my last, even though her lips were stiff with bewilderment, her arms lay numb at her sides.

And then suddenly she began to return my kisses, perhaps in spite of herself, she returned my kisses, and they were as vague and voluptuous as the thickening night.

We heard footsteps outside and I waited—although I don't know why—for them to die away before I began to unwrap her, I had been waiting seven years for this moment, I could not be expected to maintain any kind of decorum, not even at a time like this, not even at a time like this.

She stood bared down to her underclothes in the scant lamplight, suddenly immobilized again, perhaps by my haste.

Should I not be doing this? I asked her.

She did not reply.

I don't want to make things worse for you, I told her.

Oh, Max, she said.

How intriguingly the years had altered her body, I ran my hands over her breasts, tenderly disfigured by motherhood, and yet still proud and needy in my touch. Her belly was as taut, but had the feel of a cloth that knows it can shrink no further, I could spend the whole night exploring her—perhaps, I heard myself thinking, perhaps—with god's grace—I will.

What started as a gentle but inexorable need to caress each other was churned as often into moments of frenzy as the night passed, over and over again we felt that we might now part but did not.

No one will know in this confusion where I am, of course, she said, in a voice riven with guilt, when I asked her if she could stay with me all night.

Please stay with me this one night, I begged her.

She sat up and said nothing, I could feel the silent tears that were coursing down her cheeks, tears into which many griefs were mingled and were all the more tender to me for this. I pulled her back down again and held her as she wept into the pillow, kissed her forehead, her hair.

Have you been happy, Max? she asked me.

I gave that up long ago—the desire to be happy, I told her.

How pliant is her flesh in this time of great sorrow, how easily I am enclosed by it, often it feels as if we are gliding upon the peaks and the valleys of this passion, never really settling anywhere, but then we thud straight into such truths as only she and I can taste of each other, and know that it is not we who have shaped this love, rather this love that has determined us.

There is something I have never told you, she said suddenly, sitting up again.

Perhaps this is not the time to tell me then.

Do you fear that you might not forgive me?

No, that is not the reason.

I need you to tell me I did the right thing, she says.

By not bringing a child of ours into this world?

Did you know, Max?

Not until this moment.

I took her in my arms, of course it was the right thing, I reassure her.

I wish I could be so sure, she said, shaking badly.

Let us not allow these things to interfere with this moment—the life that we did not live together, the children we never had—let us leave them aside for the moment, I pleaded.

You have no idea how painful it has been to be without you, she said.

Well, you are with me now, I replied.

Towards daybreak she dressed herself but did not leave, we lay together and talked of Damini, our memories merging and diverging, and this nocturnal episode taking on the contours of a private wake.

I feel as if I am adrift without her, said Ela.

Surely you have many other things to anchor you in this life? I said.

Much to anchor me, but very little to guide me, she replied.

Where is it that you are going, anyway?

That is exactly what I do not know, she said.

How deeply aroused I was by this vulnerability, a side to her I had never seen before, I drank of it without hesitation. I am so sorry, my darling, I told her, I am so sorry, so sorry.

That such a bond would grow between them she had not imagined when Byron put her on the train to Durgapur to spend her Christmas holidays with them—her mother's eldest brother, recently returned to Bengal, and his wife and daughter, her cousin Damini, none of whom Ela had ever met. Indeed she had felt rather forlorn as the train chugged out of the station and Byron, having waved to her and quickly walked away, it seemed to her that he was rather relieved to be rid of her for a while. It was an unpleasant journey, at the end of which she was spat out from the compartment onto the platform with her huge suitcase, and there he was, in his meticulously pressed clothes, her uncle, what *have* you got in there? he had teased her as if he had known her all her life. Nothing much, she replied. It was the only item of luggage she possessed other than a small carry-on bag for her airplane journeys. When they arrived at their home, her aunt was in the garden staring into the branches of a tall tree with a worried look on her face. Ela heard her pleading with her daughter, please come down Mini, look, your cousin is here. And down she had come like the spirit of the ancient tree, her long dark limbs uncoiling to lower her to the ground. She smiled at Ela and gave her head a shake, a torrent of hair cascading over her shoulders which she quickly gathered up again into a knot, and said, come and help me feed the kittens, they must be starving by now. These were some motherless strays that she had rescued and found a home for in a corner of the servants' quarters. She had gone calmly into the bustling kitchen and asked the cook for leftovers, poured some milk from a simmering pot into a deep saucer, blowing upon it as she walked to cool it down for the creatures.

Can you play badminton? she asked Ela.

Not very well.

That's a shame. I really need to practice for the tournament tomorrow.

Ela had never met anyone whose concerns were so entirely physical, even the feeding of the cats seemed to be dictated by some basic recognition that all animals required nourishment, rather than any appreciation of their extreme attractiveness. As Damini busied herself with apportioning their food, Ela knelt down on the dusty courtyard and attempted to offer them some affection. Already, they were a team.

How pleasantly those days had passed, cycling around the leafy "colony," as they called the little oasis that housed the staff of the factory to which her uncle had recently been appointed general manager, lounging at the clubhouse, playing table tennis and board games indoors and badminton outside, sometimes by floodlight, on those crisp evenings.

Their differences too had almost immediately declared

themselves. Ela clearly enjoyed, very demurely, the attentions of the teenage boys—the looks they cast in her direction, their awkward attempts at striking up some sort of conversation—and Damini found this utterly deplorable. She also did not like how easily Ela endured the many girls whom she found to be an utter waste of time, never understand how she could engage with them in conversation about clothes and foreign pop stars. Once she had found her playing Monopoly with a gaggle of them and stormed off—how could you possibly enjoy such a stupid capitalist game? she had demanded of her later, such a stupid greedy game?

Ela was never critical of Damini but there was one habit of hers that she could not understand. When she was quite young her father had taught her to shoot, and the need for this seemed to live in her blood—every morning she would stride off with her air rifle and usually come back with a pigeon or two that she would proceed to gut herself on the veranda. It seemed so much at odds with Damini's love of animals, all this blood and feather and gizzards strewn over the concrete floor, but Ela did not try to understand it then.

Also at the time she found somewhat macabre her cousin's taste in art and literature. She relished horror films, mainly in elegant black and white, and dragged Ela to see these often after she moved to Calcutta and became acquainted with the sorts of people who would get her tickets to the little theaters where they were playing—"Les Diaboliques," "Nosferatu"—how strangely they chilled her, not so much in their content but the pleasure with which

Damini watched them, as if they connected her to a world, not this world, to which she properly belonged.

Even her favorite poem was about death—a lament for a suicide—by Jibananda Das:

The postmortem room, that was where you were taken
Last night, a spring night,
As the crescent moon, only five days old, took leave of the sky
You felt the desire to die.

How easily the words had returned to haunt Ela in these last weeks, echoing so much more than just her loss.

Do you think she might have killed herself, she said, pressing a carved wooden cheek into the hollow of my shoulder.

Why would she do a thing like that, my love? I asked.

Does one need a reason?

Surely, Damini of all people would have needed a reason.

Your wife was beside you, and your infant son,
There was love, there was hope—there was moonlight—
And yet, some phantom
Some phantom broke your sleep,
an absurd and important darkness lingered by the window,
an irresistible silence seized you by the throat,
Or was it that you had not slept in some time?
Well, now you will find generous sleep, now you will,
In the postmortem room

I would rather anything than that she might have taken her own life, she said to me.

It was an accident, Ela.

Arjun doesn't think so, she said, turning her bright tearful eyes to me.

What do you mean, he doesn't think it was an accident?

He has this crazy notion that she was killed, said Ela.

And you would prefer that to suicide?

I really do not know, she said.

Did the boughs of the old fig tree not protest
Did the fireflies not set up a commotion
Did the old blind owl not whisper this to you
As you knotted your noose:
Excellent!
Now that the wretched moon has set,
We can catch a few mice.

Is that why he is still in Darjeeling? I asked her.

Who, Arjun?

Yes, is that why he is there?

I don't know, said Ela.

I know, yes I know—
The love of a good woman—children—home—none of this is all
Neither wealth nor achievement, nor ease—
but a need for wonder
that plays in our blood
and tires us.

No such fatigue
In the postmortem room.
Yet still, every night, I stare upon the old blind owl
And with affection hear him say:
Excellent!
Now that the wretched moon has set,
We can catch a few mice.

I have to go now, she said, checking her watch.

She showed me a list of names and addresses of people that Damini had once helped scattered around the peri-urban fringes of Calcutta, whom she felt she needed to make sure could come to the funeral. Most of them did not have telephone numbers attached so she would visit them herself today, she said, as many of them as she could possibly find.

Will you let me come with you? I asked.

No, that would not be right, she said.

Why not? I have nothing else to do today.

It would not be right, she repeated.

I wondered suddenly if they too had been poisoned against me, saw me as an exploiter of their lives, their cares and sorrows, out of which no prose could lift them—not that prose on its own has achieved much for my life beyond the ability to keep the bills paid and the banks happy, but why expect any more from it than that?

She was still lying beside me in her crumpled clothes, holding the list of names and addresses in her hands, when I leaned over her and said—I want us to be together, Ela, perhaps not exactly now but eventually, I'd do anything to make that happen.

You know that can never be, Max, she replied.

But why not? I asked.

Because neither you nor I are prepared to ruin other peoples' lives, she said firmly.

We would not ruin anybody's lives, I assured her.

Be sensible, Max, she said, raising herself from the bed and disappearing into the harsh light of the day.

I lay there for a long time without sleeping, allowing myself to be encapsulated over and over again in the memory of the softness of her flesh and how it would harden to accommodate mine, feeling the iron of her desire for me rise and dissolve as it had all night, and then the starkness of her denial that there might be a life together for us somewhere in the future. How will I live past this? I wondered, what life is there beyond this for me that is not permanently stained with despair? How intensely vulnerable I suddenly felt, oh this ache, how unfaithful I had been to its memory. Part of me pleaded with myself not to surrender to it again, not to enclose myself once more within those bare brick walls in the hope that they might be flooded from time to time with an exquisite but utterly impermanent light.

Finally, I did find sleep, oily and thick, promising to enclose me deep into the day. But that was not to be for in less than two hours Piers would come barging in through the unlocked door—get up, Max, he would say to me, we have to go to Digha, we have to get down there straightaway.

Why on earth should we have to do that? I had demanded groggily.

I'll explain on the way there, he promised me.

It had better be a good one, I said, struggling out of bed.

Just do as I say, Max, said Piers O'Reilly.

The grandfather clock in the dining room chimes midnight, from time to time a breeze blows in from the sea bringing with it a faintly rotted yet tantalizing smell, like something vented from a restaurant next door.

I sink back in my chair, my head feels heavy, yet the rest of me stretched as if upon pin tacks, a need for some kind of sleep wells within me, I try and fight it off by lighting a cigarette, but it mainly burns to ash between my fingers, makes a small hole in the cover of the book on Captain Cook as I let it briefly slip, let myself be momentarily tugged into the depths of deeply desired oblivion.

Why don't you go and lie down for a while? suggests Piers.

No, no, I'll wait with you, I tell him.

You'll be more use, Max, if you've had even a few minutes of sleep.

Use? What does he mean? Of what use can I possibly be? Of what use have I ever been to anybody, including myself, including myself?

Just go and get a bit of rest, says Piers, I'll wake you up as soon as she arrives.

He pulls me up by the elbow and guides me towards the music room, where camp cots have been laid out for us and beds immaculately made upon them by Vargas. I lie down fully clothed upon one of them, gratefully bury my face against the clean cotton of the pillowcase. How I ache for her, how easily still is my flesh transported into the delight of her touch, how tightly my hopes clench around our recent encounter as though upon a note that might begin a new symphony. And yet perhaps, like me, she trembles at the thought of what might happen now, that we both might once again be plunged into that state of wild and beautiful desolation, that we might be called upon again to relinquish that small grace of being able to delight in ordinary things while our hearts are elsewhere, so very much elsewhere? The price of ecstasy, how patiently did she bear it, more patiently, surely, than I?

Where is she now, I wonder, none of us has been able to locate her, her mobile phone is inert—no doubt because she had failed to charge it last night, failed to charge it because she was with me rather than where she expected to be, last night. How has her day passed, going from household to household in mofussil towns and villages with invitations to Damini's funeral, those very same quarters that I had once visited regularly with Damini, feeling so often like a follower, a chela, of some saint. Not absurdly clothed in saffron with shaven head, but clothed nonetheless in some mixture of hesitation and despair that made me stand out as a pathetic being even to the people we had come to aid. They would try always to feed me, sticky hard sweetmeats and deep-fried savories that I could not in politeness refuse, besides which Damini would glare at me if I did, how my digestion suffered in those days, how little I cared that it did. Six years ago I had woven all these experiences, diffracted now through time into a book—and how she had hated me for it, Damini. And yet now I would not know anymore how to write such a book, all those mossy courtyards, tin pails clanking, stairs, endless stairs, and beds, rooms filled with beds, beds that we would perch upon as we were served tea—and sweetmeats and savories—while tales of extreme injustice were told and recorded, in all this all I really longed for was to be with Ela, nothing else, to simply watch her gathering up her troublesome hair from time to time so that I might kiss her upon her shoulder, to take the loose end of her sari and twist it in my palms like a mad washerwoman until it would twist no more. This, I felt they knew, the people we came to see, I felt always that they could sense that I would not be here otherwise, that my motives were never pure, never pure.

Perhaps she would have forgiven me, Damini, if she had felt that I accompanied her on these trips out of the goodness of my heart, or better still, certain stern moral convictions, perhaps she would not have taken against me so if she had not known that I came only because it was the easiest thing to do at the time.

How wretched I was then, yet how much I had gained from being so, many years later with the book that I made of these experiences coming finally to wide notice, not least because of her opposition to it, dear Damini, now dead.

Sleep, of course, will not come easily now, while I both fight and court it. I raise my face from the pillow and take in what I can of the room in the scant moonlight that filters through the slats of the shutters. The music room—that is what he had called it—why, I wonder, for it contains nothing but a tanpura, four-stringed and utterly sensual, not just in its form but in its compliance to other musical needs.

Where, I wonder, is that harp he had here, that harp from which Barbara had wrenched such clever music, where is the harp? How eagerly I cast about for its moonlit shadow, that it might eggslice my life now into manageable components, but there is no harp to be found.

Instead there are books, in this "music room" there are books, every wall is lined with bookcases, each full of books, serving gratefully to transport me to another time in my life when my parents had rented a house by a lake, where exactly I cannot remember, except that it was a different house than any that I had been in before, a different smell in it that at once beguiled me yet put me on my guard, and books, so many books, spilling out of every crevice and pleading with us to read them, even my seven-year-old sister was drawn to them, and I—yes, I—much of me was made there, I think. Here were books worth holding to one's nose between each paragraph, simply to inhale that quality of their pages that mere words could not impart, *ill-fated and mysterious man!—bewildered in the brilliancy of thine own imagination… once more thy for has risen before me!—not—oh not as thou art—in the cold valley and shadow—but as thou shouldst be—squandering away a life of meditation in a city of dim visions*, how such words filled my twelve-year-old frame and continued to tug away at me the rest of those years, while I tried to shoehorn my inclinations into the particular future that my parents had chosen for me, until I found ways to release myself from such a course, or should I say until he, Piers O'Reilly, showed me that there were other alternatives.

Piers O'Reilly, how proud I was to be within his inner sanctum, a distinction I had not acquired easily. For the first few weeks of our acquaintance he had treated me like an anthropological curiosity, a denizen of New Jersey yet possessed with the capacity to make him laugh. He had even consented to coming home with me for midterm break, and there too, in Fair Haven, had spent most of his time observing us, making mental notes, I felt, of our manners and customs, to insert later into his conversations in civilized company. Why did I tolerate him? Because I loved him, I suppose, and because I knew, like all children of recent immigrants, that these differences do not last.

For Christmas we each went our own ways—by which

I mean he to London and subsequently County Cork, and I back to Fair Haven and its nearby frozen shores. And for the first time, I realized what it was to miss somebody, yes, Piers O'Reilly was the first person I truly viscerally missed in my life.

On Christmas Day I woke up, my mouth filled with cardboard, treaded across the plastic strips set upon the white carpet of the living room for me to reach the family room from my own bedroom—a frenzy of reconstruction in the summer before I left for college having rendered me thus—and there they were, my mother and father and sister, waiting for me to open presents.

I'm sorry, I said, I shouldn't have had so much to drink last night.

Christmas Eve had been, as always, a time for my mother's Polish family to congregate at my grandmother's house, and this time I had been allowed to partake of the variously flavored vodkas for I was in college, Princeton University no less, how proud they were of me, how proud I was of myself despite my aching heart.

I returned to Princeton at the first opportunity, claiming that I had much work to do. How astonished I was to find Piers already there, lying on the lower bunk, reading Rilke.

Max, he said to me, I'm so glad you're back—my sister's here—she's dying to meet you.

At which point a wondrous creature emerged from our bathroom in a towel, her beautiful green eyes flashing, red hair cropped deliciously close to her skull, I am Barbara, she said, exuding beautiful steam, you must be Max.

Yes, I'm Max, I replied, extending my hand.

She shook it damply, I'm so pleased to meet you, she said.

Likewise, I answered, unable to check this bald response.

It's Barbara's birthday today, said Piers.

No, it's not, she said.

It is, said Piers, you are exactly seventeen and a half today.

That's not a birthday, said Barbara.

Well, it's enough of an occasion to eats lots and lots of caviar and get Mummy to pay for it, said Piers.

That I wouldn't say no to, she replied.

Well, put on your clothes quickly, there's a taxi coming in five minutes.

To take us where?

The Russian Tea Room, of course.

She grabbed a few things from what was obviously her suitcase and retreated again to the bathroom.

Will you come with us, Max? Piers asked.

If I am invited, I said.

Of course you are invited, said Piers.

Barbara stayed for a week, sleeping restlessly on our floor while I gazed down at her from the top bunk, and her brother snored happily below. How utterly beautiful she was, her pale Irish skin the highest quality of marble, her features small yet proud. She was almost as tall as myself, much taller than Piers, and moved with a broken elegance like an injured swan. I would have liked to touch her, to kiss her, to hold her all night in my arms, but that did not happen, not then. We took her to the airport, Piers and I, and still I did not kiss her, just placed my chapped lips upon her cheek, I hope I'll see you again soon, I said.

When Piers asked me if I would like to come to London for spring break I had no hesitation in accepting, even though I knew not at that point where I would find the money for the flight. I desperately longed to see Barbara again, I had found it hard to get her out of my mind, but it was not an absence that, even then, was tarnished by pain. I petitioned my grandmother, who said she was willing to pay for the trip as long as I sent her a postcard every day—which I did, I dutifully did.

And so early on St. Patrick's Day in 1975, we landed at Heathrow Airport, Piers and I, took the Underground train to Holland Park and hiked up the hill to the cream-colored terraced house that was their London home. And there she was as we lumbered in with our knapsacks, Barbara, cheerfully presiding over a row of champagne glasses, for the party had already begun, the house was full of people, Piers and Barbara's older sisters: Amanda and Georgina with their longhaired upper-class renegade boyfriends, and Anastasia—the eldest—who had married one of their second cousins, Edmund O'Reilly, and so elected to remain an O'Reilly all her life, and lived with him now on his estate in County Cork. Such happy agitation I had never experienced before, it pieced and repieced itself around me where I stood, as if in the center of a kaleidoscope, gazing at Barbara, who came forward and handed me a glass of what I supposed would be champagne.

I took a sip and almost choked, what is this? I asked.

Poor Max, she replied, have you never had a Black Velvet?

Never even heard of one, I confessed.

Guinness and champagne, she explained.

It's been around since 1861, said her brother-in-law, Edmund, slightly contemptuously, overhearing our exchange.

Leave the boy alone, said an elderly gentlemen, introducing himself to me as Barbara's father.

Brinsley O'Reilly was twenty-seven years older than his wife and well into his sixties when Piers and Barbara came into this world. How often would he and I keep each other company at breakfast in the years that followed, when I was the only one of my generation to be up at the time, and he the only one of his generation at all in the house. I enjoyed the discussions we had over our cracked mugs of coffee, all else being unwashed at that hour. He died only a few months after Barbara had left me, which had a strangely destabilizing effect on me given that I had just thrown it all away—the life to which he and I had belonged.

He had a most substantial sense of humor but would not pull such strands from it other than what he deemed essential, and that was the entire basis of his charm, the personality that he so silently hoarded, against which one could lean at any time without the anxiety of reciprocation.

Yawn a more Roman way, he offered at lunch, my first lunch with the O'Reilly family, St Patrick's Day, 1975, as we sat around a large joint of beef exchanging palindromes while Edmund attempted to carve it.

That's brilliant, Dad, said Piers.

I've a better one, Edmund interjected, I've a very good one.

Well what is it then? Mary O'Reilly demanded.

Sex at noon taxes, Edmund O'Reilly replied.

—

I close my eyes and allow myself to be invaded, like a man drowning gently, by such memories—my sister and I at Easter watching my grandmother etching patterns upon eggs boiled in dark tea, those milk-lipped afternoons with the clock ticking loudly and reassuringly while we did our homework, her proudly showing us the green cherries she had picked off the tree thinking them to be ripe—my sister. And then, much later, my father walking quietly back from the mailbox with my letter of acceptance to Princeton clutched tightly in his hand, my mother closing the curtains in my bedroom as a final gesture of possession on the night before I was to leave for college, these faintly corrugated images of hope that I have hoarded throughout my life congregate upon me now as I lie in the dark and vainly court sleep. And finally Barbara, and our many good times, all strung together in a pleasing array of something that could easily have continued and accrued more meaning, like soft snow upon the outlines of a perfect garden, but because of me, never did.

—

I am awakened by voices, hers among them, how long has she been here, I wonder, how could I have slept through it anyway? Later I will know that it is because she asked her driver to park the car outside rather than drive it in so as not to wake anybody, least of all her little girl. I sit up and run my fingers through my hair, debating whether to emerge straightaway or let the ghastly truth be told to her without me.

Don't worry, Ela, everyone is safe, I hear Piers say to her.

Then why are you here, Piers? she asks in a voice leaking a different kind of despair.

And then I hear Byron's voice, he is here to accuse me of murder, he says, perfectly pleasantly.

Murder?

He thinks it was I who was behind Damini's death, he explains.

What do you mean? she enquires shakily.

It appears that some of the baby milk produced by my factory in Jalpaiguri was found a few years ago to be a little bit impure, he says apologetically.

Impure? she repeats.

It was withdrawn immediately from the market, of course, Byron reassures her.

So then what has it to do with anything? she asks, still bewildered.

Somehow the failed batches were sent to Damini's shelter, he says, with a small cough.

Instead of being destroyed?

It was a donation, of course, says Byron Mallick.

I raise myself from my bed and walk as far as the door of the room, which opens full onto the terrace. I stay for a while in the shadows, trying to gather the courage to include myself in this absurd drama.

It is true, says Byron, that I had some correspondence with Damini on this matter, but we agreed in the end that it was in neither of our interests for this to find its way into the newspapers.

Damini was going to break that promise, says Piers, I have a copy of the article she was about to send by electronic mail to her old newspaper—except, of course, she was never able to…

But she gave me her assurance that nothing would appear in the press, says Byron.

Are you suggesting that you knew nothing about this article?

Nothing at all, says Byron.

Then how is it that it was recovered from her "Sent Items" folder marked to you? asks Piers.

I never received it, insists Byron.

You never received it? says Piers, disbelief uncurling like a lizard's tongue out of every uttered word.

Even if I had, says Byron, I would not have reacted by arranging to have her "eliminated"—if that's the word you would like me to use.

That's for you to believe and the courts to find out, says Piers with a smile.

The dog Kimbhut appears from nowhere, rushes towards me barking madly, and I am forced to declare my presence by entreating him to calm down.

Max? says Ela.

I made him come down here with me, says Piers, as if in my defense.

She looks at me despairingly and I look back, not sure of what to say, never have I more than this felt that I am failing her, that I cannot make a difference, rescue her from the situation, show her the route outwards, save her, save her, all I have ever wanted was to save her, restore her to herself and to me.

It is a relief when the lights begin to flicker yet again and eventually dim away, like a patient guardian leaving the premises—another power cut—but welcome, oh so welcome to me at this time.

For a few moments we are left in darkness with the faint sucking sounds of the sea, still in retreat from the shore, and the paltry moonlight picking out the decayed Victorian statues sequestered at the end of the garden amid the parched shrubs.

And then the power is restored, the lights shine upon our faces with an almost breathtaking vengeance, the ceiling fans whip back into action, we have hardly moved—Ela, Piers, and myself—but Byron has taken this opportunity to slip simply and quietly into the night, leaving the space that he had been occupying until this moment suddenly embarrassingly empty.

Where has he gone? Ela asks.

I think he is trying to run away, says Piers.

Run away? From what?

From the truth, of course.

And how will he do that? she says.

The same way as any of us, says Piers O'Reilly.

—

When he arrived in Calcutta last week, Piers had taken a taxi from the airport to Arjun and Ela's home on Gurusaday Road, but had been told when he arrived by Arjun's mother that her son and daughter-in-law were in Dhakuria, where Damini's body was being prepared for its final journey to the crematorium.

Dreadful tragedy, she said, wiping a tear from her eye with a corner of her sari.

I'll go there then, Piers replied.

Have some tea first, Arjun's mother recommended.

I have no need to refresh myself, Piers told her.

Very well then, I'll call the driver straightaway, the old lady replied.

When he arrived he had been ushered into the room where the body lay under a cloth so obscenely white as to be almost blue, he had knelt and taken Damini's long dark fingers, now stiff in death, in his own hands. Ela had come in, oddly composed in her grief, it's so good of you to have come, she had said to him.

The house was packed with people, she had suggested that they go up to the roof terrace, where she thought they could be alone. He followed her up the narrow stairs and lit a cigar as soon as they were out upon the rough concrete. Clothes hung everywhere, long saris draped over the parapet, socks and undergarments woodpegged upon thin lines. She began to gather and fold them and he tried to help her, cigar in mouth.

Just sit, she had said. These things are going to smell of smoke otherwise.

I'm glad you think I can compete with the pollution, Piers replied.

And then suddenly she had begun to rip what she was holding, an old white sari, to shreds, long arpeggios of old cotton shearing over and over again, until there was nothing he could do but put his arms around her.

There was a sound of flapping sandals as, pushing aside a curtain of washing, Arjun had stepped into their world.

Go and lie down for a while, he told his wife, noticing the torn sari.

And after she had gone he said to Piers: I am certain this was no ordinary accident.

What exactly do you mean? Piers had asked him, stamping on his cigar to put it out.

I am talking about Damini.

That much I assumed.

Yes, Damini.

You think she was killed? But why?

I have no idea, Arjun confessed.

But you are convinced it was a deliberate misdeed?

Yes, I am, but I need proof, Arjun said, I do need some kind of proof.

And proof it was, enough for him at least, that he had found today, the last piece of a terrifying jigsaw clicking firmly into place, when he finally tracked down Damini's lover Dhritiman in a hovel in Kurseong, found him sitting with his knees drawn to his chin on his friend's bed, still acutely griefstricken and unable to do much other than watch television from this position.

When he had told him all he had to tell, Arjun walked over to a window and pulled aside a filthy curtain to gulp in some of the damp morning air.

My wife and daughter are there with him now in Digha, he said.

I am a coward, Dhritiman said. I know I am a coward, he repeated, as if much relieved to find a label for himself in this hour.

Look, Arjun said, I am not blaming you—it is big leap from adulterating formula milk to doing away with the person who finds this out.

No, no, it is much worse than you think, Dhritiman replied, shaking his head.

What do you mean? Arjun asked.

You see I have these tapes.

Tapes?

Cassette tapes—someone left them in my mailbox.

Containing what?

Confessions.

On tape?

There are a lot of people who hate Byron Mallick…

But are too afraid to speak out?

It is possible he did not mean to have her killed, Dhritiman said.

How long have you known all of this? Arjun asked.

Since the day after the cremation.

All this time, you have known of this?

See, am I not truly vile? Dhritiman had said, burying his head in his knees.

How strange the noon sky had seemed to Arjun as he drove back to his hotel in Darjeeling, what peculiar memories it had resurrected—memories of his first encounter with Damini playing chess with Ela, his own object of desire, in the dining room of Byron Mallick's flat. Arjun had appeared upon some pretext, as he had begun to do rather regularly since he had been reintroduced to Ela at the party in celebration of his parents' silver wedding anniversary, to which Byron had brought her.

Our telephone line is down, he had explained, surveying their chess game. Our telephone line is down, he repeated, and my father wanted to cancel golf this afternoon with Uncle Byron.

I'll let him know, Ela had said.

Do you mind if I make the next move for you? he asked her.

Not at all, she replied.

Damini glared at him as it had all suddenly fallen into place in Ela's favor by his clever repositioning of the bishop, but he had not stayed to watch her kingdom crumble.

Nice to have met you, he said to her, and then turned to Ela and simply smiled before leaving them to their game.

That boy is in love with you, Damini had accused Ela.

And what if he is? Ela retorted.

He strikes me as a silly little rich boy, Damini said.

All of this Arjun overheard, for unawares to them, he was still struggling with the buckle on his sandals in the hallway.

His thoughts were simple when he finally drew the strap through—one day I will save her life and then she will be sorry, he had said to himself.

Too late for that now, too late.

As soon as he found a signal, Arjun had used his mobile phone to first try and reach Ela, and then, when he failed to get through to her, to telephone Piers O'Reilly.

Where are you? Piers had enquired.

Never mind where I am, Arjun replied, I want you to get down this minute to Digha—my driver will take you—I want you to bring my wife and daughter back, I want you to bring them back straightaway, do you understand?

I'll happily do that, Piers assured him, but I think you need to tell me why.

I'll go and look for Byron, says Piers.

He crushes his cigar into an ashtray and sets off towards the sea.

Do you believe any of this, Max? asks Ela.

Once again, I am called upon to pass judgment, when my brain—the poor pulp of my unslept brain—has hardly been able to absorb the facts.

I do not know, I admit to her, the words turning like old salt upon my tongue.

I place my hand upon hers where it rests upon the parapet, her face is turned away from me.

I need to go and see my little girl, she says.

She is asleep, I tell her.

I need to see her, she says, as if trying to communicate to a deaf-mute.

Well, go and see her then, I reply.

She twists away and disappears into the darkness, her footsteps upon the stairs fall in odd resentfulness upon my ears, was I supposed to have saved her from this? I, who should never have been here at all? I, who should now have been sitting to his breakfast of stale bread and old wine in his London flat, my loss of her floating about me like scraps of candywax, wondering how another few decades might be surrendered to such a fine delirium?

Could I have saved anyone of us from this? God knows I would have wanted to. A good word whispered in Byron's ear in those years when his love for me exceeded his trust in me, could that have altered anything at all? What proof have I anyway that his tampering with consumer goods might have led to such an all-consummate sin as the taking of a life? What am I here but an observer, an intricate piece of blotting paper, runnelling ink this way and that, but never towards any steady channel.

I light a cigarette, what else can I do, the moonlight shines with surprising virulence upon the limbs of the statues sequestered at the end of the lawn, the night around me is dense with events yet to happen, could I have changed anything, anything at all—perhaps even by one judicious word spoken at the right moment—could I not have altered the balance between right and wrong in his mind, Byron Mallick, had he not tacitly counted upon me once to do exactly that, have I not betrayed him in the end by not allowing loyalty to take precedence over love?

—

Max, where are you? I hear Piers call.

I have found Byron, he says, he seems to have twisted his ankle badly.

I come quickly down the terrace stairs.

Did he fall? I ask.

I suppose he must have, says Piers.

I'll go and tell Ela.

Why? he asks.

Because she would want to know, I reply.

She is sitting by the foot of the bed. The child lies curled on the other side in her little white nightdress, she has kicked off her meager covers during the night. For a few minutes, I stand there and watch the child, her small chest rising and falling under thin cotton, her little lips slightly parted, pale eyelids closed, for a few moments I allow myself to be mesmerized by her, feel a sudden searing and much delayed regret that she is not mine.

Byron has hurt himself, I tell Ela.

She stands up and tucks the tired end of her sari into her waist.

Take me to him, she says.

I let my fingers graze her shoulder as we come down the stairs.

Nothing can alter the fact that I love you, I bravely tell her.

Nor can the fact that we love each other alter anything, she answers.

No, that it cannot, I concede.

Just take me to him, she commands.

Suddenly I find it within myself to tighten my grip upon her, she turns around, startled.

What matters most to you just at this moment? I ask her.

Not us, if that is the answer you want, she replies.

Not us, no, I did not expect that—we can endure death but not this distension of our moralities—but what matters to you of what comes after?

Only my child, she says with absolute conviction.

We find Byron where Piers has left him only a few minutes earlier, stretched out like a monarch slumbering upon the sand.

Now I am broken—physically, at least, he says.

Just a sprained ankle, says Piers.

Ela takes his hand and begins very softly to cry.

Now, now, says Byron, it's not that bad.

I remember, says Byron Mallick, I remember the armpit scoured smell of wax polish in the lobby of your boarding school where I used to wait for you every Saturday afternoon, to sign you out for the weekend. Eventually, you would appear in your white schooldress, walk unsteadily down the stairs clutching your small suitcase, always overladen with borrowed books. Sometimes there were, among these, a book or two for me—strange volumes you had found in some dusty corner of your school library—a young lady's memoirs from the early days of the Raj, things that you thought might be useful to me, for at the time I still nourished the hope that I might turn my unfinished thesis into a book.

Every Saturday morning I would awaken amid the chirpings of sparrows to a very crisply defined gladness at the prospect of walking back with you from your boarding school—you would chatter wonderfully childishly as you skipped along on topics far beyond your own horizons: atomic energy, the problem of hunger, the inception of the universe, the existence of God. It was, for me, like looking inside a newly manufactured clock with its shiny cogs turning this way and that, trying to come to terms with the enormous responsibility of accurately keeping time. We would walk along happily, taking care to avoid the puddles from the broken hydrants, the cow dung and the clots of betel spit, and stop at the tobacco shop next to the petrol station to buy a bar of chocolate for us to split between ourselves. I enjoyed the precision with which you would break it exactly in half, and always felt that not to insist that I got my fair share would betray a lack of respect for the rules of the game.

As you grew older and I became busier, it became more and more natural that you make this journey on your own, but the school insisted that you should still be signed out, and so I gave this authority to my manservant Vargas—with your parents' permission, of course.

There was a time when I would actually tread a little faster towards the door of my apartment knowing that I would find you there, most likely still in your school uniform, resting your delicate feet upon the coffee table, immersed in a book, sipping the especially concentrated lime soda that one of my maids would have prepared for you. You would raise your lovely eyes as I entered and smile, and my heart would fill with a gentle gladness, a definite sense of how much better the room was for your presence, not an emotion I had ever been familiar with before. I would pick up the letters on my desk and as I looked through them, I would ask you about your week, and how you had performed on your various tests, I had the capacity then to keep such things in my head, and so was able to discharge my duty as your local guardian without the discomfort of having to struggle to remember these details that are so dear to a parent, and have little meaning for anyone else.

—

Kerosene oil spilling upon the paper angels that she had made in the dark, her first Christmas in Calcutta, and himself, reluctant to participate, her small efforts suddenly endorsed by the ringing of bells from St. Paul's Cathedral not too far away, lending her the courage to ask if she might hang her angels up somewhere, and him simply saying, if you like, if you like. He could not imagine that Nikhilesh would have encouraged this, but then his wife—oh, so eager no doubt to partake of every aspect of campus life—Byron could certainly see her manning the stall at some college Christmas sale, currying turkey for a Christmas lunch to which they would have invited their unpartnered colleagues, all of whom would have brought gifts for Ela, such as children's cookbooks demanding ingredients that could not be found in any local Ghanaian shop, fodder nonetheless for her imagination in all those lonely hours that still stretched before her, the darkness outside her window as innocent as the continent itself, and herself inside, turning the pages by raw electric light, wondering how it was to be enclosed instead by the noises of a family, a metropolis, others' music, others' needs.

This slender child, now part of his life, pinning paper angels to the plasterwork, wishing to be somewhere else, her small chin jutting out, her spirits clenched, later she will go to her room and lie in the dark listening to a tape of Tagore songs that her mother had made for her. That Nikhilesh's wife had a voice that was rich and sweet even Byron could not deny, but her self-consciousness was as abrasive to him as badly baked clay and he always shut his door when Ela played these songs on her little Decca cassette player, a leaving present from her parents which she was not able to keep in school but left in the room in Byron's flat that he allowed her to call her own.

In this room she would nurse her first fantasies and her first acquaintance with heartache, this he knew, and he was not afraid of it, for he had grown up with a woman's pain always close by, at times enfolding him and at other times pushing him away, was it just a lack of fulfillment or an unrequited passion that had made his mother's life so gray, Byron would never know, and yet the tides of this had been the central rhythm of his life as well as hers, and he no longer feared it in any guise. In the twelve-year-old Ela he saw the tender shoots pushing through of such thoughts that would no doubt harden and mangle as they grew, but for the moment he was content to watch them feel their way into the new wind, and concentrate on making sure they were not scorched by his own cynicism.

How happy it had made him to hear Ela's pen scratching away upon the rough pages of her journal or the sickly blue of the aerogrammes that he purchased for her to write to her parents upon—leaving the one small side for himself to fill in his own beautiful Bengali script, his ink leaching through to darken in patches her long sentences telling her parents of what she had learned and how she had eaten and whether she had won her races and how much she longed to be with them again.

—

All these years that I looked after you… says Byron.

One is never beholden to a sinner, Piers reminds him.

All this time I have protected you, says Byron to Ela.

That does not mean she has to defend you, says Piers.

You and Max, says Byron, ignoring Piers.

What are you talking about? asks Piers.

Do you not know? says Byron. Are you not aware of the grand passion between these two? It wrecked Max's life for sure, and almost destroyed your sister's, do you not know any of this, Piers?

I pick up some sand and let it drift through my fingers. Then I turn to Byron.

It is extraordinary how you are able to bespatter both truth and fiction with the same ink, I tell him.

But Ela cannot bear any more of this exchange, she rises and leaves us, walks slowly back to the house, straight and tall, holding her admission of sinning with me like a frame of wood about her narrow shoulders.

How long has this been going on? asks Piers.

Oh, years and years, answers Byron in a bored voice.

Is that why Barbara left you? Piers asks me.

I am amazed at the weight of accusation in his voice—as if a sister's honor might still possibly be a precious commodity to him.

I suppose you could say that, I admit.

You were enormously lucky to have Barbara, says Byron. And you threw it all away, he adds.

It is not as if I am terribly unhappy now, I tell him.

No—it is an existence, I suppose, dispensing every couple of years a shallow book of anecdotes about traveling in rural India, says Byron. And let me guess, says he, your new book is about returning to those locations about which you have written and captured the heart of middle-class Britain with your descriptions of the daily lives of Bengali villagers.

It is an existence, I suppose, says Byron Mallick. To rise every day around noon to an old glass of red wine, tarred around its rim, but anything, anything to quench your raging thirst. And then to stumble towards the coffee maker, your best friend in the whole wide world, gleaming chrome, and soon ready to hiss, but ultimately unable—like most others who try—to truly coax you into a state of alertness. A hot shower, no doubt, is the next step, jets of water not quite able to sluice you of yesterday, but leaving you able to journey fearless towards the day that is already half done.

Seems that you are well enough for your walk, says Piers.

Seems I have no choice, says Byron, but perhaps one of you could fetch me my pipe?

Not I, says Piers.

It is mere tobacco that I request, says Byron, most final meals are far more complex. Jeffrey Doughtie, for example, who was executed in Texas a couple of years ago, asked for eight soft fried eggs, a big bowl of grits, five biscuits with a bowl of butter, five pieces of fried hard and crisp bacon, two sausage patties, a pitcher of chocolate milk, two pints of vanilla Bluebell ice cream, and two bananas.

And did he get it? asks Piers.

That, I know not.

I will fetch your pipe, I tell Byron.

For old times' sake? he asks.

Not really, I answer.

Once I have returned with the pipe we help him to his feet, and supporting him on either side begin to walk down the hard slippery beach, towards the dark waters that will soon come thundering back.

What exactly are you trying to do to me? asks Byron Mallick, looking ridiculously comfortable in his loose cotton clothes, pipe in mouth.

Cook your goose is what first comes into my head as expressions go, says Piers O'Reilly.

Your mother always said you had bad taste, says Byron.

Bad taste in what? asks Piers.

Do you really want to know?

Perversely, yes.

Pretty much everything, gloats Byron.

And what about Barbara? asks Piers.

An average child is what she usually says of her, Byron informs us.

So we were both a disappointment to her? says Piers.

On the contrary, replies Byron Mallick, I think she had high hopes of *you*, once.

And what, after this, are the thoughts that pass through his head, Piers O'Reilly, softly steering a man he thinks to be a murderer towards his own death? It is easy for me to fool myself into believing that I know where his musings cluster for I have shared a life with him, and have also populated the many spaces of his childhood with my own fragmented images of him and his then still young and wildly beautiful mother. I see them bent upon the shore over a scrapbook filled with his deeds, all of which fascinate her, and next to them I see her pale daughter, eyes sidecast, Barbara, who learned to live with her mother's obsession with her son by colluding in it, learned to be more pure and true than anyone I know, came to love and be faithful to me until I cast her out of my life.

We begin to travel with the limping Byron over the taut seabed, the night grows old before our eyes, already dawn hangs in the air with the perfume of a sleeping virgin who will be led into an unhappy marriage the minute she awakens.

The time has come, says Byron, to talk of many

things, of shoes—and ships—and sealing wax—of cabbages—and kings—

And why the milk is mainly chalk, and whether harps have strings, Piers retorts.

And why a crocodile cannot stick out its tongue, says Byron.

What? asks Piers.

And why an ostrich's eye is bigger than its brain.

Don't even think about playing the insanity card, warns Piers.

You know I was a shy boy, says Byron unexpectedly, I did not have many friends at school, and yet quite early on I became aware of a certain quality that I clearly possessed which made people trust me.

Oh, yes? says Piers

Perhaps it was simply that I was totally untutored in the art of lying, for my life had been so solitary that I had never had any reason to employ the simple fabrications that others used as a matter of course, says Byron.

It is indeed ironic then that it was the absence of training in this area that actually prepared you to hone the art of true deceit in later life, says Piers.

What do you mean?

Well, said Piers, the first rule of the game is to win trust, and perhaps it was your natural skill in this that eventually allowed lying to become as easy for you as running your hands through your hair.

An interesting argument, says Byron Mallick, as if

advising a student rather than answering to a demolition of his own character.

But not one that I subscribe to, he adds.

For a time a silence closes about us, such as that which might surround men journeying towards one of the earth's poles, and then without warning Byron begins to sing a Tagore song.

How enchanting, says Piers.

Translate for him, will you, requests Byron of me.

I do not know how to, something about the boundless ocean, and facing endless night, all hope spent, happiness and sorrow both exhausted…

Not bad, not bad at all, Byron replies.

Ananta sagar majhe, dao tari bhashaya, I recognize it from many years ago when he had taken Barbara and myself—not long after we met him—to spend the weekend at a villa upon the Ganges which had been purchased by one of his drug companies as a retreat for its senior executives. A fleet of flimsy boats seemed always to be waiting for our custom nearby and he and I spent many an hour on the breast of the broad and sluggish river while Barbara, who had never been at ease with water, read on the riverbank. Often, like most Bengalis of his generation, Byron Mallick would break into song—refined Tagore songs mostly that he would carefully translate, but also, especially as the light softened, into plaintive fisherman's music, somehow more honest to my ears, as if learned in a period of his life when he was not who he was now, but somebody else, with no idea of where life might take him and why.

All hope is spent, all happiness, and all sorrow
Hardly a sound upon this shore
As if silenced by some spell
And how steadily the night approaches, her arms outstretched.

Ahead of us the sky is already starting to leak away from the sea, I turn my eyes away as if to escape this vastly forbidden dawn and am astonished to find forming within me, in this unlikely moment, like a deliciously dangerous act of love, the kernel of a work of fiction such as I have been aching to write, all these years.

Let me guess, says Byron Mallick, you are wondering how you might make use of these circumstances, are you not, Max? Perhaps to finally produce that great novel that has eluded you for so long?

How well you read my mind, Byron, I reply.

With myself perhaps as its protagonist?

Quite possibly.

Max, can we not go back to our ordinary lives? pleads Byron.

I do not see how we can, Byron.

Why not let natural processes of justice resolve that for us?

Is that really what you would prefer? asks Piers.

I feel my ankles starting to sink into the sand, the foam of the returning waters gently easing between my toes.

I think we should turn back now, says Piers.

And leave me here? Byron asks.

That was the idea, was it not? says Piers.

Shame there is no rock to chain me to, says Byron.

No, no, says Piers, you do not understand, we want to give you a choice.

A choice?

The choice of staying here and waiting for the waves, or walking back with us.

That won't be necessary anymore, says Byron, calmly filling his pipe.

And why not? asks Piers.

We long ago crossed the point of no return, Byron replies.

You are lying to us again, says Piers.

We will all drown, says Byron confidently.

Isn't it pretty to think so, says Piers.

You underestimate how fast the tide comes in, says Byron.

I know that from here I can easily ride the waves to the shore, says Piers.

And you, Max?

I am not so sure, Byron.

That is what I thought, he says.

so good in black

She sits unslept by her child, watching her small chest rise and fall under its sheath of eyelet lace. What has she done, where has she been, what has she left undone, the slats of her mind slowly open and close upon us, each in turn, Piers, Byron, and I—friend, mentor, and lover—have we not all in some way or another deserted her?

For where is the magic now of their friendship, Piers and hers, that led them to linger all night under the stars on the balcony of his flat in Earls Court, ten years ago, drinking his clumsily mixed cocktails, their conversation swinging from one branch to another unlikely branch in a forest of entangled interests and sensibilities. Why is it now that she is so easily overcome by tiredness in the evenings when he is visiting them, why does she feel at times a certain dread that he might extend his stay beyond his usual two or three weeks? Indeed, it is with Arjun, and even Damini, that Piers has spent more of his time these last few years in Calcutta. And in his eyes there has been disappointment, each time, and some irritation as well, when she has failed to enthuse as she might have done before about some project of his, when she has not laughed as fully as she might at one of his jokes, when she has handed back his restaurant reviews that he has cut out and saved for her to read without much comment, just a smile.

Then me, Max Gate, into whose arms she has so easily fallen after all these years, Max Gate, made no more real to her by a night of desperate lovemaking, and finally me, who never deserted her, but committed the greater impiety of allowing her to desert me.

And finally Byron, and his growing disdain for her attitude towards her career, his exasperation at her turning down the many opportunities he still creates for her of traveling abroad, appearing on stage again in the western world. Last year she had reluctantly finally agreed to spend a month in Paris, had hated every minute of it, spent the time that she should have been making contacts and giving interviews at the country home of an elderly and insignificant lady instead who had approached her after one of her performances and charmed her. Only last month Byron had telephoned her from New York with a proposal for touring on the East Coast—he had many Bengali families lined up to receive her and pack their community halls with themselves and their children to watch her dance—Byron had urged her to accept this invitation, and she had said to him, I'd rather die.

It was he who had made her what she was, she could not deny that, put pressure on the famous Odissi dance master to accept her as a student even though she was well over the age at which the guru usually took new students. It was her youngest maternal uncle, though, who took her to the lessons, for Byron did not have the time. Each time her uncle would express his astonishment that she was not lodging with them in the small house in Dhakuria that all but the eldest of her mother's five brothers shared. Sometimes she tried to imagine what it would be like to live there with a divan in the corner of the living room to sleep on, and only the stairwell in which to shut herself away from the wails of the many infants to read a book or finish her homework, and felt relieved that her parents had decided otherwise. She would visit her mother's family during the holidays for a few days at a time, and although she was grateful for their boundless and unqualified affection, she was soon bored and longed to be back in Byron's flat, longed for the quiet afternoons when she could read undisturbed and those clamorous evenings when many people—young and old—would congregate in his drawing room and exchange ideas and opinions while he sat in his leather armchair, puffing on his pipe and offering elegant interjections. They all remained welcome at his home while they were able to add to the intellectual atmosphere, sometimes even with just a well-placed nod. From about five o'clock onwards such folk would gather at the flat for their *adda*—a Bengali term for which both he and her father claimed there was no translation, but seemed to her just to consist of people talking and deeply relishing the lack of obvious purpose in their interaction. Every now and then she would be fetched to read a poem that she had written, or recite the piece that had won her first prize in the elocution contest, and they would all clap and she would quickly run back to her room.

And then one day he asked her to dance for them and her relationship with this crowd had suddenly, instantly, been transformed. For one thing they had to clear a space and so sat crowded at one end of the room, looking strangely diminished. She detected also a different kind of confidence in Byron's voice, as if he were not simply displaying with affection the talents of his precious ward, but presenting them an astonishing discovery, something they would not easily forget. Standing there, waiting for Byron to turn the tape player on, Ela looked from the expectant audience to Byron's unusually serious face, and for the first time in her life was overcome by a determination to stun them all. And so she had danced, her first real sense of performance streaking hot through her, *my eyes swoop towards the quiet light in your window like an eager bird in a storm*, and then bowed her head and absorbed their applause, instead of running away as she usually did when they began to praise her.

From then on she had joined them in their discussions and found her horizons extended simply by sitting among them and hearing them argue. But it was still the time that she spent alone in the flat that she savored most of all, as she spoke of lying upon her bed with sandalwood paste cooling upon her face, reading books that she had found upon his shelves, holding their names like mysterious lozenges in her mouth, even after she had begun to comprehend their meanings, *Exile and the Kingdom, Why I Mourn for England, Thank You, Fog.* Sometimes she would fall asleep, but then Vargas would knock on the door to wake her up with a glass of hot milk or lassi, depending on the season.

She had never denied that it was her acquaintance with Byron Mallick's unique way of life that, in the end, made a success of her father's idea that she return to Calcutta to acquire some sense of where she belonged. It was through savoring her time in his marvelous home that she came to identify with the city, time often spent alone rummaging through books and photograph albums—for Byron had been an avid photographer in his youth—listening to his records, which included a vast range of Indian and western classical music, as well as several small 45rpm recordings of his favorite Tagore songs. Time spent alone with her schoolbooks upon the broad mahogany dining table, learning to revel in knowledge and insight, learning to distill the intricacies of the universe into a few simple shapes, a few crucial ideas. Her only disappointment was in the indifference Byron sometimes displayed when she was bursting to tell him of a new concept that she had just mastered, or a new emotion that some piece of music had awakened within her. She would wait breathless to share it with him when he returned, and invariably it would get wedged between his own various stories and remain unacknowledged, it was the first intimation of his utter immorality, but this she did not know then.

She comes out onto the balcony, gasping for some air, and in the dawnlight sees us, walking out steadily towards that point in the sand beyond which absolution melts into acceptance of sin, she sees us walking towards certain death and rushes to her father's bedroom to wake him.

Nikhilesh hears what she has to say, shaking his gray head in disbelief, together they rush down the stairs and find in the garden the young boy who comes in to water the beds in the earliest hours of the morning, they tell him to run and fetch his uncles, whom they know to be professional *nuliyas*—making a living through their swimming skills by assisting seabathers who seek to risk the terrible waves—go and fetch your uncles, they tell him, there are lives that depend upon how fast you can run.

You go back, says Byron Mallick, while there is time.

But what about you? I ask.

It is too late for me now.

But we cannot just leave you here, I protest.

Byron laughs a hollow laugh. How easily you change your mind, Max, he says.

It was never my intention to leave you to drown.

What then were you thinking?

I was not really thinking at all, I confess.

He puts a hand on my shoulder—Don't worry, Max, it's for the best, as Piers says.

I close my eyes, the events of the night clatter like dull knives within my aching head.

I am finished, Max, even if they are proven wrong as they no doubt will be, I am forever damaged, says Byron.

I open my eyes and look into his face. I'll stay with you here, I tell him.

Don't be ridiculous, Max—what purpose will that possibly serve—now you go back and write that book that you so want to write about me.

Come on, Max, says Piers.

And make it good, make sure I do not die in it like this, says Byron.

There are worse ways to go, says Piers.

Suddenly I see two dark figures running towards us, who can they be? I am the only one to see them as only I am facing the shore, and before I can decide whether to draw the attention of the others to their approach, they are with us, grabbing us by our wrists, sherpas of the water, they seize us by the wrists and begin to march us to the shore, we will see you to safety, they promise us.

In the house the child wakens and tiptoes downstairs into the kitchen, where she finds Vargas, white-gloved, hovering over Byron's breakfast tray.

She wanders out into the dining room where her butterfly still flutters in its glass cage, and finds that the table has been set but no one has yet come to breakfast. Bewildered, she emerges onto the terrace, checks the sitting room for signs of life, and finds none.

She returns to the kitchen and asks Vargas: Where are they? where have they gone?

I don't know, says Vargas.

And then suddenly, most unexpectedly, he begins to cry,

his shoulders shaking as he clutches onto the tray, causing the china to tremble, a sound that will haunt the child for years to come.

The waves, when they come, like wild horses from behind, are indeed powerful and when we are finally spit by them upon the shore, there is very little energy left in us. Nikhilesh rewards the men lavishly, as Piers and Byron sit panting upon the sand I am not with them for a recalcitrant current has deposited me some distance away behind a clump of casuarina trees where I have been left to find my breath.

So what is going on here? he asks after the men have gone.

They were trying to drown me, says Byron.

I really don't understand, says Nikhilesh.

These lads are under the impression that it was I who engineered Damini's death, replies Byron.

Is that why you are here? Nikhilesh asks Piers.

I'm afraid it is true, says Piers.

How preposterous! says Nikhilesh.

There is more than enough evidence, says Piers.

To send me to the gallows? How sweet! exclaims Byron.

Nikhilesh watches as the rising sun suddenly carves hollows into Byron's wet face, he remembers how he had tried to teach him to swim, many many years ago, his pale hesitant limbs dipping slowly into the murky pond—come on, you idiot, it's not deep, just jump in—he had called.

And believing him, Byron had jumped in, except of course it was too deep, at least for him, but Nikhilesh had grabbed an arm, don't worry, he had said to his friend, I will not let go.

How can any of this be happening? says Nikhilesh.

It is your own worthy son-in-law who is mainly to blame, says Byron.

Arjun?

Yes, indeed, Arjun.

Surely you jest, says Nikhilesh.

I'm afraid he has had it in his head for a while that I am somehow connected to this ghastly business, says Byron.

What an extraordinary thought!

All Arjun has done is put two and two together, says Piers.

And come up not with four, or even five, but with some ultimately irrational number, says Byron Mallick.

And what of me? I have washed up some distance away, out of their sight. The sand that I am lying upon seems to hum beneath my head, as if richly inscribed by young children, some of whom will one day become poets. I close my eyes and try and gather my senses.

I hear someone approaching, and am overwhelmed with gratitude when I realize it is Ela. And there is no greater magic than to turn my head and lie upon an unshaven cheek to watch her come towards me, kneel at my side and say, oh Max I am so glad that you are alive.

Her eyes brim beautifully with tears, I long to kiss them, I stroke with sandy fingers the hand that she has placed upon my cheek. Sometimes I wonder whether I ever needed her to be real beyond those first few moments, so solidly was her presence established within me by that first glance, the first few movements of her lips and her fingers.

Help me get up please, I say to her.

This she does, and I stand unsteadily, holding onto her for several minutes.

Are you alright? she asks.

Yes, just dizzy—it will pass.

I notice that stuck in the sand under the casuarina trees are the remains of an old harp, can this be the same instrument that was once proudly placed in the living room, that Byron had found in an auction and lovingly restored? Barbara, who had learned the clarsach, was able to make brave and pure music upon it. And in my moments of utter desperation while trying to find, as I daily did then, a new and better path for my narrative, in these moments of thwarted aspiration I would run my hands over its pliant strings and be humbled by the sweetness that my untutored fingers could draw from it, a strange contrast to my strenuous efforts to produce a work of fiction that were coming so quietly and resolutely to nought.

What will happen now, Max? asks Ela.

You and Adrija must leave as soon as possible, I reply.

I walk over, my head still pounding, to where the remains of the harp lie, half buried in the sand. It seems as if someone has strung some of it with garden wire, their snapped ends lie curled, defiant.

She comes and stands beside me and puts her hands upon the ruined instrument.

That old harp, she says, I thought Byron had sold it.

Evidently not.

She grips the desecrated harp like the mast of a ship.

And what will happen to us, Max? she asks.

Who can tell? I answer.

She looks at me, bewildered by these words.

So strange, she says, to meet again like this.

Better this than some utterly ordinary encounter, I tell her.

No, Max, nothing could be more ghastly than these circumstances.

Go back to the house now, you need to get away from here as soon as possible, I tell her.

How hard can I prune this, I ask myself as she walks away, how hard can I prune this and still expect it to survive? And even produce that bounty of flower that only such measures can bring on?

She turns back to look at me, I smile at her, and she smiles weakly back.

What is an irrational number? Nikhilesh asks his friend, eager to find refuge in detail.

One that cannot be expressed as a fraction of integers, he replies.

Not everybody's cup of tea, says Piers.

Indeed not, says Byron, Pythagoras sentenced a man to death for suggesting that the square root of 2 might be an irrational number.

What kind of a death? asks Nikhilesh.

Why, by drowning, of course, replies Byron.

Is that true?

It is what your brother told me, says Byron.

Nikhilesh's older brother, Sandipan, eagerly they would await his arrival from Calcutta for the holidays, for he brought with him a city smell, a wealth of marvelous tales, books and newspaper cuttings, strange mathematical puzzles for Byron that he would spend hours agonizing over while Nikhilesh played his flute in boredom—shut up, you are distracting me, Byron would complain, and Nikhilesh would wander out to continue playing under the shade of a tree, digging his toes into the warm sand.

On a few occasions he almost felt a little envious of them—the wonder in both their eyes as Sandipan explained to Byron how the infinity that existed between two whole numbers was vaster than that which could never be arrived at by counting in plain integers, one, two, three. It was not just that Nikhilesh could not see how one kind of infinity could possibly be different from another, but why it mattered if indeed it was so. Sometimes he felt that he saw in his friend a fire burning that if left unchecked would consume all his material links with this world, and the magic of numbers that his brother presented Byron with seemed to propel him even further in this direction.

You know, I used to think you might become an ascetic, says Nikhilesh to Byron.

Instead of a murderer upon a lonely shore? mocks his friend.

Do you remember the long conversations you had with my brother? Snuffing out the kerosene lamp so that you might see the stars? Arguing about whether black holes might exist or not? All of it so utterly incomprehensible to me, says Nikhilesh.

Black holes do exist, says Piers. I hear you can even make a tiny little black hole now in your garden shed with the appropriate instruments.

You would be the sort of person to believe that, says Byron Mallick.

Ela finds her daughter sitting quietly at the kitchen table, drawing.

Vargas is making pancakes, Adrija tells her.

Ela seats herself on a chair beside her, tucking between her ankles the many soiled truths that have collected like mud upon her hem since she was last with the child.

When I grow up I want to be a bookmaker, says the child suddenly.

They are the first assertive words that she has spoken in a long time, and Ela does not know what to make of them.

A bookmaker? she echoes.

Like Max, says Adrija.

A writer, you mean, says Ela, and immediately wishes she had not corrected such a delicious mistake.

A writer then, the child concedes, a small hole punctured in her, but one that will heal with time as do so many such holes whose scars eventually compose us.

And here is Lazarus come back from the dead, says Byron, as I emerge sand encrusted from behind the casuarina trees.

Max, says Nikhilesh, I thought you were asleep!

No, says Byron, he has not slept at all tonight.

It hasn't been the kind of night when one sleeps, I retort.

Be truthful, Max, they are not just my iniquities that have deprived you of sleep.

What are you talking about? asks Nikhilesh, a strange despair in his voice.

I am talking about him and your daughter, says Byron.

I would rather not know any of this, says Nikhilesh.

You are simply jealous, says Byron.

Jealous that you know more of what has been in her heart all these years? No, Byron, that is something I had to get used to a long time ago. I was simply amused at first how much she spoke like you when she returned to us for her long winter vacation, I remember first being amused and later irritated at her accent, an obvious clone of yours, I even stooped to ridiculing her, admits Nikhilesh.

You ridiculed her for copying my accent? says Byron, managing to sound incredulous.

I was jealous then, concedes Nikhilesh.

Jealous of what?

Jealous that you, not me, were fashioning her, that they were your tastes in music and dance that she was adopting, that you were taking her already to film society showings of the very art films I would have liked to share with her, that you were bringing her in touch with her heritage in a way that, even if I were in Calcutta, I could never have done.

But you never gave yourself the chance! says Byron.

What do you mean? asks Nikhilesh.

You could have come back to Calcutta anytime you wanted, they would have created a position for you at the University, surely?

I was never approached, says Nikhilesh a little stiffly.

Never approached! Did you ever give them to understand that it might be worth their while to approach you?

And why should I have stooped to that? asks Nikhilesh.

Why? I'll tell you why. For Ela's sake. So that you could have been there at a time in her life when she most needed you, says Byron.

But you were there for her, says Nikhilesh gently.

I did my best, says Byron.

You did better than that, his oldest friend assures him.

Vargas comes into the dining room with a stack of slim pancakes in a round silver tureen.

Ela raises her dark eyes to him and says: Vargas, I think you should go down to the shore.

Is that where they all are, madam? he asks.

Yes, Vargas, and I think Byron may need your help, she replies.

A look of anxiety sweeps across Vargas's face—Is he hurt? he inquires.

Not very badly, says Ela.

But I have some more pancakes to fry, says Vargas, an unfamiliar helplessness in his voice.

You can make them later when everyone is here, says Ela firmly.

Yes, later, says Vargas. Later, he repeats to himself as he moves towards the door to the terrace, slips his feet into his sandals and walks down the steps, across the lawn, and down more steps, towards the sea.

And in these moments of grave anticipation much of his life compresses upon him, as it proverbially would in the eyes of a drowning man. He remembers being a child in Bandel, thirty miles to the north of Calcutta, where his father worked at the Church of Nossa Senhora di Rozario as a secretary to the Fathers, our Lady of the Rosary smiling down from the main façade, they said that her original home was the altar of the old church destroyed by the Mughals, that she had been saved from desecration by a pious merchant who had seized her and attempted to swim with her across the Hooghly river, he had been seen no more, but the statue had miraculously reappeared a few yards from the gate of the Basilica after a night of violent storm, had been reinstalled where she might be more easily worshipped, and every second week in November pilgrims would gather before her, the smell of autumn mingling with their excitement and piety, strangely soothing to him as a boy. This and more he remembers, all this and more, and how it had all been taken away from him by the death of his father and replaced by a cramped set of rooms in Free School Street in Calcutta, his mother had found a job at the Great Eastern Hotel, worked her way up the ladder, saved and scrimped every way possible to give him an education, had been disappointed when he had insisted on taking a job rather than going on to college, a petty clerkship in a small firm that was subsequently taken over by Byron Mallick—not that this had immediately changed his circumstances in any way, so little had changed in his life in the thirty years that he had been working there, except that his mother had grown too old for him to leave at home on her own and he had moved her to an Old People's Home on Lower Circular Road, which meant that there was no one to greet him anymore when he came home, meant that he had to prepare his own meals, at first a challenge and then a slightly sinful addiction, the business of attending to the small amount of mutton or chicken that he would bring home on the way back from work, from a nearby butcher's shop in a paper bag, pampering it just enough to yield its flavor without it withering into something hard and unconsumable. That he might also be a good cook was not something Byron Mallick had suspected when he approached him with his proposal of running his household, but Vargas had quickly taken over in the kitchen as well as presiding over the drinks cabinet and making sure that every other element of Byron's life was in order.

Did he know that morning, after twenty-four years of perfectly acceptable monotony, how his life was about to change, did he somehow subtly suspect in the way the light shone through the slats of his bedroom shutters, in the tune that the rickshaw puller passing at that moment in the street below was whistling, did he scent somehow that this was a different day to all the rest? He had not been alarmed when he was summoned just after lunch break by the manager; what had he—who had so dutifully given service for so many years—to fear? He had been a little surprised to find Byron there as well, and even more so when he was greeted by him with a warmth that Vargas had expected he might reserve for a great friend rather than lavish on an insignificant employee. Byron had explained that he was about to give a party, a very large party, and needed someone to take care of the arrangements—attend to every detail, he said to Vargas, rolling them around in his mouth as if reluctant to part with such a clever choice of words.

Vargas realized he was being put to a test but for what he did not quite know, nor indeed did it become clear to him until after he had satisfactorily executed the task, when Byron finally placed before him the possibility of spending the rest of his life in his immediate service. And how firmly indeed had he established himself as his familiar, journeying with him to foreign lands and learning their ways, enrolling himself in courses on butling, reading endless manuals on discharging such duties as he believed he had even though they were never really specified to him, on occasion even finding himself in a position to advise Byron on his choice of attire or an appropriate summertime menu. It was he who had broken to him the news of Damini's death in his Manhattan apartment, for Byron was out when Nikhilesh telephoned and it was to Vargas that he had spoken instead. Vargas had waited for Byron to return, given him the news, led him quietly to a chair, and poured him a large whisky, and another, and then another…

For her life to end like this, like this, oh, it is too terrible, Byron had said.

And then the telephone had begun to ring incessantly—enquiries from Bengali families in northern New Jersey and Westchester County—one after the other, their own displacement pouring dull liquid into the crevices of this tragedy, their own despair hanging like ponderous weights upon the event, so much more abhorrent to Byron Mallick than even the unclean clippings of her fate.

Ela cuts a pancake along the imaginary spokes of a wheel for her daughter, having doused it first with maple syrup, do you want me to feed you? she asks.

The child shakes her head and begins to hum a tune, the same song that she had asked for last night, the song that Damini regularly sang to her when putting her to bed, *the palace pipes are playing a tune to signal the end of the day, and here upon the road am I—a lonely wanderer—with nothing to show for myself but these few songs.* She hums it exceedingly well and for a moment Ela is caught between pride and interest in this achievement and a strangulating sorrow, she places her head in her hands and takes a few deep breaths. I think you should eat now, she commands the child a little harshly.

Before the pancakes get cold, I mean, she adds immediately by way of apology.

I watch Vargas as he slowly descends onto the beach, looks around for us and finally locates us through the gaps in the casuarina trees. He makes his way slowly towards us, I am relieved, I know that he will restore a balance that I badly want, between those of us who believe in Byron's innocence and those who do not, for although something within me has swung in his favor since our remarkable deliverance from the fury of the sea, I sense that Nikhilesh is going the other way, all the small hints of unscrupulousness that have gathered in their fifty-five-year-old friendship are coalescing within him into a terrifying whole and Nikhilesh has not the strength to dodge this, I know.

Vargas approaches, no one can see him except me, they do not know that he is coming to join us on this hard seashore, until he parts the branches of the casuarinas and suddenly stands before us.

He sees Byron prostrate upon the sand, his gray hair streaked with salt, observes the hunted and yet bemused look in his eyes.

Ah, Vargas, he says, how nice of you to come and find us, I am sorry we are so late for breakfast.

Vargas gazes upon him, unable to speak.

What I could really do with now is a good cooked breakfast, says Byron.

Very hard to find these days, says Piers.

There is a little hotel in Belgooly, says Byron, near your mother's house, Piers, which serves the best Irish breakfast I have ever had.

Breakfast in Belgooly—what a charming thought, says Piers.

Plump fried eggs dripping with goosefat, says Byron dreamily, white pudding as you never tasted before, toast poised in perfection between crisp and soggy, bacon that makes you dream of pigs fed on cloves and honey…

Vargas kneels down beside him, gingerly touches the wet clothes that cling to his spare frame.

Sir, who has done this to you? he asks.

We walk across the grass, the sun pricking our necks, the house laid out in front of us in cool white repose.

There was a man in Much Hoole, says Byron Mallick.

Sounds like the beginning of a limerick, says Nikhilesh, transported for a moment into the plainer reaches of their childhood.

Not quite, says Byron, not quite. He was one of the world's greatest astronomers. He worked out that Venus would transit again in 1639, after it had already done so once eight years before, but nobody believed him.

And so? asks Piers.

And so he set up a telescope to project an image of the sun onto a piece of paper in his house in the little Lancashire village where he had recently been appointed curate, to watch for this event that nobody but he believed would occur again so soon.

And why do you bring this up now? persists Piers.

Because, says Byron Mallick, extending an arm towards the morning sun, it is about to happen again today.

The transit of Venus, says Nikhilesh.

Last happened on the sixth of December, 1882, says Byron. I promised your brother more than fifty years ago that I would make sure to observe it carefully on this day, the eighth of June, 2004, he was certain he would not be alive to see it himself.

Well, he was right, says Nikhilesh.

It was a solemn pact, says Byron.

I can still see him, says Byron, I can still see your brother leaning out of the railway carriage window, waving goodbye to us on the day he left for Germany. Your father had been called to the side of a dying woman and could not come to see him off. Of your mother, he had taken leave at home in some ritualistic manner, and so we were left, you and I, to help him with his bags to the station where he would begin his long journey, we did not know then that he would never return.

In Germany Sandipan Sen married a Czech woman and lived with her in childless harmony until he died suddenly of a heart attack at the absurdly young age of forty-six. Byron still visited his widow from time to time, she lived in Frankfurt and kept herself by giving private yoga lessons, Nikhilesh knew that Byron had often helped her with her rent and her bills. He rarely mentioned it, and this made Nikhilesh think that Byron had not ceased to believe that he was still intellectually in debt to Sandipan, who had shown him many years ago that exile could be found more easily in the spaces between integers than in any foreign land.

There are still a few hours to go before first contact, says Byron Mallick, observing his waterproof Rolex with regret.

I expect you will be in police custody by then, says Piers.

Such terrible timing, says Byron, shaking his wet head.

First contact is not something you can actually observe, I remind him.

I have the necessary H-alpha filters, he says proudly.

But probably not the necessary expertise, says Piers with a broad smile.

Byron Mallick sighs. It is the black drop effect that I am most keen to see, he says.

By which he means the strange umbilicus by which the rim of the sun and the planet appear to be connected for a while before it finally wrenches itself free.

I put a hand upon his shoulder and say: I'll make sure you get to see it.

And how will you achieve that, by plying them with tea and biscuits, getting them involved in a long game of chess, perhaps? asks Byron.

I am silent, for there is nothing I can say.

You must learn to deliver on your promises, Max, says Byron, shaking his head.

How easily you make hollow everything I say! I exclaim.

Fine words butter no parsnips, says Byron Mallick.

Nikhilesh goes straight towards the dining room, where he can see Ela and Adrija sitting at the table, but Byron is keen to ascend to the library, where his refracting telescope awaits him with its face to the sun.

I can manage now, he says to Vargas, dismissing him.

Holding onto the parapet, he limps along until he reaches the door of the library, Piers and myself following. Eagerly, he hobbles towards his astronomical set-up, and begins to adjust the lenses. A young maid is crouched sweeping under it—you can finish here later, Byron tells her.

There, he says to us, there is the disc of the sun, safely projected onto a piece of paper so that the whole thing can be watched without suffering any damage to the eyes.

Not a bad way to spend your last hours of freedom, I suppose, says Piers, folding his arms.

I pity you, says Byron to him, I pity you because you have lived your life so much on the surface that you cannot see how such an event might move me, even in these strangest and most unfortunate of circumstances.

Explain to me then why this is of so much consequence, demands Piers.

Byron bows his silver head for a while, it appears that,

quite unusually for him he has no ready answer. Finally, after considering the question for a while, he raises his head and looks at Piers.

Imagine—says Byron, in a voice rich with the many stories it has told—imagine a young man, about twenty years of age, recently appointed curate of a small Lancashire village, imagine him waking on that morning, wondering if he would see that day what he so wished to see—just a black dot, not much else, passing over the face of the sun.

And did he get to see it?

In fact he almost missed it, Byron replies.

He picks up a book that is lying by the side of the telescope entitled *Memoir of the Life and Labours of Jeremiah Horrocks, To Which Is Appended A Translation of His Celebrated Discourse, The Transit of Venus across the Sun* and reads out to us:

> I watched carefully on the 24th from sunrise to nine o'clock, and from a little before ten until noon, and at one in the afternoon, being called away in the intervals by business of the highest importance which, for these ornamental pursuits, I could not with propriety neglect. But during all this time I saw nothing in the sun except a small and common spot... This evidently had nothing to do with Venus. About fifteen minutes past three in the afternoon, when I was again at liberty to continue my labours, the clouds, as if by divine interposition, were entirely dispersed, and I was once more

> invited to the grateful task of repeating my observations. I then beheld a most agreeable spectacle, the object of my sanguine wishes, a spot of unusual magnitude and of a perfectly circular shape, which had already fully centered upon the sun's disc on the left, so that the limbs of the Sun and Venus precisely coincided, forming an angle of contact. Not doubting that this was really the shadow of the planet, I immediately applied myself sedulously to observe it.

I need some coffee, says Piers, heading towards the door.

To think that he only lived to the age of twenty-two—Jeremiah Horrocks—and was the son of a Lancashire farmer, says Byron, ignoring Piers's abrupt departure.

I thought his father was a watchmaker, I say to Byron.

And where did you get that information?

Probably courtesy of Justin, I reply.

For I had been obliged to look up the transit of Venus on the internet for him while we waited in the flat for his grandmother to pick him up, last week, after having returned so hastily from the exhibition on Calcutta.

Don't you find him rather a priggish child? asks Byron.

Justin is a wonderful boy, I retort.

Such a tender age, fourteen, says Byron Mallick dreamily.

And what does he remember any more of being fourteen, I wonder, of jolting along still upon the bullock cart with Nikhilesh to school, trying to get him to see how easy it was to prove the Pythagoras theorem, if only one encased the square on the hypotenuse in a bed of right-angled triangles instead of chopping it up with senseless lines? Does he remember that only two years later, on the fateful day that they were trying desperately to reach the examination hall in time to take the exams that would determine whether they were bound for Calcutta, huddled pale in one corner clutching his pencil case, having barely recovered from a terrible attack of pneumonia which left him prone to all manner of other infections that year, they were late, fearfully late, and just as they were nearing the town the bullock cart hit a cripple.

Do not stop, Byron had pleaded with the driver, whatever you do, do not stop, he is not badly hurt and someone will take care of him, but if we get embroiled in this we will miss our exams, and no one will be able to help us then.

And Nikhilesh had not said a word, had only asked pardon for this many years later when his wife and unborn son lay in a critical condition in a West African hospital, he had clutched the hand of his ten-year-old daughter and prayed to the Lord to be forgiven. And when news came that his wife would live but their child would not, he had in his confusion, caught between relief and despair, confessed this past sin to Ela—and this moment of pain had remained part of her life long after it had ceased to trouble him anymore.

Piers finds Nikhilesh on the terrace, drinking tea and staring out into the gathering heat.

So, what will happen now, Piers? he asks him.

Ela and Adrija should leave straightaway, says Piers.

I would prefer to go with them, if that is possible, says Nikhilesh.

No longer interested in defending your friend? asks Piers.

There is very little I can do to help him now it seems, Nikhilesh replies.

Or later, says Piers.

There will no doubt be a trial, says Nikhilesh.

And you will stand by him then?

If I think it is the right thing to do.

And if you do not think it is the right thing to do?

Then I will have to let him go to hell, says Nikhilesh.

Something strange, like a crucifix, seems to move very rapidly across the white disc of the sun.

Just a low flying aeroplane, says Byron.

What a beautiful shadow it casts, I remark.

You know, says Byron, Nikhilesh and I used to wait with breathless anticipation, when we were boys, in the courtyard of my house to gaze upon the Imperial Airlines aircraft that flew over us at an appointed hour every week, carrying mail from London.

I marvel at how composed he seems, the sea salt has dried upon his features, giving them the look of well-honed limestone, he pats his damp breast pocket and shakes his head and smiles.

I have lost my pipe, he tells me.

I'm sorry, Byron.

Do you suppose they will let me smoke? he asks.

You'll be bailed out before long, I assure him.

And then?

And then you can smoke all you want.

I was thinking of prison rather than custody, says Byron.

I do not know about prison, I reply.

Ela, coming out of the dining room to talk to her father, finds him reciting to himself from Tagore's poem "Karna Kunti Sambad." Why he has chosen this poem to soothe him now in his state of extreme distress she cannot guess, and neither really can he, except that he remembers how, many years ago he and Byron had argued wildly about it on their journey back home by bullock cart after they had been called upon to dismember this unique work of art in their Bengali literature class. Karna, a character in the epic Mahabharata, had fought with the losing side and elected to stay with them, even after he realized he was a half brother of the Pandavas, being the lovechild of the Sun God and the Pandavas' mother, Kunti, and thus entitled to occupy the moral highground from where they would eventually achieve victory. He who has always known himself to be the son of a lowly charioteer suddenly finds that his ancestry contains both the kingly and the divine, and that he is born of the same woman as his mortal enemy, Arjun, the third of the Pandava brothers. In battlesweet darkness he swiftly makes his choice, he does not submit to his mother but begs instead from her leave to remain in the company of those who have trusted in him, and whom his own kin are sure to destroy. Must you, who once refused me a mother's love, tempt me with a kingdom? Karna asked his mother.

It was impossible for Nikhilesh to comprehend why Karna had not changed sides on the eve of the defining battle, knowing that he was connected to those in the right by blood. Nikhilesh felt that his decision not to join them came from wounded pride, not much else. Byron saw it differently, loyalty—he argued—loyalty and dignity come before ties of blood. All these years Karna had dragged his lowly origins about him, concealing them to gain a place at the school of archery that only accepted Brahmins, but betraying himself to be of the warrior caste in his stoicism when he endured the pain of a bee sting simply so that his master might sleep upon his lap undisturbed. It was only Duryodhan, the eldest of the evil Kauravas, who ever treated him with respect, so why should he not be faithful to such a man?

I am ready to leave, says Ela.

So am I, says her father.

But I would like to say goodbye to Byron first, she says.

She reaches towards a rose bush in full bloom in a large pot, and twists off one of its blooms.

What did you do that for? her father asks.

It is almost dead, she replies.

Still an hour to go before first contact, says Byron. And then he coughs, and it is a truly wretched sound.

I can't seem to get rid of this, he says.

You might need antibiotics, I tell him.

Started when I got caught in a shower in Central Park last month, he says.

A Pakistani vendor had offered him an acrylic "I Love NY" cap as he sheltered under the meager awning of his stall, and when Byron reached into his pocket to pay, the man had said to him—No, no, it is a gift, you look so much like my grandfather, please accept it as a gift.

The day that Damini died, says Byron Mallick.

The door opens and Ela enters, she holds an exquisite bleached pink rose of an advanced age between her fingers, a color that for some reason I always associate with the petticoats of seventeenth-century Frenchwomen.

You have brought me a rose, says Byron, you have brought me a rose, how apt.

It was drooping sadly, says Ela.

You have brought me a damask rose, says Byron, gathering the dying flower in his hands.

Byron's mother had loved roses, she had always grown them in pots where they demanded constant attention, and when he moved her to his flat in Calcutta, she insisted that they go with her. Vargas had helped her to look after them, and continued to tend them after she died. Ela had taken great interest, as a child, in the many potted roses on the balcony that Vargas fussed over so much, and that would only occasionally yield a most exquisite bloom. Byron had been delighted by this, and together they spent many evenings poring over the books that he had once brought back from England for his mother, color photographs of old English varieties that she would never see and elegant passages on how well they associated with lavender and santolina.

Some of his mother's roses he had brought down to Digha, where despite the salt wind one or two had miraculously survived under the loving hands of the old caretaker whom they had inherited with the place. The old man had lived until very recently above the garage in the room that Vargas had now made his own. About a week ago his grandson had appeared and taken him away, he told Nikhilesh—for he and the child were the only persons there at the time—because he would not have any relation of his work for such a man as Byron Mallick, although he refused to explain why.

The morning light falls full upon her face as her dark eyes softly trace the curve of the projected sun. That brow, those eyes, those lips, of what sand are they sculpted that it flows so easily into every crevice of my soul? I long to touch her, to let my fingers run aimlessly down the length of her body, I long to touch her without any purpose other than that of touching her, not to heal her or to hold her near, not to further any interests at all, but just to touch her, to touch her without the need to acknowledge our past, or the horror of this moment, and certainly not the murk of our immediate future. I long to touch her and cannot.

And suddenly the paltry incongruence of our fates takes on a new bitterness for me, it seems painfully ridiculous that when she was born I was merely a ten-year-old boy shooting hoops against my parents' two-car garage in Fair Haven, New Jersey, that while she was riding her tricycle under the blue skies of Africa I was learning how to coax girls to bring me to a climax in drive-in cinemas, and while she languished in her Presbyterian boarding school in Calcutta with Byron's intoxicatingly refined existence as her only oasis, I was gaining in self-importance at Princeton University, luxuriating in the liberty of not having to conceal my love of poetry, and trying to find a way to liberate myself from the study of medicine, which I had, up till then, seen as the only suitable trajectory for my life.

Whereas once it filled me with wonder, it tires me now to think that I had no idea while I waited, perspiring profusely by the baggage conveyor belt in Calcutta airport, that somewhere out there in the terrible August heat was Ela, who would soon totally alter my life, somewhere out there was Ela quietly pawning her wedding jewelry so that they could afford to send Arjun's brother to Vienna to finish his training in orthopedic surgery. Arjun himself was in Delhi at the time, working at an international bank, and she spent much of her time traveling back and forth between the two cities, and so remained hidden from me while my friendship with Byron grew and grew, until Arjun suddenly resigned from the bank and took a job as deputy editor at one of Calcutta's more overtly left-wing Bengali newspapers, and their lives had permanently knotted themselves around the house in Gurusaday Road.

I have tried often to picture her there, in the well-proportioned colonial villa that Arjun's great-grandfather had built for himself in the early nineteenth century. It has never been my privilege to visit its interior, and although it is a space that negates every claim I have on her, I often feel I would have liked to have known it, if only to be able to imagine her within those thick walls, her in-laws in retreat from her silence, her daughter under the constant supervision of an army of housemaids, Arjun dashing in sometimes, grabbing a bite to eat, making a million phone calls, and then rushing out again, sweeping up the frenzy of his existence from their midst. Somewhere within all this, she had had to nurse the pain of being apart from me, except that was before the child, and before the garden full of roses. Somewhere within all this, she will have to face the same pain again.

Byron places the rose beside an old magnifying glass, I see his fingers arranging it, almost by habit, at a pleasing angle to the tortoiseshell rim.

Come and kiss me, he says to Ela. Before they take me away, come and kiss me.

I have never kissed you, she reminds him.

Soon I will be sitting in the cold cell, says Byron, remembering how it was once between us, how much we laughed together, how happily we argued about the meaning of a work of art, how eagerly you listened to the essays that I sometimes stayed up late to write. I usually read them to you just after breakfast on Sunday mornings, you in your nightdress, arranged demurely upon a chair, your face smeared with the sandalwood paste that my maid always ground for you. You said it was to improve your complexion but I could see nothing wrong with it, it carried none of the blemishes so obvious in other girls your age. Indeed, the whole of you seemed utterly flawless to me, from your large bright eyes to your perfect little feet, every movement of yours was music to me, and often I would feel a great sadness for I would never be able to protect you from the ravages of time.

Time is no enemy of mine, says Ela.

It has not claimed any part of your beauty yet, if that is what you mean, says Byron.

No, that is not what I mean, she replies.

But your best days of performance are over, I suspect, says Byron.

That does not bother me, says Ela.

And why does it not bother you? asks Byron.

I do not know that I have that much more to learn from dance, she replies.

Did you ever?

Of course. It is dance that made me into who I am, she asserts.

Byron pats his pocket for his pipe and does not find it there.

You know, he says to Ela, I used to wonder sometimes what it was that you were missing. You danced so passionately, so perfectly, and yet some ingredient was lacking which I could not quite lay a finger on then. But now I know what it is—you have never cared enough about your audience.

I cared enough to be devastated by even slightly critical reviews, she reminds him.

Ah, but that was because they were an intrusion into your private relationship with dance, says Byron.

Then why was praise too not an intrusion?

Because praise never has any meaning.

Is that why you are always so generous with it?

Clearly not generous enough, says Byron Mallick with a mirthless smile.

I remember, says Byron Mallick, I remember watching you dance when you were a little girl, I marveled to see how your little feet moved to the music that your father played on his rather primitive cassette player, she has an unusual skill, I remember telling him. It was I who convinced him that he should arrange for you to receive proper training in dance, sought out for you the best master in Calcutta, made sure that one of your wretched unemployed uncles regularly took you to your lessons as I did not have the time then, nor even the means to provide the transport. It was I who arranged for your first performances—after all, how many girls find themselves on stage at the age of fifteen, however talented they may be? It was I who used my connections to get you the necessary auditions, the rest perhaps was a combination of grace and good fortune but none of it would have happened—at least as it did—without my intervention.

And then, just as you started to truly flourish, your parents removed you from the scene, banished you to cold

England, how you managed to evolve your talent during those fallow years I do not know, but when you returned you had somehow become a very mature dancer. I had been waiting of course for you to come back, I had prepared the ground for you to launch yourself when the time came as the most astonishing new performer to have emerged in the last twenty years. I lined them all up—critics and patrons—to love you.

And in these last seven years, I have painfully had to watch all the opportunities you had—that, truly speaking, I had given you—lie wasted, unnoticed. I have watched you exchange them, one by one, for all those things that you have come to treasure more—your daughter's laughter, her first dry crop of baby carrots, a fresh laid egg—even the sight of a pink helium balloon rising high into the bright blue autumn sky, I fear, fills you with more joy than the unbridled applause of a discerning audience, and this is sometimes more than I can bear, says Byron Mallick.

Before she leaves she whispers to Byron, Goodbye.

Goodbye, Ela, he says, and the memory that returns to him at this moment is of racing with her in the park outside what would later be her father's home, at that point just a building site, she was only eight years old then, wearing a red and white poncho which flapped mercilessly around her narrow hips as she and Byron ran between a row of recently planted trees. Later these same trees would arch over and become a holier space, but at the time they were like gangly adolescents waiting in line for nothing in particular to happen.

She halts briefly by the door and looks towards me, and I can see that she no longer believes that interruption can inject dignity into our desire, all those long and excruciating pauses that have lately begun to smell to me in the same way as death, not unpleasant, but final—I can see that suddenly it seems pointless to her to punctuate our passion with such bleach.

And yet I know, even as we part, that I will not be there—as she hopes—later today when Piers steps into the hallway of her home in Calcutta, I will not be there, and something inside her will finally capsize.

Is Max not with you? she will ask Piers.

He wanted to go back to London, Piers will reply.

Back to London, she will repeat.

Back to London, Piers will confirm.

We hear them leave, Byron and I, the roar of the engine, and the crunch of gravel—and then she is gone, and her sweet child, she is gone, and so is Nikhilesh, who has left without coming up to say goodbye.

I watch Byron Mallick as he stoops over the blank disk of the sun, there is only half an hour to go before the transit of Venus commences in this part of the world, I pray that they do not arrive to take him away before then.

Suddenly he says to me: You are a coward, Max, you should have made her stay with you, it would have done you both good, it was how it was meant to be.

I tried, Byron, I tried.

Oh yes? Some weak pathetic plea to run off with you, start a life without coordinates somewhere else? Wait restaurants in Manhattan while you struggled to be a writer?

What else had I to offer?

You were thirty-five, Max, you had a career, prospects, personality, everything, all you had lost was a wife. You had much to offer her, but you chose not to.

I wanted her to make her own choices.

You gave her none.

That is not true.

You would have had a few years of bliss, at least, that I know, says Byron.

And afterwards?

Afterwards, you would both be more alive than you are today.

Surely she is better off in her current circumstances than she might have been with me.

That is questionable, says Byron. It is true that Arjun adores her, but he has also managed to reduce her to nothing but a glorified housewife. He has never nurtured her spirit, never attempted to prevent her from retreating from all that had once mattered to her, giving over her attentions to rescuing the garden—which of course had once been splendid—of the Mitra mansion, and keeping the house in reasonable condition.

For Byron knows that most of her day now is spent in tireless direction of their many servants to dust and polish, and dust and polish yet again, wash the floors three times a day with a drop of dettol and a drop of kerosene, rinse the mosquito nets in bleach and hang them up from the balcony to dry, iron her husband's socks and handkerchiefs and fold them into neat piles, take the larger items to be pressed by the man on the street corner with his heavy coal-warmed iron. Then there are the meals to be prepared and served exactly as expected by her father-in-law with the right balance of variety and routine, the supervision of the washing up afterwards, the putting away of the right things in their right places, tablecloths and napkins to be washed, more water to be purified and milk to be boiled, ice to be made and leftovers that were not going into the refrigerator to be placed upon platforms with their legs in water to discourage insects. There are certain tasks she clearly likes to reserve for herself, ironing her child's clothes for instance, he has come upon her once or twice in this task and watched her inhale the hot and fragrant steam with the same lust with which she absorbed the incense in a Tibetan monastery on a trip they made to Sikkim, just Byron and herself, just before her parents sent her off to finish her schooling in England.

I remember when they came to tell me they were getting married, says Byron Mallick, he bumped his head against one of my wall lights, he was so tall, her suitor Arjun Mitra, whom I had known since he was knee-high to a grasshopper, grown now into such a handsome young man, his manners were perfect, his conversation amusing and polite. I felt a twinge of envy, but this was quickly replaced by an expansive avuncular pleasure in watching the two of them sitting side by side, so very much in love. But then I also felt a certain pity, thinking of the yards and yards of their lives still stretching ahead, that they might put an end to all possibilities by committing themselves to each other seemed a little tragic to me. You see, I did not know then how easy it would be for her to be unfaithful to him…

I do not think it was that easy for her to be unfaithful to him, I say boldly.

That is not an argument that would go down well with Arjun, says Byron with a small laugh.

No reason why it should.

He has absolutely no latitude in his morality.

What do you mean?

He possesses a vertical morality.

A vertical morality?

Yes, one that straitjackets all creativity, not just in himself, but in all of us. And with this he has crushed all of us, first his father, then his mother, his brother, Ela—and now I am his victim, his ultimate victim, says Byron.

That is an interesting line of defense, I remark.

I watched him mock his father when he was a young man, says Byron, I watched him sneer at the gifts and favors bestowed upon his father, as if he—young Arjun, then hardly out of his teens—could tell whether they were bribes, as if he had not benefited himself from these offerings, so often made in peace rather than to influence the old judge.

But surely he was right to question this?

I was able to accept it then as part of the natural history of a boy born into extreme affluence, but his utter intolerance of his mother's obsession with religion was shockingly unkind, says Byron.

Even though the Swami concerned was the cheapest of fakes?

Nobody knew that then, retorts Byron.

He was right to act by a suspicion, even if that was all that was available to him then.

But for him she would be yours, so I do not know why you are defending him, says Byron.

Because that is not a good reason to not defend him.

Perhaps, like him, you too desire my descent into hell, suggests Byron, his eyes narrowing.

I do not believe that either of us desires that, I reply.

Only once had I been alone for any length of time with Arjun Mitra, and that was when he had replaced his father in a game of golf that I agreed to play with the retired High Court judge. Instead, Arjun had turned up, for his father apparently was feeling terribly unwell, but had thought it would be impolite to cancel the game. I won easily for I had played regularly with my mother while in high school, and such skills as I had acquired then were still in place. I had easily beaten Arjun, trying all the while not to let the thought that I was in love with his wife blemish the contest.

It is suddenly so chilly, Arjun had remarked, and I had given him my sweater to wear as we made our way back to the clubhouse. He was so tall and young, so full of purpose against the pale winter sky, his eyes shining bright, I knew then that territory would never become even a subtle issue between myself and this young man, that he would never allow himself to be aware that it might be so. Watching him that morning as we sipped our cold drinks and ate freshly made samosas in the clubhouse, watching him that morning enquiring gently after the families of the various men who served us, I realized that the metal he was made of would not easily twist under the weight of others' wrongs towards him, and if this did peel at least a thin layer of dignity off me, I thought it but a small price to pay at the time.

I do not know if you know, says Byron Mallick, that she was carrying your child when you saw her last.

She told me so herself last night.

I helped her get rid of it, says Byron.

Why do you feel the need to tell me this now? I ask him.

Because it may be my last opportunity.

Your Parthian shot?

I have no need, Max, to make you suffer.

Such information, in any case, leaves me cold, for human life for me is human life only when it is granted the privilege of consciousness.

Do you not feel even slightly cheated? Byron probes.

Cheated of what?

Of the ability to stop her, I suppose.

I would not have stopped her, Byron.

No, I don't suppose you would have, he replies.

In fact, she had come close, very close, to telling me, seven years ago, that the life that was quickening within her was hers and mine, that the clockwork nature of the process firmly indicated that it could not be otherwise. Except she had not told me, for while boiling the kettle for tea in my kitchen she had suddenly found all possible consequences of this intolerable, whether it be some sordid trip to an abortion clinic, or a lifetime of fighting to find a way to bring up the child on my meager and unpredictable income, a lifetime of knowing that she had disappointed Arjun. He was likely to recover, of course, being so strong in spirit, but this she knew, that equally well he might by degrees collapse, end up like one of Damini's old journalist friends—slumped over a bottle of cheap rum at the Press Club—and this she could not bear. And so she had telephoned Byron Mallick instead, who agreed that her condition was most inconvenient and arranged a speedy termination in surrounds so secluded and comfortable that they resembled a well-appointed country house hotel rather than anything else she might have imagined, where he had insisted that she should stay and be pampered for a whole week afterwards.

And quite soon another life had taken residence within her, another life that would never have come into being otherwise and now, somewhere out there she is sitting with an arm around this other child in the back of the car that is taking them both home, warm wind in her face, the wet fields of southern Bengal streaking her senses an unforgiven green, somewhere out there she is composing her inclinations towards me into a tight petalled shape that she can pin onto her life, but I will not let it be so for I am done with that now, I cannot spend what is left of life to me in perennial heartache, and so, this evening when Piers returns to her home I will not be with him, even though her intentions are pure and beautiful and crystalled in the highest quality of desire, I will not be there.

Where is Max? she will ask.

He thought it was best if he went back to London straightaway, Piers will reply.

And upon hearing this she will at first freeze, fearing that the steadfastness of our love has turned the skies within me to gray instead of rose, that the proportions of pain in seeing her again have begun to outweigh the bliss, and her desire to be desired will remain brimmingly fulfilled. But perhaps she will also know that at that very moment I am thinking of her with my head pressed against the airplane window, I am remembering how it was to kiss her shoulder, and how her breasts had heaved and condensed to primordial clay under my touch when I lay with her, how it had been for a few moments at a time as though such a harmonious darkness would never exist again until the sun eventually folded in upon itself and relieved us finally of our every burden. Perhaps she will sense this and unlock her inward gaze to meet Piers's eyes and ask, did they come for Byron then in the end? these words blindly tumbling out of the bitter sap within her throat.

Yes, they came, and he went without a fuss, Piers will answer.

And so they had, who exactly they were I cannot say, but we heard them only minutes after Byron had drawn my attention to the small dot that had appeared like a potentially malignant mole on the surface of the sun.

The object of his sanguine wishes, he called it, young Jeremiah Horrocks, Byron said, shaking his head in deep wonder.

And as I looked upon this insignificant black mass struggling to pull away from the rim of the sun, I too felt deeply moved, as if gazing upon some infinitely gentle, infinitely suffering thing.

We heard a car pull into the driveway, footsteps on the gravel. The door was pushed open and Piers came in.

Time for goodbyes, I think, said Byron, reaching for the sill to steady himself.

Finally, yes, said Piers.

But this was not how you wanted it, said Byron.

Oh, it'll do, said Piers.

After they took him away we wandered slowly back towards the sea, Piers and I, our moods suddenly altered.

We should try and get some sleep, Piers mutters. But instead we move closer and closer to the sea, as if inexorably drawn to the scene of these last several hours' unreal events.

Were you really her lover? he asks me suddenly.

I do not reply.

How extraordinary, says Piers.

He kicks at the sand and shakes his head. To me she always seemed as if she was made of porcelain, he says.

You were not in love with her.

She must have been very much in love with you, says Piers.

To have submitted to my touch?

No, it's not that, says Piers. It's just that I realize now just how deeply it must have pervaded her life, the way she talked about you, not that we talked of you often. It all makes sense now.

Does it? I thought she had rooted me out of her heart a long, long time ago.

That would not be like her, says Piers.

And the tone of his voice reestablishes in an instant the void within me of never having known her as well as the many people who surrounded her, nourished her, admired her, and yet never had the same access to her soul as I did.

You know her so well, I say bitterly.

And you hardly know her at all, he agrees.

I close my eyes and remember the harsh afternoon light suddenly turning to orange upon her heavy lids, the damp folds of cotton rising and falling against her neck in that moment when she turned her dark eyes to me and I fell in love. And what exactly do I mean by that, I wonder, what beyond lust could have lent such dignity to my feelings that when I returned home with them, I remained all evening simply wrapped in awe of my own emotions? What indeed can be so crucial, and yet eventually, pass?

What do you think will happen to Byron? I ask Piers.

Criminal prosecution, he replies confidently, criminal prosecution and disgrace.

Prosecution, yes, but not followed by disgrace, not for Byron Mallick, and by November of the same year he is acquitted of all charges, his assets diminished, his various properties under auction, but enough remaining to maintain him in his flat in Calcutta, surrounded by penitent acolytes and those who had played a more prominent role in his recent ordeal, all of whom he is ready to utterly forgive.

The shock of the events still hangs over us, but we are determined not to let it intrude upon our jollity when we congregate at the O'Reilly's family home in County Cork for Christmas: Piers, Barbara and her family, their eldest sister Anastasia and her husband Edmund, and the matriarch herself of course, Mary O'Reilly, made recently Baroness of East Grinstead or somesuch. For a while it had united us as nothing else could, Piers, Barbara, Mary, and

I, our every muscle at every moment attuned to Byron's fate and nothing else. Barbara had arranged to spend most of the year in London, and even when she was in Kenya we had spoken daily, a habit her husband appeared to tolerate with extraordinary ease. Indeed, something has been reborn between myself and Barbara that evades definition, a friendship, a dependency, in which somewhere deep the erotic is embedded, or perhaps just embalmed.

The thought of spending Christmas with her was extremely tempting, not simply to savor the irony of it as I might have done some years ago when irony was still an antidote, but because I sensed genuine sympathy within her, and genuine sympathy is what I dearly needed. Still, I had hesitated when Piers telephoned me the week before to suggest it.

You're not going to refuse are you? Piers said, you are not going to fucking refuse having Christmas lunch served up by the world's greatest food critic, are you?

Throwing down the gauntlet, are you? I said.

More like the oven glove, he replied.

It was Barbara who was there to meet me at Cork Airport, clad in a long green cape and sunglasses—why sunglasses? Helps me see through the burning mists, she explained later in the car—Justin was with her, as well as his two younger brothers, I imagine that Mary had persuaded them to accompany their mother in the hope of having a few hours of quiet in the house. They chattered amongst themselves and with us in a manner that was almost painfully cozy, and indeed when we turned the bend and saw the house before us, rising white and pale-eyed against the winter sky, I could not but for a moment imagine that we were approaching it as we were *meant* to, Barbara and I, in our happy middle-age, with *our* boys in the backseat, excited by the prospect of wandering loose along the various wooded tracks, or descending the steep path to the bay where the boats that they used in the summer lay sleeping in their wooden vaults, the waves glinting a patient silver as they tentatively advanced towards the rocky beach. I believe the same thought might have crossed her mind as she came sharply off onto the little road—tarred now, after a fashion, I noticed (but not feathered, some perverse part of my consciousness added)—that led to the house, but what I knew also was that it was a thought that would have left her with a searing regret, whereas for me it was simply a life not lived, that was all. That it was perhaps the best one to have lived was of small consequence—to me, at any rate.

Mary O'Reilly was standing on the steps to greet me, wrapped in a shawl but shivering still. I'm so glad you could come, she said to me, planting kisses on both my unshaven cheeks.

I'm very glad to be here. Now, let's get you inside, I said to her.

And you—you must be exhausted—flying is such an ordeal these days—I have a lovely pot of tea waiting by the fire in the library and Piers appears to have baked some scones—never thought I would have a son who took such pleasure in making scones, she said.

Scones! the boys chorus.

You are to have yours in the kitchen, their grandmother tells them.

I am allowed first to take my bags up to my room, it is Barbara's old bedroom that I have been somewhat unexpectedly assigned, up on the second floor. I notice, as I walk up, that the sill of the landing window on that level is still cluttered with the antique sandglasses that interested Mary O'Reilly for a time. And there is the familiar view of the orchard, still sheltered by a tall hornbeam hedge from the salt breeze. Who delights now in this garden? I wondered, who delights in it for most of the year? It was a garden that Mary O'Reilly's great-grandmother, Alice Nagle, had created when her husband built this elegant house by the sea for her. Mary O'Reilly—once a Nagle herself—had inherited it from her father in the mid-sixties. By then, her three older daughters had more or less left home, but Piers and Barbara were still young and the house had quickly become their summer home. Mary had siphoned much of her husband's money into restoring the garden to its former glory, indeed it had been the most exciting project of her middle years, she told me once, puffing away on her couch, for it is at that time when life is not quite past all projection, that the creation of something that might possibly endure may occupy you, so it was for me anyway, she said.

And now, Mary? I had ventured to ask while refilling her champagne glass.

And now, I don't give a toss—she had replied gaily.

Only two bedrooms on this floor, Piers's old bedroom and Barbara's. I halt first to catch my breath before Piers's, which he is clearly currently occupying, judging by the open suitcase on the floor and the various flamboyant waistcoats laid out upon the bed, visible through the open door, as are the tin soldiers of his childhood and his matchbox cars, his airplanes and fire engines, all gracefully inhabiting the shelves above. And then I take the few steps that lead me to Barbara's room, which is still arrayed with tasteful and seemingly careless displays of her porcelain dolls and stuffed animals. I can see why her boys refused to sleep in there—that is, assuming they had been offered the choice—for it has the forbidding atmosphere of a toy museum.

I set down my bags and proceed to quickly unpack, in the closet where I place my few shirts and spare jacket are some old ballgowns, belonging to whom I wonder, so timeless and mothworn are their contours, Barbara most likely, but equally possible is Mary, or some previous ancestor—a Nagle perhaps, declaring her deep roots in this soil through the remarkable dignity of her attire, even as the Ascendancy are in their twilight, and there are no more battles of any sort to be won.

Max, says Piers, as I enter the library, somewhat better groomed, so good to see you—will you have a scone?

Yes, I will, thank you, I reply.

Barbara hands me a cup of tea, very lightly brewed, as she knows I prefer.

Jam and cream? asks Piers.

Yes, please, but no butter.

Then I'll have to start over, but never mind.

I'll have the one you've just buttered, Barbara volunteers.

Oh, perfect, says Piers, handing her the plate.

Let me attend to my own scone, I say to Piers, setting down my teacup.

As you wish, he replies.

I take a sip of my tea and sink back into the armchair that I am occupying, the very same one where I had sat and devoured the entire works of Samuel Beckett—when would that have been now, twenty-five years ago, I suppose—a time when I still thought I might write fiction, and that this isolated house upon the Irish coast was the best place to pupate these ambitions and yet, in my many attempts to create here the conditions that might propel me in that direction, found myself instead transformed by the literature that was available to me in this very room, one of the four generous chambers that symmetrically occupy the ground floor—the others being the kitchen, the dining room, and the drawing room, the latter two having fine views of the bay while the others look out onto the walled garden, Mary's joy and Mary's delight, and now a winter sculpture of frosted box and careful thistles, and in the middle of them an umbrella pine, its spokes in sorry disarray—to see it so brings tears to my eyes but Mary does not seem to mind, this is her preferred room in which to light a fire and take tea, whatever the season.

How was your journey? asks Piers.

No more unpleasant than usual, I reply.

So, it is to be small talk then in the wake of his acquittal, and the end of these six months that have seen us so tightly knotted around the circumstances of Byron Mallick's trial, watching from afar the evidence against him erect itself and then crumble, and the speech of the young barrister leading the charges against him suddenly veering into pathetic hyperbole as he tried to show Byron up as a plain villain, ruthlessly exploiting the Indian economy to support his own international lifestyle, not hesitating to draw any lines at eliminating any person who might get in the way of this ambition. It had not been obvious to any of us at the start that he would survive this, and yet, one November morning, I had woken to a wonderfully blue autumn sky and walked through Hyde Park, where the trees seemed so cheerfully to be clinging on to their last leaves to meet Piers for lunch, and I suddenly had known in those dripping moments that Byron would emerge from this unscathed, known that some incomprehensible dynamic was now steering the whole procedure towards a different steady state, one that was remarkably close to just how things had been before.

I have a feeling that Byron is going to get away with it, I told Piers as I sat down at his table.

Strange, said he, I have had the same thoughts myself.

I cannot imagine what odd cues we might be relying upon, I said, black in thought.

Well, I think this calls for a celebration, said Piers, calling the waiter and ordering a bottle of champagne.

A celebration of what?

I don't know—our deductive skills, perhaps?

We have no idea that we are right.

All the more reason to celebrate now, Piers O'Reilly had said.

Barbara sets down her cup of tea and announces that she has to drive into Cork to meet her husband, who is due to arrive by train from Dublin, where he has been visiting an elderly relative.

I'll take the boys with me, she says, sensing that this is what her mother, yet again, desires.

Yes, do, my darling, I fear there is not that much to entertain them here, says Mary O'Reilly.

Barbara departs, although not before filling my teacup once more, and the rest of us sit for a while, sipping more tea as the afternoon light peaks and begins to wither, speaking of such things as the weather and the merits and demerits of the Christmas choices of favorite books by noble persons in noble newspapers, and we do not mention Byron, whom Mary had been minded to shelter under this very roof to shield him from his troubles, if that were possible—which it clearly was not. We do not speak of the recent news that no charges remain against him, that his name has been cleared, and that next year he might indeed be here instead of my taciturn self in this wonderful house for Christmas, be buttering one of Piers's delicious scones himself to offer to some lady guest.

Eventually, Mary excuses herself to make some phone calls.

Piers raises himself from the sofa—I'd better start preparing supper, he says.

Isn't it rather early for that? I ask.

I think we'll have a Polish Christmas Eve—lots of fiddly little eats and flavored vodka. It'll take a while.

I know, I tell him.

Oh yes, he says, I forgot.

What he means is that he ought to have remembered that I am no stranger to a Polish Christmas, my grandmother having insisted throughout my childhood on maintaining this tradition. I remember her small elegant hands placing colored glasses around the table where we—my mother, father, my sister, and I—sat with sundry Polish friends and neighbors of hers, our Christmas presents from her already opened and so a sense of mystery already in decline, but with plates of delicious and exotic little morsels to still look forward to, and tales of her life in Poland still to be told in greater and greater profusion as she continued to consume her various vodkas, and Polish tunes to be played on her creaky piano, and Polish songs to be sung, with us smiling and applauding until such time as we were able to extricate ourselves from such immigrant merriment and return to our house in Fair Haven, pin up our stockings to our beds and settle into sleep, Christmas Day, neat and ordered, still ahead of us.

I think I will go for a little stroll, I tell Piers, while there is still some light.

Be careful on the steps to the bay, he says, they are very treacherous at this time of the year.

I nod and head into the hallway, put on my overcoat and boots and emerge into the damp cold. The garden has certainly matured in the time since I last set eyes upon it, the shrubs stand tall now on this top terrace, rubbing raw shoulders with each other, almost blocking the views to the sea, which is a shame, I think to myself, remembering the many happy evenings Barbara and I had spent lolling on the grass, with her reading, and myself mainly staring out at the boats in the bay, the odd ship in the distance. It was not far from here, in pretty Cobh, then called Queenstown, that the *Titanic* had made its last stop, and I would wonder if the inhabitants of this house—whoever Mary O'Reilly's father, Hugh Nagle, might have installed here at the time—I would wonder if they might have gathered here to see the great ship sailing to its doom. A drunken microbiologist with more than a passing resemblance to the actor Kevin Spacey had told me, at one of the many Christmas parties I had recently attended, that the *Titanic* had now effectively turned into a giant saltwater battery, powering the numerous microbes that still chewed away upon it, primitive life forms that have, in these hundred years or so since it went down, evolved into super-organisms complete with circulatory and immune systems, drawing energy from the complex chemical entity the wreck itself has become.

I walk down the steps to the lower terrace—here again the shrubs that were only knee-high to us are now tall and full, sullenly guarding the view. I push past them as one might through a barricade of grown sons and walk down a few more steps to an area of scrubland from where the sea is clearly visible, finally, and the rocky strip of beach, reachable from here by the steps that Piers had just described to me as treacherous, or by simply scampering down the easy slope, studded with small boulders and heather.

The sea again, staring balefully upon me now, and cold weed snaking about booted feet, I had never liked this shore, never felt that it welcomed me. I find a jellyfish splayed upon the mean pebbles, and for some reason the memory returns to me of my grandmother, by then a little old woman in a linen nightdress, hopelessly infirm, asking me to run a bath for her in her little apartment still full of Bohemian glass—make it hot, Max, and put some lavender oil in it, you'll find it in the cabinet, she had said. I helped her in, she insisted on keeping her nightdress about her, nothing more disgusting than an old body, Max, she said to me.

Now go and wait outside like a good boy, she had said.

Which I did for a good half hour, trying desperately to make some progress on the term paper that was due the following day. When I came back in she was lying like an aged Ophelia, her face submerged, bits of old lace from her nightgown floating around her like flowers. I did not scream but simply pulled her up by her arms, she was not dead, just trying to be.

She took a deep breath: why did you not let me drift away? she asked.

How could I? I asked in return.

It was what I wanted, surely you knew that.

But I cannot let you die, not while you are in my care, I protested.

She gave me a withering look and gathered the wet folds of her nightdress about her.

You were always a coward, Max Gate, said my grandmother.

I walk back up by a different path, one that takes me by the coach house, a smart little Georgian abode which I know that Mary O'Reilly has recently been forced to sell to an old friend, Byron having called her up on at least part of the huge debt she still owes him. In my time here it was occupied by their old gardener, for a long time effectively the caretaker of this property. I do not believe it had central heating then, but I am certain it does now as I catch a glimpse of children frolicking in their pajamas within. I look quickly away, something about its cheerful glow shames me, I feel like an intruder but stay rooted to the spot, looking towards the darkening sea.

A soft click of a door and then a voice through the thickening fog—hello—a woman's voice, sweet and soft, a Dublin accent, and then I remember that it is Julia who is staying here, her mother having been the one of Mary's various acquaintances who had purchased the coach house from her in October. Julia, pretty Julia, whom I remember as a lithe college girl, I know she is divorced now and in her early forties, with three children, but in relatively happy financial circumstances, Julia, Julia—I turn around to meet her—I don't know if you will remember me, I tell her, my name is Max Gate and I used to be married to Barbara once.

Of course I remember you, she says.

I certainly remember you.

Will you come in for a glass of mulled wine? she asks.

I really should go back, I tell her, checking the illuminated dial of my watch.

But the others are due here soon anyway, she says.

It has been the plan all along, it seems, for all of us to congregate here for mulled wine and mince pies as darkness falls, sing a few carols for the benefit of the children, and perhaps ourselves as well, so she tells me, twisting a strand of her long hair between her fingers, her lips moving like an oracle in the shaft of light that is cast from within.

Well, I'd better phone to let them know I am here, I say to her in acceptance of her delicious invitation.

Oh, yes, do, she replies.

Just in case they are waiting for me to return, I explain.

Yes, yes, she says.

And to my surprise, I find that my heart is more than ready for this as I follow her inside, watching her re-gather her honey-colored hair into a stern clip upon the nape of her neck, her manner robustly untainted by the trauma of a recent divorce, her cherubic children tumbling happily upon the sofa, a steaming wineglass handed to me, and her eyes, oh yes, yes her eyes, still green and still so piercingly beautiful, oh yes, was my heart suddenly ready for this.

When I telephone through, Piers tells me that they are likely to be late as Barbara and the boys are still at Cork Station waiting for Gerard's delayed train. I relay this information to Julia, who simply smiles and refills my glass.

Come into the kitchen and tell me about yourself, she says, putting on a video for her children.

And as soon as we have escaped to such a sanctuary as a small fitted kitchen can offer, unchanged as yet from when Mary O'Reilly had graciously ordered it to be provided in this manner with an electric oven and a washing machine, all for old Barry in the late seventies after his wife passed on and he was forced to cook and clean for himself as well tend to the gardens and the various needs of the main house, as soon as we have closed the door and made such small talk as is appropriate under these circumstances, I find myself kissing her with a passion that fairly bursts with our unknown histories and yet is secure enough to be eventually purged of them—why are we doing this, I ask her, when our lips briefly unlock, why are we doing this?

Maybe because we have always wanted to? she suggests.

I don't remember wanting to. I remember thinking you were very pretty, that's all.

But you want to now?

Oh god, yes, I tell her, reaching under her fine woolen shirt to feel her warm breasts, and quickly thereafter to the buckle of her belt, the glorious yielding of her trembling wet self to my incantate fingers.

The doorbell rings, they are here, she whispers into my hot ear.

They would be, I answer.

Gather yourself, she says, while I let them in.

She is, naturally, within an instant, cool as ice, she walks out and greets them, I hear them enter, Mary, Piers, Barbara and her three sons, Gerard's voice booming, bloody trains, he complains, sorry to keep everybody waiting.

And then there is more warm wine to be served, clove and cinnamon smells, and carols loudly sung by the boys and their father, Piers chiming tunelessly in at times, and Mary's silver tinkly voice always hovering slightly above. Barbara casts many a suspicious glance in my direction, all of which I happily ignore.

Is Nora not coming down this evening? Mary asks, referring to Julia's mother, whom she had clearly been expecting to be present at this gathering.

That was the plan, Julia explains, but Sally has suddenly to be on call this evening, so they'll be driving down tomorrow, and hopefully be here by lunchtime.

Sally? I ask.

My youngest sister, I don't think you've met her ever, she replies.

Not much traffic, I imagine, Christmas morning, booms Gerard.

I hope you are right, says Julia.

Well, if you find yourself on your own just come and join us, says Mary O'Reilly.

Oh, I wouldn't want to intrude on a family Christmas.

Darling, you'd have to try very very hard to be an "intrusion" in this family, says Piers, leaving me to wonder whether it is his family he is disparaging or extolling by these careless words, or if they are her limitations that he is covertly drawing my attention to, a despicable ability to be easily assimilated into her surroundings, never stick out. Suddenly I feel ill at ease and am glad when it is time to leave. Still, I slip back on the pretext on having left a scarf behind and assure her that I will be back, later, if she is willing to let me in at a late hour.

I'll be waiting, she assures me.

I'll be here as soon as I can, I tell her.

But when I do return nothing is quite the same anymore, even though I have taken care not to drink a drop of vodka all evening, and not fill myself too much with Piers's insidious delicacies, still something has already been lost and even though we make generous love to each other all night, it has the flat edge of a honeymoon that will lead within days to only a comfortable marriage. Finally, as we lie together after a strenuous bout of mutual satisfaction, she strokes my cheek and complains, almost cheerfully, that I am too far away.

You are right, I tell her, taking my arms away from around her and folding them over my chest.

Let me guess, you are actually still in love with somebody, she said.

I wish I knew what you meant, I replied.

You are just too accustomed to unhappiness, she said.

And you?

I have my children, she said.

And they make you happy?

For the moment, they anchor me, she confessed.

Meaning what?

Meaning that they do for me what your ex-wife still does, said the laughing nymph.

You think she anchors me?

Most certainly so.

In what way?

Oh, I don't know, it's clear to me, though, that you don't want to displease her.

Well, of course I do not.

But you have been unattached to her for more than fifteen years.

Yes, yes, but one still bears certain responsibilities.

You intrigue me, she says.

I intrigue myself, I confess, finding myself suddenly aroused again by this conversation.

But this time she pushes me away. I am afraid I have an old-fashioned respect for what actually resides in your heart, she says.

Will you give me breakfast, anyway? I ask.

I don't think so.

Not even coffee?

Not even coffee. Go back now, Max Gate, go back and try to be happy, she says with gentle affection.

I'll try, I answer, pulling on my clothes.

And you really ought to wear underclothes, she advises me.

Whatever for?

So that your kidneys do not catch cold, as my grandmother used to say.

Do you really believe that?

It must be a metaphor for something, she says assuredly.

I make my way back to the main house, let myself in through the kitchen, where I find Piers at that early hour, attending to the goose with a large hairdryer of a shape and particular hue of orange that I have not seen since the 1970s.

Like some bubbly? he asks.

It is Christmas, I suppose, I reply, reaching for the glass he has already poured for me.

You know I always used to wonder why Arthur Koestler described a girl's breasts as champagne glasses, I tell him after a few sips.

Until I introduced you to the right kind?

Until you introduced me to the right kind.

I notice a dark shape, perhaps a squirrel, bounding across the dimly lit lawn and vaulting onto the old brick wall, it skips like a harmless phantom across the tops of the overgrown espaliered fruit trees, and then dutifully disappears.

You wouldn't mind peeling some parsnips and carrots, asks Piers, pulling out a peeler from one of the many tall collector's cabinets that line one end of the kitchen.

At this hour?

There is much else to do, Piers replies.

These are filthy, I tell him, inspecting the pile of root vegetables that had been thrust upon me.

They do grow in the ground, said Piers.

The flower says, I am beholden to this earth, that I am, but can you not let me forget that I have been born out of dust, for there is no dust within my soul?

I'll peel the vegetables, says Barbara, coming unslept into the kitchen.

Thanks, Barbara, I tell her.

So, have you two been up all night? she asks.

Not I, said Piers.

I, naturally, do not reply. And then for a while we are ensconced in a sort of medieval coziness, with peeling and scrubbing and the rinsing of the insides of birds large and small, and pepper and salt ground over and into them, while the vegetables boil or suffer swift blanching, we work so swiftly and with such unearthly dedication that the goose has already been an hour in the oven, stuffed with sweet mash and all manner of herbs, when finally the Christmas dawn began to break through the old limbs of the horse chestnuts buttressing the eastern sky.

The hellebores are out already, Barbara remarks, rubbing her eyes as she stares out of the kitchen window.

They do call them Christmas roses, you know, says Piers, wiping his hands on his striped apron.

Yes, but…

Yes, I know—that corner of the garden has its own particular microclimate, I have given up trying to understand it.

He looks over at me, standing with my elbows propped upon a cabinet, cupping a glass of champagne in my hands.

You will stain your collar on those lilies, Max, now come and help me with the goose.

You should always cut off their stamens, says Barbara.

You mean neuter them, not on your life! replies Piers.

The dangers of lilies, say I, shaking my head.

Come and help me with the bloody goose, Max.

We are a large party and the bird that is to feed us is commensurately substantial, it is no easy job to hold onto it while Piers decants the hot fat into a glass jar, a job I perform with the pair of black gloves of some indeterminate rubbery material that Piers has handed to me, assuring me that they are totally heat resistant. This they are indeed but also rather slippery, and I am glad to let the partially roasted creature drop back into its tray and be shoved back into the oven to consummate its own splendid flesh and release some more of its delicious reserves.

Am I working you too hard? asks Piers.

Not at all, I reply, shaking my hands out.

You are not regretting this, I hope, says Piers.

Barbara looks sharply up from the peas she is shelling. I smile reassuringly in her direction. No, I am not regretting this, I tell them both.

I think you need some sleep, Max, says Barbara.

You're probably right, I tell her, swallowing the rest of my champagne.

Sweet dreams, says Piers, as I head out of the kitchen.

You are too kind, I reply.

—

Christmas morning, I am not in evidence until nearly noon, when I am offered a cold boiled egg by Justin, which I receive with grateful cupped hands, there is coffee still in the percolator that could possibly be microwaved, but the call of a half-empty bottle of champagne is greater, where are they all? Down at the beach in scarves and sunglasses apparently, just to breathe a bit of salt air before the orgy commences, and was he satisfied with his Christmas presents I inquire of him, oh yes, he says, oh yes, and then rather blushingly confesses that he has something for me, a small brown paper bag he produces and hands to me, on it he has scrawled my name, and then his—With affection—no mention of Christmas, 2004 being the occasion, which is a relief to me, although I do not quite know why.

I hope you haven't spent any money on this, Justin, I start to say.

No, no, they threw it in free with the book that I got my father on big-game hunting in the Rann of Kutch—not that I wouldn't have paid the 50p for it if they had let me, he says.

Well, I much appreciate it, I tell him as I extract it from the paper bag, a little red book, its binding intact, etched with what might be a double menorah of barleycorn, and above them the words ESSAYS ON THE BRITISH RAJ. I open it to the first page, which contains a fairly detailed map of undivided India, and next to it the

Contents in letters too small for me to make out anymore without the aid of my reading glasses.

This touches me immensely, I tell Justin.

I hoped it might, he says in a slightly shy voice.

Well, you were right, I reply for want of any better words.

We hear voices in the hallway as Edmund and Anastasia O'Reilly arrive, somewhat early, having set out "in good time" from their estate in the Blackwater Valley hardly a hour away.

They greet Justin and myself cordially, but where is everybody? Edmund asks, his popsicle eyes moving from me in my dressing gown to Justin in his jeans and T-shirt, while he tugs at his waistcoat and wonders, unlike us, if he has actually made a faux pas by arriving so unspeakably early.

I look at him kindly, for in our various attempts at trying to set ourselves up here, Barbara and I, in this house near Kinsale, Anastasia and Edmund O'Reilly had genuinely tried to look after us, inviting us often to their perfect home, trying to interest me in fishing and hunting rather than frittering away my time trying to write a novel, which they suspected I was incapable of, an opinion they have yet to exchange, on good grounds, for any other.

We would visit them often, eat and drink handsomely, read by firelight in the evenings, and during the day go on endless walks. Not far away were the ruins of the castle of Monanimy, under whose walls was the open-air hedge school that Edmund Burke had attended, having been sent away to Ballyduff from smoky Dublin as a child for the sake of his health. "Open air" so that no trace might be found if they needed to quickly disband, for a Catholic education was illegal in Burke's time. How had it shaped his language and his imagination, I used to wonder, to be flipped like an eel between the English of his lessons at the hedge school and of distant Dublin where his parents lived, and the Irish that he spoke with his cousins and at playtime with his schoolmates, does early bilingualism always sharpen the senses to the many shades of meaning, or merely leave them prey to a ruthless detachment between word and object? I knew very little at the time of Burke other than that he had championed the cause of American Independence, despite his abreaction to slavery. And despite the overt anti-Catholicism of many of the revolutionaries, he had wanted for them their liberty. The O'Reilly family claimed to share some kind of ancestry with him, deep Norman roots, although their family, they proudly claimed, had survived the wretched years of the Penal Code without converting to Protestantism as the Burkes had, their family had simply lain low within the green folds of Munster until the horror passed. Many a dinnertime discussion at the O'Reilly's would fall and rise to this subject. What recourse did Edmund Burke have but to claim the Protestant faith if otherwise he would be denied an education at Trinity College and the opportunity to practice law afterwards? one party would submit, while the other would hold doggedly onto the view that this was, in its ultimate analysis, morally reprehensible. It amused me to watch them argue with such passion, and I never dared then to examine myself to determine what I might have done in those circumstances, or even whose side I would now take among the O'Reilly's and their spectacularly immutable points of view.

Strange, several years later, to meet with Burke again in Byron's salon and have my ears filled this time with his florid denunciation of Warren Hastings. Hastings had pleaded that his actions be judged by different moral standards than those that applied at the time in Britain; Burke had scoffed at such an idea, accused Hastings of hiding under a "geographical morality"—as if all morality is not geographical, Byron commented when reading me this part of Burke's four-day opening speech at the trial. Byron had taken pains to present Burke to me as a man for whom language rather than thought was the putty of his imagination, a man of so rigid a sense of right and wrong as to be effectively without morals himself.

Indeed, in later years, when Byron became a regular at Mary O'Reilly's table, he too was inducted into the ritual of disagreement over Burke. I remember a particularly furious argument erupting between Byron and Edmund O'Reilly at Mary's seventieth birthday, which she had chosen to celebrate at her home in Holland Park with an intimate dinner for family and a few close friends, it was not clear to me which of these I was, but I had certainly been invited. Her other four children were there, Piers of course, Amanda and Georgina, who now lived with their successful corporate husbands in London, and Anastasia, who had driven over from Cork with Edmund for the occasion. The subject of their battle quickly became Hastings rather than Burke, whom Edmund O'Reilly saw in the words of the latter as "a captain general of iniquity," a phrase he kept repeating throughout their unpleasant interchange, while Byron continued to lay his arguments like bars of ice in front of a roaring beast.

The crimes of the East India Company, Byron posited, were nothing compared to the crimes of the Empire that came in its wake, for these were committed within the framework of accountability that men like Burke had helped put into place.

Are you suggesting that you would have done better in a system without accountability? Edmund O'Reilly barked.

It depends on whether you prefer formal discrimination to informal extortion, Byron Mallick replied adroitly.

Well, I believe Mr. Warren Hastings to be a perpetrator of both, Edmund O'Reilly bravely advanced.

On what grounds? Byron asked, smiling a victor's smile.

Edmund O'Reilly flung his napkin onto the table and stomped away, and Byron had turned to his hostess and said brightly: I have never tasted a more perfect syllabub, Mary!

To which she had replied, all froth, my dear Byron, all froth.

Anastasia and Edmund O'Reilly, I have not seen them for many years, and here they are again even more gracefully aging, still playing out their lives as best they can in their Georgian farmhouse in the Blackwater Valley, perpetually hosting their friends and family on their visits to this part of the world, their every gesture slightly inflected with the self-righteousness of having never left the homeland.

Max, says Edmund, good to see you again, old chap, it's been years.

How does it feel, asks Anastasia, to be back here?

Well, the plants have certainly grown, I reply in attempt to deflect her real question, which is rabbit-holed with all kinds of suggestions, mostly the disappointment of Barbara and myself not having decided to settle here and become involved in the management consultancy that Edmund so successfully ran, with offices in Cork and Waterford and Dublin—from hedge school to hedge fund, he had joked to me once, that's the history of my family—but I was not willing to whittle down all options to this—a great house by the sea and a stream of income from business that was meaningless to me, and therefore that I was unlikely to perform at. I had tried to explain this to Edmund but all he said was, I have been observing you now for a while, Max, and I can tell how much you like to win and that is why I know I can bank on you.

Everyone likes to win, I had retorted, it is more the measure of a man how he loses, surely.

Oh, you will never lose, Max Gate, you are too much of a coward for that—Edmund O'Reilly had replied.

We sit down to our Christmas meal, a festive table laden with birds, big and small, partridges stuffed with pears, baby turkeys braised with bacon and cabbage, quail spilling charred grapes and pine nuts, and in the center, a goose, splendidly aching with mashed potato.

Barbara and I have not been together for Christmas since our last painsoaked experience of it in Calcutta, shortly before she left me, a day I had made sure to fill with one engagement after the other so as not to have to confront my own self too fully, as I surely would have had to if we had sat down as we usually did, in smug delight, to a Christmas meal for just the two us, the prospect of which suddenly at that moment filled my mouth with ash. And what clearer signal could I have given Barbara that our life together was over than to avoid this, our sacred just-the-two-of-us Christmas meal, using some pathetic excuse about the Vice-Consul having suffered a disappointment and needing cheering up. Whatever it was she went along with it, and we endured instead a very boring luncheon at their house in Alipore, and a trip on a steamer with a number of other colleagues afterwards. And now, here we are again, sixteen years later, in circumstances so different that they could barely have been conceived of then.

The first course is samphire with quails' eggs. My boys won't eat this, Barbara says.

Give them a chance for god's sake, Piers barks.

It was George Washington's favorite dish, says Mary, as if this dubious historical fact might somehow serve to tempt them.

... half way down hangs one that gathers samphire, dreadful trade! quotes Gerard, spearing four miniscule eggs in one go and popping them into his mouth.

Gloucester in *King Lear*, says Justin.

Edgar, his father retorts.

Gloucester, Justin insists.

Edgar, confirms Piers wearily, *Methinks he seems no bigger than his head: The fishermen that walk upon the beach, Appear like mice; something something Almost too small for sight: the murmuring surge...*

What am I paying all these school fees for? Gerard asks his son.

Leave him alone, says his mother.

I cannot imagine such a conversation taking place between myself and my father and for this I am grateful, and yet, it is oddly liberating to watch them, they have turned Shakespeare into a tribal dialect and rely upon it to fulfill the same function as my father and I had done with sports, or even general knowledge, the specifics as irrelevant as the pine nuts in the quail.

Crackers are pulled and small, marginally useful, objects appear—for myself, a set of miniature screwdrivers.

Did you know that at least three arms are broken in Australia every year from cracker-pulling accidents at Christmas? says Justin.

We all laugh.

Or that thirty-one Australians have died since 1996 by watering their Christmas tree while the fairy lights were plugged in? Justin continues.

We laugh again, and this time Justin follows it up with:

Eighteen Australians had serious burns in 1998 trying on a new jumper with lit cigarette in their mouths.

Why are we talking about Australians? Gerard asks.

Piers places a dish of parsnips and red onions on the table and sprinkles them gently with balsamic vinegar.

My boys won't eat them, says Barbara.

Well, they can have baked beans then, says Piers.

Do we have any baked beans? asks Mary O'Reilly.

Plenty, says Piers.

His mother makes her way into the larder. This place is full of cobwebs, she complains.

I like cobwebs, says Piers O'Reilly, I like cobwebs whether they reside in the mind to trap your unwary thoughts or upon your Christmas lights to catch the dregs of the Christmas spirit, so abhorred by us all.

Well, my opinion of spider webs is that they are like gray hair—perfectly arranged, there is nothing more beautiful, but anything otherwise is ghastly, says Mary.

And the ones that stretch here in your own neglected home do not meet your standards?

Most definitely not, his mother replies.

Christmas lunch over, Mary O'Reilly retires to her bedroom and the rest of the party embark upon a long walk. I am the only one who chooses to stay behind, I am simply too tired still, I give them as my excuse.

I take my coffee into the library and pick from my modest pile of presents still gathered there Justin's little book, and find within it, like a hidden letter, Macaulay's essay on Warren Hastings, vastly abridged, which suits me well. I locate my reading glasses and start to flick through it, swallowing small pieces rather than trying to gain a sense of the whole—*Hastings had clearly discerned, what was hidden from most of his contemporaries, that such a state of things gave immense advantages to a ruler of great talents and few scruples...* and later in the same paragraph... *in every controversy, accordingly, he reverted to the plea that suited his immediate purpose, without troubling himself the least about consistency...*

A man of the moment he might have appeared, then, Warren Hastings, and why not, knowing that his truths were anchored to something quite beyond the immediate gains of empire, commerce, or society?

I turn the pages and find this—*The influence of Mrs. Hastings over her husband was indeed such that she might easily have obtained much larger sums than she was accused of receiving... he seems to have loved her with that love that is peculiar to men of strong minds, to men whose affection is not easily won or widely diffused...* I close the book rather quickly and begin to sink down into the comfort of my armchair, absorbing such refluent thoughts as whether I myself had been afflicted with a love that was peculiar to men of strong minds, and yet not being of strong mind myself had squandered such an opportunity in the stupidest of ways, thoughts that should have caused me to tear out my hair but instead lulled me into that kind of sleep with more than one clock ticking and the dark outside hauling itself into comfortable shapes, and human company awaited, if not quite desired.

When I wake, I feel it fit to return to the kitchen and start to clear away the remains of the feast, no easy task, and what can she be doing now, I wonder of Ela, a constant companion still to my thoughts, what can she be doing now, as I scrape the remains of parsnip and red onion from the bottom of a roasting pan, it is late in Calcutta, perhaps they have held as always their Christmas party at Gurusaday Road, a tradition that started with Arjun's grandfather when he had first acquired the house, and was carried on by his father, the High Court judge, an occasion that Arjun himself apparently abhorred but—like much else in his life of that nature—managed to tolerate for his family's sake. Would they still be hosting such an event in 2004 with his mother now hardly able to leave her bed, and Byron freshly acquitted? Somehow I imagine they would, relying on social obligation to fill the cracks that have been opened in their lives by all that had happened this year, justifying it all for the sake of their daughter perhaps, her excitement at seeing yet another tired conifer dragged in and stationed in the hallway and decked with old tinsel and some of the extremely tasteful ornaments that Byron always brought back for her from abroad at this time of year, trumpets and cherubs in matte gold, the three wise men bearing gold, frankincense, and what she used to call "mirth" but now knows to be something bitter and vowel-less, and of use in embalming butterflies.

The door creaks open, and there is Barbara in her waxed jacket and walking boots, her cheeks wonderfully colored by the wind.

I suddenly realized that we had left you to do all the clearing up, she says.

I hadn't any real intention of attending to it, I confess to her.

I had a feeling, though, that you might feel obliged to try, she says.

You know me so well, I reply.

She turns to me smiling, not so very different to how I remember her as she was when I first set eyes upon her, emerging from behind Piers into the sunlight, her blond hair cropped close to her delightful skull. I had thought in that moment that life could produce nothing better than this, about which I was wrong, and am grateful to be, for what could be worse than to have adhered to such an impulsive judgment on the quality of erotica?

Why are you looking at me like that? she asks.

Just thinking how beautiful you are, I reply.

I thought we were done with flirting about thirty years ago, she says.

I'm not flirting with you, Barbara, I'm just telling you how beautiful you are.

As any kind ex-husband would, she says smiling.

I hand her a dishcloth and hold her gaze for a while.

I wonder if you could love me again, I say to her.

What do you mean? she asks.

I don't exactly know, I answer, I think I am simply trying to understand the nature of love.

As if there is only one kind of love, Barbara exclaims.

No, it is painfully obvious there is not, but perhaps I am more concerned with the residues of love than love itself, and there is some unity there among different kinds of love, I suspect.

There are those, she says slowly, for whom, quite frequently these days, love turns to hate.

And that has never included us, I gaily pronounce.

No, says Barbara. I have watched your love turn not to hate, but into pity.

Into pity?

Yes, Max, and that was worse than watching it turn to hate.

Except that now, Barbara, when it is your turn to pity me, there is some hope, is there not, of neither pity nor hate but something else?

What else? she asks, smiling like a Madonna with no care except for the deliverance of this world.

Just something to lead me into this imminent night? I suggest.

It is no good, she spells out suddenly harsh and cold, it is no good trying to call upon me again now.

You were never my insurance policy, I assure her, I would never have been so honest with you at the time if you were.

Dust to dust, Max, she reminds me, ashes to ashes, and flesh to flesh.

And what can she be doing now, late on this Christmas Day, does their guest list still include Byron Mallick, the Mitras of Gurusday Road, with her now, Ela, as their hostess, her mother-in-law having been bedridden since early October of a stroke, what can it be like now, the last flares being lit, the last rum cocktails served, the remaining samosas put away, what can she be doing now but perhaps settling her daughter to sleep, or wandering among the detritus of the party, and thinking perhaps of nothing but me.

You are thinking of her, aren't you, says Barbara.

How well you know me, I reply.

I could always recognize that dreaminess, she says.

That dreaminess that descended upon me in the summer of 1988, and never passed.

I wonder why it still hurts to think how much more you loved her than me, says Barbara, her smile suddenly dissolving.

Oh, Barbara, I'm so sorry.

No reason for you to be, she says, dabbing her eyes with a used napkin.

My feelings I could not control, but my actions I could have.

Why, says Barbara a little bitterly, why are feelings not in the same jurisdiction as actions?

Don't complicate things for yourself, I advise her. You have come this far and done so well, don't complicate things for yourself now.

Gerard would be quite happy to let me go, she says.

How do you know? I ask her.

He has been seeing somebody else for years.

That does not mean he would let you go.

We have discussed it.

And would you come and live with me again?

Would you want that? she asks anxiously.

I would want it very much.

I wouldn't want to live in London, she says.

No, not London again, I agree.

In the country, somewhere.

A small rectory perhaps?

Where I might make a garden, I long to say, where I might make a garden filled with various shades of box and a few marble urns purloined from Eastern European cemeteries to fill with my unspent desire for another woman.

No, Barbara, I say to her instead, you have worked long and hard at this life, now give it it's due.

And leave you to fill yours with candyfloss, she says pointedly.

By which she means that she had indeed jerked awake the previous night beside a snoring Gerard, as she heard my footsteps, stealthy but not stealthy enough for her trained ear, the crunch of gravel as I made my way to the coach house to be with Julia.

I sigh and look away, I have nothing to say to her on that matter, nor even to myself in fact, we find ourselves eventually sitting at the kitchen table drinking the peppermint tea that she has just brewed, a multitude of roasting pans soaking in the various sinks, an army of dishwashers chugging away in the scullery, Mary's poodle sunk on the sofa stupefied with leftovers, we sit and sip our tea in silence, waiting for the others to return.

And soon enough they are back, the thrill of the cold

and the saltbitten wind still in their footsteps, the boys troop straight into the kitchen in search of more food, Piers and Edmund follow them, I offer them tea, and Piers sniggers.

What I want right now is a large glass of Madeira, he says.

How peculiar, says Edmund.

What would you like? asks Piers of his brother-in-law.

I'll have a coke, says Edmund, a clear submission of alcoholism, and indeed the care with which he adds to it just the right amount of crushed ice and lime suggests that he is investing in it all the ritual of making a perfect cocktail. He sits down at the other end of the long table and picks up a copy of *The Spectator*. The boys, having stuffed themselves with odds and ends of goose and gamebirds, leave to set up a game of Cluedo, encouraging us to join them when we are ready.

So, says Edmund O'Reilly—as if finding a cue in the suggestion of playing a murder-mystery board game—so, that Bengali scoundrel managed to buy his way out of it then, he says, while still leafing through *The Spectator*.

He has always categorized Byron as an upstart, a man of new money who acquired such refinements as was necessary to place him above his true station. I remember the final exchange of words between them some years ago at Mary O'Reilly's seventieth birthday party. Edmund and Anastasia had taken their leave early as they intended to spend the night with friends in Warwickshire.

It will be a long hot drive, Edmund said.

Surely you have air-conditioning in your car? Byron asked.

Can't stand that sort of thing, he replied.

Too middle class? Byron taunted.

Too unnatural, Edmund O'Reilly answered.

More unnatural than throwing all those fish whose lips you have ripped back into the river? said Byron.

What would you know about fishing? replied Edmund O'Reilly.

As much as any native is capable of knowing after a few years of exposure to the habits of their colonizers, said Byron.

I am an Irishman, we played no part in colonizing you or in reducing your culture to a state that could easily produce men so lacking in grace as yourself, responded Edmund.

Byron Mallick looked him in the eye and smiled.

Well, now I am truly crushed, he had said.

Why do you not answer? asks Edmund O'Reilly, looking accusingly at Barbara, Piers, and I, gathered at the other end of the table like a silent subcommittee, Can it be that you actually believe that a verdict of not guilty should have been returned?

It's just something we thought we would not discuss today, explains Barbara.

A moratorium on the subject? Why? To preserve the spirit of Christmas? Or because your mother still owes him so much money? asks Edmund.

That will be paid back, says Barbara calmly.

Oh, I know, says Edmund, I know it will be paid back, it is I who will be doing the paying.

I thought we had agreed that we would all contribute, says Barbara.

And out of what funds will you do that? You and Gerard cannot have much left after you have paid your boys' school fees, I suspect Piers's income does not quite match his expenses, and the other two will find some way to wriggle out of it, no doubt.

I do not wish to carry on this conversation, says Barbara, standing up. She places her teacup in one of the sinks and leaves the room.

I think it's time for us to leave, says Edmund, setting his Waterford crystal coke glass down on the table with a heavy thud, I'll go and find Nan, he says, meaning his wife, Anastasia.

After Edmund has departed, I tell Piers—You are not going to approve of this, but I have decided to go and see him.

You must be joking, he replies.

I'm not joking.

You are talking about Byron, aren't you?

It is Byron that I am intending to visit.

Surely you do not believe in his innocence? says Piers.

No, I tell Piers, I do not believe in his innocence.

Then why are you going?

Because I cannot also bring myself to believe in his guilt.

So how will going to see him resolve that?

I do not know, I confess.

Poor Max, said Piers, when will you ever get over him?

And indeed, only a few weeks later, I find myself in congested slumber upon the Eastern Calcutta bypass in a taxi on my way to see Byron Mallick. The year before, Byron had—without my knowledge—furnished me with an upgrade, but this time I had no such patronage and so arrived, utterly exhausted by ten hours in cramped steerage. No car was there, either, to meet me, so I had climbed into a black and yellow taxicab, given the driver the address, and promptly surrendered to thick and sticky sleep.

I jerk awake as the car turns into the courtyard of Byron's mansion block apartment building, and suddenly there she is, Adrija, half a year older, walking ahead of us with her mongrel dog, she turns to see who it is and then, instead of waiting for me to get out, hops in beside me when the driver stops and opens the door.

You remember Kimbhut, she says by way of greeting, hugging the dog to her thin chest.

I certainly do, I reply.

The creature has lost some weight since I last saw him, more of the caravan hound in him than the setter now. As soon as we draw up into the parking area and the driver opens the door, the dog scrambles out from her arms and she rushes away after him. I step out of the taxi and make my way up the familiar broad stairs, the driver following with my bags. They are heavy, for even on a journey such as this, I carry in my suitcase a pair of antique standpipes that he had intended to take back with him last year, but for obvious reasons could not.

There is no immediate sign of Byron, but the girl reappears with her dog.

Come into the kitchen, she commands me.

I marvel at how easily she accepts me as part of the constellation of adults in her firmament, come on, she says, laying her small fingers upon my damp sleeve.

Are you sad about something? she asks me.

No, just confused, I reply with unnecessary truthfulness.

Oh, she says, utterly unconcerned.

She skips her way to the kitchen and I dutifully follow. Vargas is there, quietly peeling carrots by the sink.

From the refrigerator the child extracts a plastic bag, and from it a large block of ice. She places the monolithic object upon a wooden tray.

Look, Vargas, it has turned to ice, she says.

Yes, memsahib, it has, says Vargas.

I clear my throat and say: Hello, Vargas.

Good afternoon, sir, he replies.

I filled this bag with water, the child tells me.

And it has turned to ice, I remark.

Isn't it wonderful? she says.

It is the most wonderful thing in the world, I tell her.

I hear a cough and turn to find him, framed within the doorway, Byron Mallick, tapping his pipe against the peeling green paint, I am shocked to see how much he has aged, particularly his eyes, the gaze that had once pinned my entire existence onto a bed of dry wax, where within those watery depths will I find it now? Why do I long to find it again? What did it ever bring me but chaos and harm?

Being acquitted has restored my reputation Max, but not my health, he says, noticing how I look at him.

I'm sorry, Byron.

So you should be, Max.

That is why I am here today.

Not to ask my forgiveness, surely.

No, not that.

Byron Mallick smiles, and it is not a smile that I recognize as ever having seen upon his face.

Where is Kimbhut? he asks the girl.

Running around somewhere, she replies.

You had better go and find him, says Byron.

The girl runs off, leaving the block of ice to melt in the tray.

Why exactly are you here then, Max? asks Byron.

Were you hoping I would come all this way just to apologize?

Perhaps.

I lay my fingers upon the ice. What I have come here to gain is faith in some version of events, I tell Byron.

Which you do not yet have?

Which, I am afraid, I do not yet have.

So, in your head, I may still be a criminal, is that correct? asks Byron.

I have to acknowledge that possibility, I tell him.

Then you are taking a grave risk, are you not, by being alone with me here?

It is a risk I can afford to take.

Not knowing the truth is eating you from within, then?

In a manner of speaking, yes, I confess.

The scandal has naturally diminished him financially, a state from which he is unlikely to recover, but I do not read the regret that I expect in his voice as he says this, he certainly has enough to retire on comfortably, enough to carry on living the same life, now that his friends and acquaintances are ready to accept him again.

Come into the dining room, says Byron.

The sitting room, he explains, is still piled with unpacked boxes from his properties in London and New York which he has been obliged to sell.

Will you have tea or coffee, sir? Vargas asks, as I make to leave the kitchen.

There is something about his manner that is a little

more confident, no doubt the balance of power in his relationship with Byron has been altered by how staunchly he has defended his master and tended to his needs during the trial.

Tea, please, Vargas, I tell him.

In the corridor outside the kitchen there still hangs a large and grainy reproduction of Joshua Reynold's portrait of Omai, the Tahitian.

Whatever actually happened to Omai in the end? I ask Byron.

Joseph Banks felt the experiment was over and sent him back, he replies.

The experiment of introducing him to British society?

There he was still very popular, but for Banks he had served his purpose, says Byron, he starts to laugh, but then a fit of terrible coughing overtakes him, dry helpless coughing.

And did Omai ever settle back into his own culture? I ask, when he has recovered.

No, he never did—died within a few years, killed probably, says Byron.

A victim of his own international success? queries Piers.

If you like, says Byron.

Of course, Cook never came back himself from that voyage, he adds.

Vargas brings my tea, and with it some buttered cream cracker biscuits, not something I can imagine Byron allowing him to serve me before these recent changes to their lives.

Are you working on another book, Max? asks Byron.

I'm afraid I have not quite recovered yet from last year's events to be able to concentrate on anything.

You haven't yet recovered, eh? says Byron with sarcasm.

Nor do I feel that I will until I can trust in a particular version of what really happened.

Do you not have a favorite?

No, do you?

The verdict, Max, why not simply trust the verdict.

You cannot have faith in a verdict. A verdict may map closely onto your idea of the truth, or it may not, but you can never have faith in it—by definition.

I do not know what you mean, Max.

A verdict is just the best we can do as a society in the absence of access to the truth.

So you still think I was responsible? says Byron bitterly.

I'd like not to, god knows I'd like not to.

Byron bows his head for a moment and then looks up, his face horribly hollowed by uneven sunlight, but his eyes flash brightly as he says:

I'll try my best, Max, I'll try my best.

So what does Piers think of this matter now? asks Byron.

Piers thinks nothing. Piers is bored with you, bored with it all, I reply.

And Mary? asks Byron, what does Mary think?

Mary believes in you, always has.

She still owes me quite a lot of money, says Byron.

Barbara is seeing to it that she pays you back.

Barbara?

Yes, my ex-wife Barbara.

But, Barbara was never on my side, says Byron Mallick.

Barbara may not have liked you, I tell Byron, but for her that would be all the more reason she would want to see your money returned.

Yes, I can believe that, says Byron.

You say it with such disdain!

That is because disdain is what I feel.

But why?

I see her as yet another victim of one-dimensional morality, says Byron.

Like Arjun?

Indeed.

And what does Arjun think of your acquittal?

He is deeply suspicious. In fact, I am sure he is always thinking of other ways to catch me out. I really have to keep my head down these days, Max, it's a stultifying existence.

Can you not return to your academic pursuits?

The sense of purpose in that dried out a long time ago for me, Max. No, the only thing I can do without arousing suspicion these days is charity work. I have been spending a lot of time up at the shelter in Darjeeling. Arjun—naturally—thinks it is some twisted form of atonement but Ela believes that I want to actually achieve something, which I do, and it is really the only arena where I can.

Well, I suppose that is at least slightly noble of you, whichever way you look at it.

Besides, I did sink a fairly large chunk of money into it once, says Byron Mallick.

So he had, so he had, in a vastly different time to this, magnanimously handing over large checks signed in his beautiful hand to a supremely uncomfortable Damini while Ela smiled by her side, pleased that she had been able to persuade her cousin to make this petition, happy to see Byron exhibiting such a great generosity and clinging to the hope that such a gesture might finally create an understanding between two people she so loved, who had not been able to abide each other from the moment of their first meeting, if not actually earlier than that, for Byron had started to openly mock Damini's vision of the world as Ela presented it to him long before he actually set eyes upon the dark complexioned and in his opinion, rather ungainly, maiden who treated his flat quite insolently as a place to which she might come and go as she liked, intrude upon his precious time with Ela, and worse still, induct her into a way of thinking whose framework was dubious and language crass, very crass, to Byron's ears. No love was lost between them in those years while Damini was in college, forming her convictions and allowing them to sink into the foundations of her personality, and Byron was sandpapering his inclinations and ideas to fit into a different role than that which he had originally envisaged for himself, as his business expanded and brought him within sight of other goals. And tossed between the two of them, Ela, finding solace nowhere in the end other than in dance.

Piers is writing an opera, I tell Byron.

About me? he asks.

Why would it be about you?

I imagine that neither of you has had the time or energy to think of anything else, says Byron.

Well, if it pleases you, you might consider yourself the template for the main character, I tell him.

And what does he do?

He abducts a child, in cold daylight, while her sister plays the wonderhorn nearby, oblivious.

Does anybody see him?

Yes, a young burglar who has been keeping vigil for many days with a completely different intention.

And how does he react?

He records the license plate.

And so they are easily tracked down?

Indeed.

But where?

Legoland.

Byron fills his pipe cautiously.

Does it have a title? he asks.

I believe it has a working title.

Which is?

"An Ornery Sod," I reply.

Yes?

Or "Dreary Noons"...

Why the latter?

Just an anagram of the former.

And why the former? he asks, coughing badly.

I have no idea, I tell him.

You will be happy to know, says Byron, that all this fuss has at least had a positive effect on Ela's career, people are flocking to see her, pretending that their interest has no connection to the great scandal.

I was under the impression that her performances were always sold out, anyway.

Yes, but the eagerness of the crowd is now tinged with the energy of prurience, and this has made her take an interest in them after all.

I don't believe you, I tell Byron.

She has certainly started to perform more regularly, anyway. She is in Bangalore at the moment.

Is that why her daughter is here?

She does not know that her daughter is here.

Where does she think she is?

With Nikhilesh.

He explains to me that Nikhilesh has had to move in with him because of some serious plumbing problems at his own home. He had been looking after Adrija, both her parents being out of town, when the taps suddenly ran dry and so they had come to seek refuge in Byron's apartment, the past clearly put behind, rapidly and firmly put behind.

And where is Nikhilesh? I ask.

Deep in afternoon slumber, I suspect, replies Byron.

Sleep, what a precarious friendship I have had with it lately, with it sometimes smothering me in a much wanted oblivion, and at other times denying me its embrace, but most often spreading itself upon me like the folds of a tattered shroud, as if intent on revealing to me that it is but a poor relation of death.

So Nikhilesh believes in your innocence then? I say to Byron.

I am sure Nikhilesh has given up on believing in anything, he replies with something like a laugh.

And why would he do that?

Because there are bigger things in life than believing, or even knowing.

Like what? I ask him.

Like her, he says, gesturing towards the child, who has conveniently darted into the dining room in pursuit of her puppy and rapidly darted out again.

And what I see upon his face for some reason illuminates for me how my mother must have felt all her life in her immaculate New Jersey kitchen, fixing meals for us, breakfast, lunch, and supper, day in and day out, ferrying us to and fro from our activities, our parties and sleepovers, I realize suddenly that the look of great love that I always imagined I saw upon her face was, in the main part, of abdication from belief in anything other than us.

I had not realized, until now, what a luxury the

pursuit of truth was, what an enormous luxury, I tell Byron.

Well, at least it is a luxury you have been able to indulge in most of your life, Max, he consoles me.

Unlike yourself?

I lost faith in truth, Max, when I realized how much truth had merged with surveillance in the modern consciousness.

I do not understand you.

So what is new?

Indeed.

What I am trying to say is that I have no problem with truth, says Byron Mallick, as long as there are social mechanisms in place for the proper concealment of truth when it is necessary.

And why is that so?

I thought you of all people would understand this, Max.

Me, why me?

Because it was your inability to conceal the truth that led to the chaos in your life.

You mean the fact that I was unable to cover with sand what was etched upon my heart?

Precisely that, says Byron Mallick.

The shadows of the early afternoon lengthen and congeal upon the dead walls, and I am in the grip of that same tropical stillness that had once brought me a delicious peace and yet eventually came to mock the very notion that I might find respite anywhere other than in the silence that rushed over our hands and lips as we drew them apart under our own watchful and penitent eyes, so many years ago.

So she does not know her child is here? I repeat to Byron.

I do not think she would mind, he replies.

Because she trusts you again?

Byron Mallick turns to look at me, I notice that his irises are outlined in a cloudy blue, as if slowly being rinsed by age of their natural color.

Do you really think I could ever have done her any harm? he asks.

I never imagined that you could do anybody any harm, once.

And now?

The jury is still out, I reply.

I hear a door creak as Nikhilesh comes out to join us, fanning himself with a slim newspaper.

So you are here already, Max, I hope you had a good journey, he says.

Very pleasant, thank you, I reply.

Unusually warm and muggy for this time of the year, says Nikhilesh.

It is supposed to rain later, says Byron.

And no doubt hold up the repairs to my plumbing, groans Nikhilesh.

You cannot have it both ways, says Byron.

Something in the banality of their interchange brings a lump to my throat, I excuse myself and get Vargas to show me to my room. My suitcase has been laid on a walnut wood coffee table under the window, I open it and have to remove the several books that I have bought to read in the five days that I intend to spend here, before I can gain access to the rest of my things. I make my way to the adjoining bathroom and turn on the shower, but the water from the overhead tank is already unpleasantly warm, and so instead I take one out of a line of full buckets that stand against the marble wall and tip it over myself. There is a rush of wings as the birds roosting under the eaves fly away, terrified by the sound of water crashing from my shoulders onto the bathroom floor.

I lie down under the ceiling fan in my boxer shorts, it is indeed very warm for January. I take from my wallet a little notelet that Ela had sent in response to the postcard I had written to say that I was coming, she has agreed to meet me the day after tomorrow at the Grand Hotel for lunch, her handwriting is like an impenetrable shield whose surface is somehow achingly familiar. I put it back in my wallet and drift into a steel slumber with my head buried in a pillow, and am awakened some hours later by the roar of thunder, lift my eyes to the window to see that the sky is knotted darkly now into stormcloud, soon there will be rain, and relief, and the eager smell of soaked earth rising to meet our nostrils.

And if she does not come, after all? I suppose I shall drink a quantity of gin and tonic and then go for a walk to see how it has all changed in the last fifteen years, the old street names will perhaps have finally vanished now from use, Hungerford Street, where Barbara and I lived, I know, has experienced much demolition, so it is just as well that it calls itself something entirely different now. I will take refuge in the emptiness of revisiting, and despite myself will see the kernel of yet another meaningless book beginning to form within me out of such an experience.

I dress myself, then take out of my suitcase the standpipes sheathed in bubblewrap and immeasurable yards of sticky tape, and my own gift for Byron—a ticket to the trial of Warren Hastings—which I had chanced upon on eBay while carrying out my usual searches before settling down to serious work, as necessary to me now as my morning ablutions. It had cost me a mere £60, despite being over two hundred years old and a relic of one of the most extraordinary public events of the time, but it is no longer a name that sends the fabric of the nation atremble, Warren Hastings, pale and alone in the hungry crowd, Burke leading the charge against him—flanked by Sheridan and Fox—eloquent Burke, over-eloquent perhaps on this occasion, accusing Hastings of desecrating an ancient culture in order to advance the interests of the East India Company without a thought as to where such rules might have been laid down in the first place, not least where within his own heart, Edmund Burke. Later, he would revile the French Revolution on the same terms and reveal himself to be a champion of aristocracy rather than culture, and the fallout from this, among other things, would lead to Warren Hastings finally being acquitted of the several articles of impeachment, seven years from when the charges were first leveled against him.

Pale and alone in the hungry crowd, and yet somewhere

among them, flamboyant in her eastern silks, his wife, Maria. Days together waiting for the trial to recommence, days spent in the restoration of the family home in Gloucestershire that money from the colonies had allowed him to be lord of again, days spent waiting waiting, the hourglass turning round and round, the fritillaries too early that year and the roses with their petals singed by a late frost, but always Maria, never any other music in his life but Maria, hidden from him now in the sea of faces eager for his disgrace.

They are already at the table eating curried chicken when I arrive, my senses still slightly in disarray from this sudden and unexpected exposure to fresh rain.

So you have brought my standpipes, observes Byron.

They have been sitting in Mary's hallway for well over a year now, I reply.

I wonder what she would have done with them if the verdict were different, says Byron.

Returned them to Chadder & Co, no doubt.

And kept the refund?

You seem not to trust her at all.

I have seen how badly she needs money, says Byron.

That does not mean that she will stoop to anything to procure it, I say in defense of Mary O'Reilly, who had once cut many sandwiches for me with her bejeweled fingers in the kitchen of her Holland Park house, for no reason but to show me that she loved me and that she was in charge.

I have brought you this as well, I say to Byron, handing him the ticket in its plastic zipcase.

He wipes his fingers on his napkin before reaching over to accept the gift. I see a grim mist settle upon his eyes, you are very thoughtful, Max, he says.

Just something I found by chance, I protest.

Do not diminish yourself, pleads Byron Mallick.

That was not my intention, I reply.

You have an unfortunate addiction to honesty, says Byron.

It is just an addiction, I console him.

A corkscrew crookedness, Mark Twain credited him with, says Byron.

He said that of Warren Hastings? Nikhilesh asks.

Apparently so. Clive he said was crooked enough, but as straight as a yardstick in comparison to Hastings, replies Byron.

Is that so? says Nikhilesh, relishing his own incredulity.

If you will pardon me, sir, says Vargas, I believe that he also said that, despite these deeds, Warren Hastings saved for England the Indian Empire, and that was the best service that was ever done to the Indians themselves.

Thank you, Vargas, says Byron, I wonder if you could close the shutters now.

For a wind has started to rise and drive the rain into the room, more thunder, more lightning, and soon the power fails and kerosene lamps are brought in. How regal he had once looked in this light, Byron Mallick, as he sat telling stories and puffing away at his pipe, I would almost welcome the atmosphere that was created during the many power cuts we were subjected to in Calcutta in the '80s, I would let myself quietly drown in the shadows cast upon the high ceiling by the blades of the still ceiling fan, the edges of towering bookcases, the claws of the antique betel-nut slicer sticking out from the bookshelf, a corner cobweb suddenly brought into relief, and Byron's voice, like that of a good innkeeper, holding us in a travelers' harmony.

How splendid he once looked in lamplight, Byron Mallick, and yet how cruelly it carves his flesh now into sallow deathly trenches that I long to fill with a different clay. Once it had picked from his eyes a fire that made it impossible for any but himself to live other than in utter pursuit of the truth, today they are like the insides of old refrigerators, cold and underlit.

You look as if you have just sucked the poison out of a dead snake, Max, he says to me.

It is just the weight of the fifty years that I have spent on this earth, I answer.

A weight that dances lightly upon you yet, he says.

What do you mean? I ask.

You do not look a day over forty. But time will catch up with you, eventually, and reduce you to this that you cannot quite bear to recognize as me, says Byron.

I will not pretend that you do not look old, but that is not what frightens me, I tell him.

What then?

You do not look as if you are at peace with yourself.

I am sorry you do not find me in a state of saintly desiccation, says Byron Mallick.

The rain abruptly ceases, like the sudden end of a torrid love affair, there is only a wet silence and no promise of anything ever to take its place. I begin to wonder if it has not been a mistake to come here, what could I have possibly been hoping to achieve? And what value is there anymore in reestablishing a friendship with Byron, who clearly has no room anymore for any of us in his heart. That life is over now for him, of meeting Mary O'Reilly at the Palazzo Gritti for a quick martini, a water taxi waiting to whiz him across to the airport to catch a flight to New York, that life is sealed and put away in a place where such memories can rustle like old ballgowns never to be released again from their cedarwood hangers, that life is no longer of any interest to him, but part of me longs to believe that our friendship lies very much outside of it, wants to reaffirm that the best part of what existed between him and me was in the magic of our days in Calcutta, the eagerness of our spirit to feed off each other's very different histories, an enchantment in another which so rarely forms outside the boundaries of desire.

After dinner, we play Snakes and Ladders with Adrija, still by lamplight, the dice clinking softly in the dark and counters moving in and out of columns and rows, up the ladders, down the snakes, it is all strangely harmonious and imbued with a false sense of this being the rhythm and substance of our lives. I have not felt so comfortable in a long time, and let myself be seduced by the darkness, the calling of frogs and night insects, the easy turns of fortune in our game, until he coughs, Byron Mallick, and it is a desperate cough, its bite penetrating every inch of its bark.

My god, you sound ill, I say.

I am ill, he replies.

And so saying, gets up and takes himself off to bed, rasping a small goodnight, leaving me and Nikhilesh with the girl to finish the game.

Later, after a few whiskies, I stagger to my room and fall into long dreamless sleep. When I awaken, it is to that strange feeling of knowing where I am and yet more particularly, knowing where I am not. I haul myself unwashed towards breakfast, which I know that Vargas will soon cease, out of principle, to serve. Adrija is still at the table eating cornflakes, liberally sprinkled with sugar. Nikhilesh has had his whey, perhaps with puffed rice, and is reading upon the balcony stretched out on an old sofa with arms designed, once upon a time, to accommodate a multitude of East India cocktails, but being used instead at the moment to support two separate piles of books. Byron has yet to emerge from his bedchamber and Vargas is flapping around, obviously worried about his master's condition, but too proud to inquire whether his fears are rational.

I'll go and see how he is, I tell Nikhilesh.

I find him propped up against his pillows, eyes closed but not asleep.

I think I have a fever, he says.

We'll fetch a doctor.

It can do no harm, I suppose.

You need medical attention, Byron.

He opens his eyes, made starkly luminous by his high temperature.

Tell me Max, how can you tent-peg your life so that it is not too much swayed by the wind, and yet not so firm as to be effectively tethered by brick and mortar to your ideals? he asks.

I have no answer to that, Byron.

I did not think you would, Max.

I place a hand upon the noble curve of his forehead, feel his temples throbbing.

Try and rest now, I entreat him, please try and rest.

The child is playing on the piano as I emerge from Byron's bedroom, Corelli's Sarabande, I find it oddly soothing, the competence of eight-year-old fingers utterly unsupported by an emotional understanding of the piece.

Nikhilesh, who has been sitting reading on a nearby sofa, puts down his book as the child finishes her practicing and skips away in search of the dog.

I have a feeling that he is not ordinarily unwell, he says.

There isn't any reason why he should be, is there? I reply.

Well, surely the stress of the trial—and those dreadful people he was locked up with.

Not for any serious length of time, I remind him.

But could he not have caught something off them?

Not easily.

What gives you the confidence to say so?

Something of an education in risk, not a complete one, but better than most, I venture to say.

There is no crack in the odds so narrow that one might not snag a toe in it, says Nikhilesh.

And you think that is what has befallen him?

He was acquitted, says Nikhilesh.

And so?

He was acquitted, he repeats, as if this might somehow also improve Byron's chances against a life-threatening illness.

I am sure it is simply a bad bronchitis brought on by this freakish weather, I reassure him.

I hope you are right, says Nikhilesh.

By mid-morning Byron is worse, his breathing tortured, eyes sunken, fever high—a local general physician has been and gone and left a prescription as long as his arm for every kind of antibiotic known to man.

Vargas brings the list out to us, bewildered. I had better go to the pharmacy straightaway, he mutters.

Has he had anything to eat? I ask him.

I have made him some chicken soup from last night's leftovers, sir.

But when Nikhilesh and I tiptoe into his room he is asleep with his back to us, and the soup sits cold and untouched on the table beside his bed.

Best not to disturb him, says Nikhilesh.

We walk cautiously back into the sitting room.

Would you like a whisky? Nikhilesh asks.

A little too early for that, wouldn't you say? I reply.

I always take something before lunch, he replies.

The child wanders in again, the dog in tow, and this time sits and bangs out Abba's "Super Trooper" on the piano, and then with slightly more effort proceeds to tackle the "Ode to Joy." Then, she is gone again, slipping off the plush stool like a lithe spirit exiting a waterfall. Suddenly she is gone and her grandfather has consumed three whiskies in the meantime.

Why are you here, Max? he asks me slurrily after a few minutes.

Why should I not be? I respond.

Do you know how much he has suffered? A man like him? Nikhilesh asks.

We have all suffered, I retort.

Oh, yes, all of us, he says sarcastically.

What do you mean, anyway—a man like him?

Whatever his flaws, whatever his faults, a man like him, that's what I mean, says Nikhilesh.

A man like him, Byron Mallick, his gray head bowed before a perfect shaft of light in the dusty courtroom while counsel for the prosecution steps forward: My Lords, he says, I am obliged to make use of some apology for the extent of depravity I have to present to you, of oppressions upon property and oppressions upon liberty—

Nikhilesh takes a deep breath, he must be clear now, and cogent, he faces the task of reporting certain details to me that may influence my understanding of what has happened in the last few months, for he has gleaned from my simple movements that I am not convinced, and realized also with some horror that it is a state I am happy to exist in for a long, long time.

You should have seen him, he says to me, you should have seen him standing there, the steel fence of his nobility deflecting everything.

Including the truth? I venture to ask.

Nikhlilesh buries his head in his hands.

Why are you here, Max Gate, if you do not believe in his innocence? he asks.

Do you?

Do I what?

Believe in his innocence?

I cannot believe you are asking me this, says Nikhilesh.

Vargas knocks gently as he appears with a tray bearing two filled champagne glasses and some cashew nuts. He sets them down and leaves, unwilling to explain why we are to be indulged thus when our host lies seriously ill.

He was acquitted, says Nikhilesh, reaching for his glass.

It is the job of the court to determine whether, beyond reasonable doubt, he was responsible for the crime.

Which they did, quite, in spite of that rabid maniacal Harvard-educated piece of hot-brained eloquence that

Arjun managed to put in place as counsel for the defense.

But our job is different, I mention to Nikhilesh, the bubbles from the noisy wine hitting my brain.

Which is what? he asks wearily.

In my opinion, it is to figure out, beyond reasonable doubt, that he could not possibly be responsible for the event.

Well, it's clear in my head that he had nothing to do with it, says Nikhilesh.

But not yet in mine, I confess to him.

And yet you are still here, he points out to me.

Yes, I am, I concede, I am.

Lunch is served, says Vargas.

We file into the dining room, the child behind us and behind her the dog, and seat ourselves at one end of the table where we are served curried lamb chops and deviled eggs, like the remains of an Edwardian breakfast, with only a tureen of overboiled spinach to soothe our intestines.

The dog, Kimbhut, is given rice and spinach, and later the bones of our chops, he does not complain, and neither do we, even though none of it is up to Vargas's standards, which indicates that he is worried for Byron, as are we, albeit along different axes, all of us.

Vargas refills the champagne glasses we have brought to the table and brings in a jug of water, ice clinks sonorously as he pours. For Adrija, he provides milk in a glass decorated with Disney figures, Beauty and the Beast, perhaps, from the look of them.

Why can't I have Sprite? the girl asks.

You need your milk, Vargas insists.

I hate milk, she protests.

Do you remember the story from the *Mahabharata* about Dronacharya's son Aswathama? Nikhilesh asks his granddaughter.

He saw his friends drinking milk and wanted some for himself, but I can't remember how the rest of it goes, says Adrija.

He cried all night for a taste of milk and it broke his father's heart, great warrior that he was, Dronacharya. And then in the morning he had a brilliant idea, he obtained for his son a tumbler of water mixed with rice dust and it was the color of milk, and Aswathama danced with joy upon tasting it because he thought he was drinking milk.

That was a bit silly of him, says Adrija.

The reason I am telling you this story, says her grandfather sternly, the reason I am telling you this is to make you aware of how lucky you are.

To drink milk with every meal?

Yes, indeed.

I'd rather drink water with rice powder in it, she replies.

I really don't think so, says Nikhilesh.

At this she becomes silent, gulps down her milk, finishes her meal with alarming rapidity, and asks to be excused. Permission is stiffly granted and she slips off her chair and quickly vanishes, the dog following, bone in mouth.

Rice dust, eh? I say to Nikhilesh, once I am sure she is out of earshot.

Pituli gola jol, he says, back from the comfort of his own language.

Better than chalk?

More nutritious, I imagine.

By a margin, no doubt.

Nikhilesh takes a long gulp of iced water and then he says: What is it that you are made of, Max Gate? How can you be at the same time so affectless and yet also as a man flayed raw?

Both are, I suppose, in my constitution—to feel nothing or to feel too much, I confess.

But what is it that you *believe* in? asks Nikhilesh.

All the usual things, I'm afraid: compassion, loyalty, love.

Nikhilesh emits a hollow laugh.

And which of these has brought you here today?

All, I should think—and in equal measure, I reply.

Vargas enters, bearing a pot of coffee and a plateful of a Bengali sesame seed confectionery for which I had betrayed a great affection many years ago when I had so regularly been a guest at Byron's home. It was a delicacy that only appeared at wintertime, when a man with several basketsful of the stuff would ring the doorbell, clearly having made a long journey, the entire contents would be purchased and the man would leave happy, with another long journey ahead of him but some serious cash in his pouch.

Vargas, what an unexpected treat, I tell him as I help myself to a piece of the gloriously chewy substance whose name I struggle to remember.

Sahib was keen that we should have some in the house for you, sir.

Does our old friend still arrive in November with all those baskets of it upon his shoulders?

Oh no, he is long dead.

So, how did you find it now?

With great difficulty, sir.

You should not have gone to such trouble for me, Vargas.

It was no trouble, sir.

A patter of small feet and padded paws as Adrija rushes in, followed by Kimbhut.

There's a woman on the stairs trying to take pictures of me, she says breathlessly.

Vargas rushes out and I follow, and there indeed is a young woman, camera slung around her neck, I meant no harm, she says, I'm just taking some pictures for a brochure, the top floor flat is coming on the market soon and we think we may be able to attract an international clientele.

Tall and dark, attired in skinny jeans and an elegant white shirt, she reminds me suddenly of Damini, as though a vision of the life she would have had if born twenty years later, a photographer for an international real estate firm rather than an investigative journalist with a corrosive mission of her own.

So you are not from a newspaper? says Vargas to the dusky nymph.

No, I am not, she firmly replies.

When I return to the dining room, the girl is still sitting with her face buried in her grandfather's chest.

I am sorry, Max, but you do not know what a time this has been for us with the press regularly on our doorsteps, hounding all of us, even the child, says Nikhilesh.

I am truly sorry to hear that.

Well, it's over now at any rate, he says.

Yes, it's over now, I repeat.

The dog barks and the girl raises her head, go and play now, her grandfather urges.

Do you not realize, Max, that he may have been hanged? he says after they have gone.

It's a thought that has tormented me as much as any of you, I reply.

Hanged for a crime he did not commit…

He never even came close to such a verdict, I remind him.

But you know that they have started to hang people again, says Nikhilesh a little blearily.

Yes, I do.

Last August, they had strung up a man in Calcutta jail, the country's first execution since 1995, it had chilled me to read of it, and what strange details I retain of doing so—that he had been given a new set of pajamas for the occasion, and curds and sweetmeats as requested for his final meal, he had bathed and prayed and walked without any resistance to the gallows, where his life had been terminated by an 84-year-old hangman with his 21-year-old grandson serving as an assistant. After the execution, the hangman, who had been drinking heavily for the preceding three days, had to be taken home on a stretcher with a saline drip.

Human rights protestors had held a candlelit vigil outside Alipore jail with anti-death penalty banners. Some had sung "We shall overcome." The convict had asked for his kidneys and eyes to be donated after his death, but the family had refused to give consent.

Nikhilesh checks his wristwatch, we should be setting off soon, he says. He is intending to meet Ela at the airport when her flight arrives from Bangalore.

Vargas brings us a selection of cigars. I pick out a small panatella, and Nikhilesh, after the slightest hesitation, follows suit.

So, how did it happen, this dismissal of charges, this quashing of the case that we are kindly referring to as an acquittal? I ask him.

The murder charges fell apart almost instantly, replies Nikhilesh.

And those of adulterating formula milk?

A case of arbitrary power winning over law, he replies.

What?

Law and arbitrary power are at eternal enmity, says Nikhilesh.

Says who?

Burke, of course.

Yes, it would be, wouldn't it.

Nikhilesh wipes his lips with a khadi napkin.

Burke, yes, he replies.

> My Lords, I will venture to say of the governments of Asia that none of them had an arbitrary power; that is, they cannot delegate it as to leave them unaccountable upon the principles upon which it is given... I am to speak of Oriental governments, and I do insist upon it that Oriental governments knew nothing of this arbitrary power... I do challenge the whole race of man to show me any Oriental governors claiming to themselves the right to act by arbitrary will...

Arbitrary power, granted to those above the law, was he not of that manner of angels, Byron Mallick, whom he had seen pelt frogs to death with stones when he was a child only so that his mother might be spared their raucous croaking, and not be woken a minute too early from her flimsy sleep?

Was he not above such paltry jurisdiction as that which had failed to appoint blame to him on the lack of evidence alone, exacted merely a small fine from him for not having disposed of his failed batches of baby milk correctly—how the judge had wagged a finger at him for not taking more care to see that they were not destroyed instead of being dispatched as slight seconds to Damini's shelter, where so many unfed mouths were waiting, mouths that without his generosity would have remained sucking desperately on air or the dry nipples of their unfortunate mothers.

Who were they to judge his actions, men bewigged and of another time, still clinging to rules that had never quite applied to their own checkerboard lives? What business had they to lend an ear to the upstart counsel for the prosecution, whose various resentments against the globalization of economies came to be concentrated upon Byron Mallick during the course of the proceedings, but eventually backfired and granted the verdict that they had been praying for—that Byron was exonerated of all charges but mere carelessness, his friend Byron Mallick, no longer to face the gallows then, metaphorically or otherwise.

Max, says Nikhilesh to me, it is your turn to care for him now.

I am certain that he is no danger, I reply.

He was forced at times to spend the night in proximity of people of very poor health, says Nikhilesh.

And what of it?

Could he not have contracted something from them, like TB?

I very much doubt it.

Of course, he has had it once already, says Nikhilesh.

Yes?

Almost died of it as a child, but this was before I knew him.

But he recovered then.

With the help of a long vacation in Darjeeling, I believe.

As he will now if he is dogged by it again, besides which there are drugs now to help him, I reassure Nikhilesh.

I'll go and look in on him, he says, laying his unlit cigar aside.

We both rise from our chairs and I head towards the balcony, where I might smoke in peace, just for a while.

Adrija is playing with the dog in the courtyard below, throwing a ball for him to catch and bring back to her. At one point she loses her aim and it bangs into a tier of flowerpots assembled against the wall, threatening to destabilize them. She watches fearfully, trying at the same time to restrain the dog, who is eager to hunt for it, and is relieved when nothing happens. I notice two rabbits cowering in the corner within a large wire-mesh enclosure and wonder who they might belong to, I have rarely seen children in this courtyard or indeed any of the common areas of this mansion block, it is almost as if there were some tacit agreement that whatever children might have been dwelling there they were neither to be heard nor seen when I was a regular visitor in the '80s.

Suddenly, a car backs into the courtyard and I find myself shouting down to her—watch out! She looks up and smiles but pays no heed to my unnecessary warning, the car stops a good distance away from her, it is their car, come to take her and her grandfather to the airport.

Nikhilesh comes out onto the balcony to say goodbye. Byron, he tells me, is still sleeping, but breathing more calmly, as if on the mend.

I'm glad to hear that, I reply.

I expect I shall see you again, soon, says Nikhilesh.

Well, I hope you'll allow me to take you both out to dinner once Byron has got over this illness…

That would be splendid, he says.

I stay on the balcony still watching Adrija and the dog frolicking downstairs until Nikhilesh appears and leads them towards the car. Before she climbs in, she looks up towards me and gives me a small shy wave, I wave back. And somewhere within me a deep sorrow gathers for the unborn child that her mother had discarded from her womb only months before she herself had taken residence there, the child that was ours and whom I imbue at this moment with the same qualities as this other little girl, her unburgeoned womanhood so quiet within her, so intact still within the membranes of her uncomplicated needs.

Can the exorbitance of peonies sicken instead of pleasuring the senses, peonies that will thicken and withstand every late frost and this year emerge late, vying with her roses in Mary O'Reilly's beautiful Holland Park garden. Only a transient luxury—the perfect peony—the rest of the year will be roses, roses, roses all the way, and the church spires spilling bad bellringing.

After I finish my cigar, I wander in again, wondering what to do with myself. In the sitting room the grand sofa is littered with framed prints and lithographs from one of the boxes that he has been attempting to unpack, they will surely not all fit in this apartment, what will he do with them I wonder, dispatch them perhaps to Digha, where he still holds to his house by the sea, and indeed hopes soon to remove himself there permanently, be done with Calcutta and all metropolitan living, so he has told me.

The servants have all retired to their quarters for their afternoon siesta, even the threat of Vargas with a quiet glass of chilled water at my elbow is dim, and so I wander, as I never have before, effectively alone, through rooms that have made and undone me. None of it is, as I might have predicted, too consequential, these old spaces become ransacked of memory by the very condition of my being there again, my passing my hands over the teak that Ela and I had both breathed upon once, the wall still bleeding chalky distemper against which I had first pinned her to take her face in my hands and kiss her lips, the same crow-calls and rude noises of transport that had somehow insulated us in this haven.

But her old room is a shock to me with all the posters of her performances still tacked to the wall, a photograph of her receiving her undergraduate degree in London—which Byron had traveled to England to witness—framed certificates of successes in elocution contests and watercolor competitions.

Here is one in French, with only the sweet arch of her shoulder in plain focus, her face is turned away and her neck is elegantly twisted, that neck, I have kissed that neck, I think to myself, I have kissed every inch of that neck and my kisses have drifted down to those eager breasts, it is the miracle of the desire to kiss that neck staying with me for so many years that I wish to conserve, sluiced of pain this time, the desire that I eventually nailed shut somewhere inaccessible within me, unable to survive the agony that came with it.

How I wish I were able to take it and kiss those long fingers, untainted by being bent constantly into meaning, now a fish, now a flower, now a spiteful serpent, kiss those long fingers and let them drift across my face, god, how I want this still, how I want this so much, still.

The cathedral clock chimes four, and with a gentle knock Vargas enters.

Sahib is awake and asking for you, he says.

I shake myself out of reverie and make my way to his bedroom, where Byron Mallick is sitting, propped up against many pillows, sipping some reheated chicken soup, or so I assume.

Did it ever pass for you? he asks. Your obsession with her, did it ever pass for you?

No, it did not pass, it became something else, but in doing so gave the impression of passing—at least for a while.

It never passed for me, says Byron.

Byron Mallick hands me his empty cup. When she was nine years old, he says, I took her to play at the Mitras' house with their son, only a little older than her. Some kernel of a relationship must have been born then, while they shot each other down with their imaginary pistols, for when I reintroduced them more than ten years later, these memories must have fed their attraction to an extent. How well they looked, walking arm in arm, our future, the future of Bengal, how satisfied was I in having played a part in bringing them together, nothing could have made more sense than them, what hope they gave us, such a divine posture they took in their robust and pure young love.

And then he leans over and vomits with dignity into a metal pail. He dabs his lips with a linen napkin.

Max Gate, he says, you have broken my heart.

The doctor is called out again, and this time advises that Byron be removed to an exclusive private residential clinic nearby, just a precaution, he assures us, given his advanced years, it may be wise to put him on a drip if the situation deteriorates and that is best done there rather than at home.

Vargas goes to fetch the driver while I help Byron into his brocade dressing gown.

Has it got colder, or is it just my imagination? he asks me.

I think it is considerably chillier, I reply.

Will you come with me, Max? he asks.

It is what I was intending to do.

Have they managed to get me a suite?

Vargas thinks a regular single room would be more prudent.

Yes, of course, he says with a sigh.

And after we arrive at the clinic, while Byron is still sitting in a wheelchair waiting to be taken to his room, Vargas approaches me and confesses that he does not have the funds to pay for the estimated expenditure of the first seven days of his stay, which is what they require. I walk over to the desk and peel out my credit card from my damp wallet—it is not only cold now, but humid, the air is thick with winter smoke—my card is handed back by an attractive young receptionist, thank you, sir, she says, the patient may proceed now to his room.

I notice that there is a florist and a gift shop on this floor now, as well as a café.

Why not? I ask myself, why not?

A person, suitably attired, arrives to wheel Byron to his room. I walk beside them while Vargas follows a few paces behind. Eventually, we reach his allotted cabin and it is clear, the moment I hold the door open, that it is not to his liking. The view is of a grim new apartment block across the road rather than the park on the other side, of which there were generous views from the suite he is used to occupying at this clinic for his various minor illnesses and medical investigations.

I can get you a better room, I quickly assure him.

No, no, he says, it's bad enough that we have had to rely on you to put up the deposit.

Not at all, I protest.

You'll get it back, of course, says Byron.

We'll sort that out later, now let's see what else you need, I reply.

We settle him into bed and then confer amongst ourselves, Vargas and I, as to what should be fetched to make him as comfortable as possible. Vargas departs with a mental list of these, and I pull over a chair to the foot of the bed and sit down.

Byron is leaning back against the pillows with his eyes closed. I am thinking about the first time I visited you in London, he says to me suddenly.

There is a constriction in my throat as I recall that happy time myself, when he arrived almost unannounced to my flat in Notting Hill Gate, about six months after I had quit Calcutta and still fancied myself in extended transit to New York.

I was still living out of boxes at the time, and the flat itself was in a shabby state, decorated in late '70s style, and bearing every hallmark of having been let to young professionals for a long period of time.

Max, Max, how can you live like this? Byron had asked, shaking his head congenially.

I'm not intending to live like this much longer, just need to tie up a few loose ends and then move on.

Will you sell this place?

I'll have to.

But this is such a bad time to sell, I'd hang on to it, Max, straighten it up a little, rent it out again for a while, just until the market recovers.

I'll think about it, Byron.

Meanwhile, what do you say to a trip to Oxford?

When?

I was thinking of going right now—you have a car, don't you?

Yes, Barbara's mother has lent me one of hers.

And it's not more than an hour from here, is it?

Less.

Well, shall we go?

Yes, of course, if that is what you feel like doing, I had replied.

Byron had visited England only once since he returned with his accountancy degree to Calcutta in the late '60s. Soon that would all change as his business exploded internationally, leaving him richer than he had ever imagined he might be and in possession of properties in both London and New York by the time the new millennium arrived—all liquidated again now to meet the heavy costs of his defense and to pay his many creditors, who were no longer willing to extend him their trust.

He had not been in the country since the early 80s, and there was an excitement in his eyes which I liked, felt thrilled by even. My first six months in London had been a little dreary despite Piers's valiant attempts to rehabilitate me, prevent me from seeking a different life in New York, and Mary's constant attention, her determination that I should not sink into a depression, or starve.

We settled into the little orange Mini that Mary had lent me, Byron's knees close to his chin, I should have warned you about the car, I said to him.

No, I'm enjoying this, Max, he replied.

The day had started off bright, clouds scuttling gaily

across a blue expanse, but as we made our way into Oxford we were accosted by the proverbial gray skies and drizzle, still we parked in St. Giles and proceeded to walk around the colleges, and for once I found myself the guide although my knowledge of any of these places was woefully superficial, but Byron seemed satisfied with what little I was able to tell him.

When we entered the grounds of Christ Church, he smiled and said, This was Halhed's college.

Nathaniel Brassey Halhed, who under the patronage of Warren Hastings, had produced a Bengali grammar, the first book ever to be printed in Bengali script, again with Hastings's support, the year was 1778, the characters had been cast by none other than Charles Wilkins, another company servant who would himself later translate the Bhagvadgita and produce a Sanskrit grammar.

Of course, William Jones was also in Oxford then, said Byron pensively.

William Jones, the great Orientalist, who also eventually ended up in Calcutta as a puisne judge in the Bengal Supreme Court and founded, in 1784, with the help of Halhed and Wilkins, the Asiatic Society, Warren Hastings was asked to be its first president, an honor he declined. Within a year, Hastings would depart, and Halhed and Wilkins soon after, but Jones remained in Calcutta until his death in 1794, laboring away at his various tasks of translation and philology, as well as his judicial duties—a man with too much on his plate, you would be inclined to say, no wonder he keeled over when he did, not quite fifty yet, but having done enough to merit a monument in St.

Paul's, London, and a statue in Calcutta—William Jones.

It is Jones who is credited with pointing out the affinities between Sanskrit and Latin and Greek, yet Halhed had already made such a connection, albeit not quite as gracefully, in his preface to the Bengali grammar, continued Byron, as we headed to University College, where Jones had been an undergraduate, and of which Byron was obviously eager to breathe the air again, having only once visited Oxford before in the mid '60s, when all had been seen in the light of more immediate involvement in these histories, a baleful reminder perhaps of his recently abandoned thesis.

Of course, Halhed might never have become interested in Oriental Studies if he had not met Jones here, said Byron as we made our perambulations.

I had heard him before on Halhed and Jones and suddenly felt disinclined to endure yet another riff on this topic, one that would no doubt end with him making the ironic connection between Halhed and Sheridan, and Jones and the whole lot of them—Dr. Johnson's Literary Club—particularly Burke of course, men who would struggle to bring down Warren Hastings not long after Jones found himself in Calcutta and Hastings, only a year later, back in England. Halhed, who had once been so intimate with Sheridan as to sign his letters to him LYD for Lazy Young Dog, found himself now on the other side of this complex breach, defended Hastings all he could, but fell out of favor due to his tendencies towards mysticism and his frank support of the French Revolution, while Burke suffered for his condemnation of it.

But I did not want on this day to be an audience to Byron Mallick's tender dissections of this subject matter, and once we had done a turn around University College, I suggested a pub lunch at the Turf, which turned out to be relatively empty, the undergraduates having departed already.

Did I ever tell you, asked Byron, still steeped in his own contemplations, did I ever tell you that Warren Hastings tried hard to establish a Chair here in Persian?

I don't think you did, I replied, digging into my steak and ale pie.

It was a major chapter of my thesis, his efforts at establishing such a professorship, Henry Vansittart was all for it and Dr. Johnson promised to draft the regulations, but it all came to nought.

Why do you think?

He didn't play his cards right, he should have emphasized, as he originally had, that this would enable men who were interested in entering the Company's service to better equip themselves for dealing with the natives of Hindustan, but instead he became distracted by the value of scholarship for its own sake...

A common trap, I said to Byron.

And one that he was prone to fall in, over and over again, he replied.

Vargas returns with a basket of items for Byron's immediate use, and also a tiffin carrier with some hot food in case he has recovered his appetite. But Byron shakes his head at the offer of soup, I'd like to sleep now, I think, he says.

I'll call in tomorrow morning, I tell him.

No need for that, he says, I'm sure I will be discharged by noon.

Well, let's hope that's how it will be.

Come in the afternoon, if I'm still here.

If you are still here, I shall definitely arrange for a better room, I tell him firmly.

This is fine, Max, he says wearily.

I'll see you tomorrow.

It's better than a jail cell, anyway, says Byron Mallick.

Vargas and I return to the flat, less than fifteen minutes' walk from the clinic, it is dark now and foggy, something pleasantly ghostly about the atmosphere, car horns cajoling each other like fond toddlers in play, and—almost disjointedly—lines of pale headlights patiently progressing down the Lower Circular Road or whatever other name it may have by now, having started life as a ditch, a moat dug by the East India Company in 1742 to ward off the fearsome Marathas, the Circular Road, Acharya J.C. Bose Sarani, the Maratha Ditch, who cares now as we cross its fume-ridden face and make our way back to Byron's flat.

There are people waiting for us, his various acolytes mainly, standing around in the sitting room between piles of boxes, making uncertain conversation with each other.

How is he? they ask, almost as we enter.

He is not able right now to receive visitors, Vargas informs them.

Is his condition grave? somebody asks.

No, he simply needs to rest, says Vargas firmly.

This has not been an easy year for him, says an elderly member of the assembled company, vigorously fanning himself with a large theater ticket.

An understatement, that, says someone in Bengali.

I feel suddenly as if I am facing what could easily become a lynch mob and quickly excuse myself, I make my way to my room and fall gratefully upon the bed, tightly swaddled in a Rajasthani cover, the pillows smell somewhat soothingly of napthalene. Sleep shakes over me like the remains of a rusted pylon, and when I suddenly sit awake again, it is four thirty in the morning, and I have still to digest the contents of my strange dystopic dreams.

I tiptoe out, cautious not to wake anyone, not that there is anybody to wake, for the servants all have lodgings in the quarters down below, all but Vargas, who has a room next to the kitchen, once a storeroom of sorts, but easily adapted since to his purposes, a comfortable room, despite its prison-like window, its shelves lined with books rather than groceries. This I know, for there have been occasions when I have actually intruded upon his privacy, when neither he nor Byron were obviously in evidence despite my having been invited to arrive for dinner at such an hour, I have found myself knocking on his door in these moments and casting him into confusion and embarrassment, Byron obviously having forgotten to relay to him his plans for the evening. I would by then have myself taken the sting out of such embarrassments, and happily spent an hour drinking coke and rum in the sitting room until

Byron apologetically arrived, having been mercilessly detained by some Bombay businessmen on whom his plans for the expansion of his business crucially depended.

I do not wish to disturb Vargas at this hour, no need to anyway as he has thoughtfully left some sandwiches out for me on the dining table and a bottle of red wine, I rapidly consume vast quantities of both for I am overtaken just then by that kind of hunger which comes of being recently thrust into a new time zone, something that my body should have learned to cope with by now, you'd think. I pick up a tuna sandwich and run my tongue along its edges to catch its excesses, there is a tincture of coriander paste in the mayonnaise, Vargas again, exercising his brilliance, I bite into its perfect interior, it so happily renders itself to my basic needs, and yet most of me is removed from this, most of me just wants to go home.

Home? What is that? How much time and taxpayers' money have we devoted to set about defining home for those obviously not of the correct hue or persuasion to easily consider the United Kingdom their rightful abode, but what of me, neither distinguished by my skin color nor the tatters of my rituals as being outside the majority? Home, what is it for me but to have enough in the bank to just carry on as I have for over a decade now, in full acceptance of all my quirks and irresponsibilities, my terrible reliance on the British institution of the off-license, what more can the concept of "home" offer me?

Home, Nikhilesh had said ironically to me yesterday—the context of which I fail to remember—home, it's easy to find home, it's exile that so resolutely eludes us, he said.

Home or exile, scarcely have I desired either, only somewhere to be sustained by my own thoughts and what little they did to enrich the lives of others, to be in a position to offer a roof to those in need of it, and to be offered one when I was myself in the same position, to not be so mindful of my own solitude as to find the company of those who required mine to be oppressive, and yet to adore that solitude when it was available to me, whether at home or in exile, any one of them would have done.

Yet, sitting here, a sticky dawn starting to probe through the heavy lidded window slats, I know that I have neither the energy nor the courage to face the day that is to come. Byron, I am certain, will be sent home by the afternoon, but in need of rest rather than entertainment, I wonder if it might be prudent to remove myself to a hotel or whether that would simply make him unhappy, I am booked to depart on Friday, three days, that is, from now.

I pour the last of the wine into my glass, my head eagerly accepting any brokenhandled thought now that the early morning has to offer to such a fool as I, come so pointlessly to these Gangetic shores. I drain my glass and my grandmother, smiling indulgently, arrives again in my memories, in her mid-fifties, upright and elegant, a small woman fighting for her dignity, widowed, displaced, her only daughter miraculously married to a young doctor already established in his father's practice in Fair Haven, New Jersey, in easy distance of her house in Brooklyn, and just as well, for it was she who brought me up while my mother struggled and struggled to have another child, suffered a series of miscarriages, and then finally produced my sister, a child who swiftly and painfully delivered her of the possibility of having any others, almost dying herself of course in the process of securing such a freedom for her mother.

My life with my grandmother, what do I remember of it, except that strange comfort that emanated from our understanding that winter afternoons were to be spent in silence, lamps lit, both of us reading, and something bubbling on the stove that would eventually and indifferently feed us. Summer days were different for she had a goddaughter on Long Island who insisted that we both occupy their gatehouse while she herself was in Europe, and we would revel there, my grandmother and I, with the marvelous grounds open to us, and the beach deliriously populated with horseshoe crabs and other prehistoric beings, the house was locked up, but I liked to see what I could through the windows and imagine what kind of life might be lived there, and sometimes she would stand with me also peering through the cracks in the curtains, my grandmother, a strange smile upon her face, it was her family who had taken her in, the young woman who would eventually be the mistress of this mansion, when she had arrived from Poland, a distant relative, for five years she had been sheltered by them, and then suddenly—because of a party where they insisted that rather than hiding herself away she appear in one of my grandmother's outdated, but still perfectly glamorous and quite distinctive dresses—she had found quite inadvertently a very rich husband for herself and this new life. Not that Marta has ever neglected her responsibilities since, my grandmother told me as we walked back to the little gatehouse where we had happily spent a number of weeks already, and would again the following year and also the year after, this time with my squealing little sister, and my mother indisposed, quietly lying upon the couch downstairs, waiting for something to lift her out of a misery that contained far more than I would ever comprehend. Later that year, the cousin in Long Island ran off with a Swiss photographer and no more summers were spent there again, and indeed no longer so much time with my grandmother anymore, for the hours that I spent at school lengthened and looking after my baby sister proved to be no trouble to my mother after a while, suddenly we became a family, eating supper together, laughing at each other's jokes, but how I missed her, my grandmother, forced now to amuse herself otherwise, how I missed her, how I ever will.

—

A tap on my shoulder, some hours later, for I have predictably fallen asleep at the dining table, head upon folded arms like an obedient schoolboy, it is Vargas, he has already been to see Byron at the clinic, he tells me. I look at my watch, it is just past eight in the morning, is he any better? I groggily inquire.

It is possible that he is, says Vargas.

Well, that is good news.

Yes, but… he trails off

Yes, but what?

He commanded me to bring him a cockatrice, replies Vargas somewhat helplessly.

I bury my head for a while in my hands. And if we do, do you think he will finally eat? I ask.

I think he might, says Vargas.

Surely you have a chicken in the icebox?

I do, sir, but we still need a piglet, or at the very least a rabbit.

I know where to get a rabbit, I tell him.

And indeed within a few moments, I have returned with a suitable specimen, a fat white albino from one of the hutches below, the children who own the creatures having served them their morning feed of puffed rice and grated carrots and gone off to school.

Did you get that from downstairs? Vargas asks.

Where else did you expect me to go? I demand of him.

It needs to be killed and skinned and gutted, he reminds me.

I can do that, I assure him.

I try and remember how my father did it, when he would take me with him in late November to hunt cotton-tails and the few hares and jacks that might come our way, I hated these frozen excursions, how much would I have rather been at home sipping hot chocolate and reading, and how very much more did I hate how he insisted that I come to help in the basement after they had hung there for a week as he skinned and gutted the creatures to deliver to my mother to braise for Sunday supper.

I manage to kill the poor domestic pet that sits unconcerned upon the kitchen counter with a blow from the cleaver, I gut it with ease, skinning it is another story, I am nonetheless almost done with it when the doorbell rings, Vargas answers it and returns to the kitchen to tell me that it is Ela.

To see me? I ask.

I think so, he replies.

The rabbit is prepared now, I bring the cleaver down again to separate its hindquarters from the rest of its lifeless self, and watch Vargas as he deftly rinses it out and begins to sew it into the cavity of the hen, I splash some water on my face from the kitchen tap, run wet fingers through my hair, then come out to see Ela.

She is standing in the hallway scrutinizing the artwork as if at a private museum that she has never visited before, I would rather that we had met her somewhere else than within these walls that heave so carelessly with our past, I would rather have met her at the Grand Hotel today at lunchtime as previously agreed, but it is only for a moment that this prevents the color from flooding back into my desire, I kiss her forehead and then her eyes. I am so glad to see you, I tell her.

All that is left of her youthful arrogance wraps around me like weathered lace as I behold her now, beaten by fate and more deliciously dignified than I ever imagined she could be, fifteen years ago, when I first gave my heart to her.

How did you know to come in the hour of his death? she asks.

He is not dying, I assure her.

I know he is, she insists.

We walk into the sitting room and stack the framed etchings that litter the large sofa on the floor so that we can sit down somewhere. They are all by Solvyns, a Flemish artist who had lived in Calcutta in the late eighteenth century for thirteen years. Solvyns has been a long-time interest of Byron Mallick's—he painted ordinary people, Max, he would tell me over and over again—he painted ordinary people at a time when Kettle and Zoffany were painting nabobs, and the Daniell brothers their pathetic panoramas, while they were engaged thus Solvyns painted instead cowherds and soldiers, jugglers, weavers, potters, confectioners, lime workers and toddy tappers, and all manner of boats, fakirs, and palanquin bearers.

Why it mattered so much to Byron Mallick that he painted ordinary folk I could not fathom, when his own life—it seemed to me—had been dedicated to the avoidance of them. And what had he feared more in his youth than that his life might become ordinary, what more can he have feared, lying on the top bunk in the hostel room he shared with Nikhilesh, experiencing the transience of his passions, what more can he have feared than that this might link him to the ordinary. For nothing had lasted very long with him at the time, no lust for a ravishing damsel—even when uncategorically spurned by her—no obsession with a particular poem or a controversial historical incident, no object of art or piece of music had for him any enduring appeal, all this he had had to painstakingly cultivate within himself. By the time I met him, however, he had more or less perfected the inclination to be totally absorbed in certain topics—Bengal in the late eighteenth century being the principal of these, and what he lacked in passion he had taken care to make up for in erudition, as so many do, but hardly with such grace and charm.

Do you really think he will pull through? asks Ela.

I'm sure he will pull through, I answer.

What makes you think so? she asks.

I don't know. He always does, doesn't he?

That is irrelevant, says Ela.

Ela picks up a book from inside a box that has been opened but not yet unloaded.

Calcutta, Past and Present by K. Blechynden, she reads.

I remember Byron giving it to me to read, many years ago, when he had managed to awaken in me an interest in the history of the city far beyond the superficial need to locate myself rapidly and economically in my new cultural circumstances. I take it gently out of Ela's hands, and leafing through it am briefly transported to the time when he and I would sit and talk, late into the night, of life and art and all that mattered to us, and also of what did not matter to us, like why we have eyebrows or what color a chameleon would turn if you put it in a roomful of mirrors.

He loved you very much, she says.

Perhaps he still does.

Perhaps, she agrees.

She walks over to the window and throws open the shutters that are still closed against yesterday's furious thundershower.

You are like the prodigal son, she says.

If you like, I reply.

Why do you sound so weary? she asks.

Because if there is anyone I am trying to come back to, it is you, I tell her.

I see, she says.

And for the first time I realize how deeply I have disappointed her, all along, in not having the courage to pull her away from the life that arranged itself around her and brought her security, motherhood, and fame, none of which I felt I could offer her, ever.

I am not asking you to come away with me, I reassure her.

Why would you do that? she says, almost bitterly.

It is not as if I have not before, I protest.

When? she demands.

In our little schoolroom in Howrah, I remind her.

Curlylocks, curlylocks, wilt thou be mine, thou shalt not wash dishes nor feed the swine, but sit on a cushion and sew a fine seam, and feed upon strawberries, sugar, and cream.

Oh, that, she says, all I remember of that is how relieved you were when I declined.

That is grossly unfair, Ela. You are all that has ever lent any completeness to my life, I tell her.

And yet I can still smell your relief as if from a flower crushed recently in my hands, she replies.

Perhaps you are right, for I was uncertain of my future at the time, and although the pain of leaving you was great, to see our love destroyed by sordid practicalities would have been far more unbearable, I say to her.

The story does not change, she says.

No, but neither does my need for you.

And what do you propose to do about it now? she asks.

Simply to entreat you to be part of my life again.

And how would that happen?

Just as it did before when you made it your business to travel to London frequently.

But all that was arranged by Byron, she says, with a tragic smile.

But it need no longer be so—you have Piers and myself, and nothing would please either of us more than to help you perform internationally again.

I stroke her long hair, which has fallen out of its knot, I love you, I tell her.

You know, she says, in these last months I have realized that to not have your friendship and your regard is like death to me.

Those you have always had, I assure her.

But I no longer expect undying passion, she says.

Even though you know it is there?

What does it matter if it is there, if it bubbles to the surface under only the most unpremeditated circumstances?

You can be very cruel to me, I tell her.

It's what you deserve, Max, she replies.

A servant comes in to tell us that tea and savories have been laid out for us in the dining room. Normally, she would have served us in this room but there is hardly anywhere to set down a tray among the partially unpacked boxes.

The dining room, by contrast, is almost bare, it is

possible that Byron has had to auction some of the ornate Victorian lamps and candlesticks that he inherited from his mother's family, the chandelier is certainly missing, and a very reduced collection of china sits forlorn in the glass cabinets.

We sit down at right angles to each other at one corner of the dining table and she pours me tea, having dismissed the servant. I take her free hand and trace the weariness in her fingers, something is ended between us, but I cannot but hope that it is only so that something better might take its place.

All I ever wanted was for you to delight in me, she says.

And I did, I reply.

Yes, that is true, she concedes.

And I will again—if you can bear it, I say to her, enfolding her wrist in my long grasp.

And some part of me cannot but indulge in the peculiar possibility that if I had somehow convinced her to make a life with me, that we might be sitting somewhere very similar now, perhaps in a house in Georgetown, Washington DC, discussing which shade of neutral to paint the study, and whether it was box or yew with which we wished to punctuate the borders of our narrow garden.

Near us is a pile of papers that nobody has dared move, geometrical theorems and riders that Byron has spent the last six months solving as a distraction from his trial, I hope she will not notice these scribbles for I know they will move her to tears.

And why do I demand of her an incessant composure

when it is clear that some turbulence is much more likely to carry us to the port where we both really want to be, perhaps because I would wander those streets only as a coward, unsure of how to keep her and make her happy, even though that is all my heart has ever desired.

I keep my eyes upon her, so much at an incline towards me, so exceptionally endowed with beauty and grace, and my fingers radiate along the lines of her palm as if to receive her arrogance as an antidote to despair, my despair and her own, both to me good reasons for life not to continue beyond these precious moments.

Piers has asked me if I will sing in his new opera, she informs me suddenly.

Can you sing? I ask her.

Yes, I can sing.

I run my finger along the line of her collarbone where her talcum powder has morained in this sticky heat.

I hope he finishes it, I tell her.

Not that he has never seen any of his projects to completion, Piers O'Reilly, with his habit of suddenly and precipitously losing interest, as he has done in many things, including women, in the thirty years that I have known him. When I met him he was intent on becoming a film-maker, and while still an undergraduate, produced a number of short black and white avant-garde films that Mary O'Reilly would screen for her friends in her living room, over Sauterne and figs. Then, for ten years he had worked in television, raced his way up that ladder and then elegantly stepped off, wandered the world teaching English for a while, and then returned to London and eventually became a restaurant critic, exactly by what trajectory I do not know.

He has finished it, says Ela, I received it from him by e-mail last night.

Is it any good?

I have not read it yet.

Vargas enters bearing the cockatrice on a silver platter, it has on a head and wings and a golden egg between its ungilded feet.

Ela shudders to see it, what is that? she asks.

A favorite dish of Byron's, he has asked for it specially, which is why Vargas has spent all morning making it, I tell her.

It's ghastly, she says, once Vargas is out of earshot.

And indeed it is, with its dusty decorations and the golden egg held in its withered claws, clearly Vargas had not been prevailed upon to produce such a thing in a while, he returns now with a cover for the peculiar conceit, it needs a collar, he says ruefully.

I'll make it a collar, says Ela, fishing some crepe paper and a small pair of scissors out of her handbag, such things as mothers keep in case of suddenly having to amuse their children, I imagine.

How did you manage to cook it so quickly? I ask Vargas.

He confesses to having squeezed it first into a pressure cooker, then cooled it with ice water, glazed it and put it in a very hot oven, the whole process had taken just over an hour.

You really are a genius, I tell him.

I'd better rush, visiting hours will soon be over, he says.

He slips on the collar that Ela has so swiftly fashioned and disappears with his hybrid culinary feat under its silver dome, I imagine him weaving cautiously with it through the unpredictable skeins of traffic and the dismal smog, thicker today than ever before, for it has become colder, much colder, since I arrived and drops of condensation that settle on the surfaces around us are heavy with exhaust and other grime. I hope that Byron—even in his much diminished accommodation—is breathing something more purified, air that has at least been filtered if not sweetened in any other way.

He won't want to eat it, says Ela somewhat smugly.

That is surely not the point, I say back to her.

Then what is? she asks.

Letting him know that we care, I should think, I answer.

Just caring for them never saved anybody, she says.

We hear a bark and a shuffle and, a few minutes later, the dog Kimbhut wanders in with a chewed book in his mouth. It is poor Kathleen Blechynden's *Calcutta, Past and Present,* badly mauled, I rescue it from his jaws without much effort and it opens in my hands to the page bearing the inscription—From Hugo, Dec 12 1905—now heavily bleeding under dogspit after having remained legible these one hundred years.

I should never have taken it out of its box, says Ela.

I stroke the wounds of the mutilated book, it is only the covers and the first few pages that have suffered, the reproduction of the engraving entitled "General View of CALCUTTA, taken near the Sluice of Fort William" by W. Baillie 1794 is now pulp—I remember that I had once urged Byron to frame it, he had been horrified at the thought of separating it from the book, besides it is just a reproduction, he had said.

I did not know you had brought the dog with you, I say to Ela.

I have to take him to the vet later, she replies.

One of the servants apparently had taken him for a walk but lost control of him upon returning to the flat.

Byron will not be amused, I say to her.

Byron will never know, she replies.

I run my finger down the naked spine of the book before putting it gently aside.

He is dying, I know he is dying, says Ela.

It takes him another two days to fulfill her prophecy, and in the end we do not know exactly what kills him, just that he is found curled up and dead, an image that I cannot separate from a poem of Jon Silkin's, *Something has ceased to come along with me, something very like a person: something very like one. And there was no nobility in it, or anything like that.*

Nikhilesh sits, unslept, by his side, holding his hand.

What was the real cause of his death, I ask a doctor.

None of us knows, he replies.

Did he not respond to the drugs you were giving him?

Too early to say, says the doctor.

So why did he die?

We will have to open him up to see if we can determine that, he says.

Is that really necessary? asks Nikhilesh.

No, says the doctor. He died in hospital, there should be no problem issuing a death certificate.

Then leave it, says Nikhilesh with vehemence. There is nothing to gain by this, Max, he turns to me and says.

Perhaps he died of a broken heart, I find myself saying.

If so, that was what he deserved, says Nikhilesh.

And so saying, he buries his eyes upon Byron Mallick's lifeless arm, and is overwhelmed by the memory of a late summer afternoon when they had been playing chess quietly in Byron's bedroom, their peace suddenly broken by a shrill but strangely tuneful cry they had rushed to investigate and seen upon the road outside, a girl of about ten in an intensely yellow sari being taken away by her new husband. Byron's beautiful mother had come and watched with them, poor child, she had said, poor child, and the quality of her sympathy had touched Nikhilesh, isolating him briefly from Byron, who had simply turned away, anxious to resume their game.

There is a knock at the door, it is Barbara's old friend Arunavo Haldar, come to see the invalid, I signal for him not to enter, and step out into the corridor. He has brought with him his newlywed wife with a vast acreage of vermillion in the parting of her hair. I give them the bad news.

Arunavo shakes his head in disbelief, how did it happen? he asks.

Probably a heart attack, I reply.

We heard that he had attempted suicide, says his wife.

This is my wife, Archana, says Arunavo quickly.

Byron would never take his own life, I tell both of them, reading his hurry to introduce her as an endorsement of the opinion she expresses.

Not even after this disgrace? says Arunavo.

He was acquitted, if you remember.

Only because he had all the judges in his pocket, laughs Arunavo.

You must not speak ill of a dead man, Archana chastises.

I am forgetting myself, Arunavo admits.

He was very kind to you once, Archana reminds him.

That is why we are here, he says.

For it was Byron who had finally found for him a decent students' hostel after Barbara brought Arunavo's plight to his attention, and a sort of friendship had developed between them, with Arunavo distilling for him some of the more exciting advances in the physical sciences, for Byron no longer had the time to sift through this information himself. Not much of it made sense to him anymore but he liked to hear the young man talk about it, liked to inhale his enthusiasm, hold it within him for a few seconds before letting it escape into the marshy air. Shortly after I left Calcutta, Arunavo actually boarded with Byron for a few months while he finished his Master's degree, typed his letters for him and persuaded him to buy a computer, which he fixed up with simple word-processing and spreadsheet facilities before leaving for the United States on a graduate scholarship for which Byron had encouraged him to apply, not least because he had friends on the awarding committee.

Ten years later he had returned to a lectureship at Jadavpur University armed with a PhD and respectable length of postdoctoral training, dutifully married the young woman his parents had selected for him, and settled with them and his new wife into the flat that had been purchased for this purpose in one of the southernmost suburbs of the city. While living abroad, he had been encouraged by Byron to send regular popular science bulletins to a Bengali newspaper, and this has now developed into a weekly column, he has brought his most recent one to show Byron expecting to find him not just alive but in a condition to read and absorb his musings on superstrings and sparticles, on how easily beauty can strangle truth.

I owe him an awful lot, says Arunavo, wiping a small tear from his eye.

But it does not prevent you from doubting him, I say in a cold voice.

No, he replies, should it?

A figure, tall and heavy-shouldered, clad in a gunmetal gray kurta and jeans, becomes visible at the end of the long corridor. It is Arjun, I feel myself gathering Arunavo and Archana like a shield around me as he approaches, and yet what have I to fear from him, and what has he to fear from me, I have only made love to his wife once these last eight years and he has most likely made love to her this morning, so his easy and satisfied movements would suggest as he strides towards us, streaming stern compassion, he has already received the news on his mobile phone from Nikhilesh.

Max Gate, he says to me, it is you, isn't it, how you have changed!

Fifteen years will do that to you, I reply.

As it has with him, thickened him into manhood, replaced luster with depth in his gaze, how handsome he appears to me, how perversely handsome.

You look well, I tell him.

Arunavo places his palms together in a gesture of farewell.

We had better go, he says.

It was good of you to come, I tell them.

But we were too late, says Arunavo with a vaguely philosophical smile.

They troop off and we are left alone, Arjun and myself, looking at each other, unsure of what course to take, with Byron lying dead behind the pale door in front of us and the woman we both love watering her roses somewhere in this city, before the heat of the noon sun turns her efforts to salt.

She does not know yet, he says of his wife.

The doctor returns, I am afraid a postmortem is necessary, he says.

That is not what you said a moment ago, I challenge him.

That is not what I said a moment ago, but I was wrong, he replies.

He opens the door to Byron's hospital room and shuts it behind him as he enters, he knows that he will meet even more resistance from Nikhilesh and does not wish to deal with our combined protestations.

Should I intervene? asks Arjun.

What do you mean?

I could probably prevent a postmortem if that is what you wish, he says.

My wishes surely do not count.

No, I am thinking of Ela, he admits.

As you did when you arranged for Byron to be acquitted? I say suddenly, a strange gamble, made possible only by the incongruent energy of the situation.

You overestimate my powers, says Arjun, a silver trace of pity in his voice.

Anyway, he is dead now, I say, desperately drawing a line under this verbal exchange.

But not yet beyond dissection, says Arjun Mitra.

The doctor emerges, holding a very shaky Nikhilesh by the arm, the body will be ready in five hours, he tells us, unless of course any further investigation is required, which is unlikely, very unlikely, he adds hastily as he meets Arjun's clear cold gaze.

We walk through the muddy streets back to Byron's apartment in Bishop Lefroy Road, it has rained all night, the monsoons have finally arrived, the pavements are filled with goatscum and parchment, but the earth around it breathes again.

Vargas answers the doorbell, sees our faces, and freezes for a moment as the implications of the event order themselves in his mind, and then he unlocks himself from this position and tells us—I know already he is dead, it was foretold in one of maid's dreams.

I did not realize you believed in such things, Vargas, says Nikhilesh.

I do not think I do, he replies.

But you are right, says Arjun, Byron is no more.

Vargas bows his head, Hail Mary full of grace, he remembers sitting starched by his mother as his father's coffin was borne solemnly out of the church in Bandel, how that death had changed his life at the age of nine for they had moved to Calcutta afterwards, to some rooms in Free School Street and his mother had worked at the Great Eastern Hotel supervising the waitresses and the novice maids. Often, after school, he had helped her set tables and polish wine glasses, how quickly these skills had resurfaced when Byron Mallick selected him to be his manservant and rescued him from the prospect of spending the rest of his life as a petty clerk.

I will go and see about breakfast, he says to us.

What we do not know is this—on the day before his trial started, Byron Mallick had presented Vargas with a large check and given him the option to quit his job, I do not wish to drag you through this with me, he said to him.

But, sir, I cannot leave you now, Vargas protested.

I was hoping you would say that, Byron told him, I

was hoping you would say that, but I want you to stay entirely of your own volition, so cash the check and invest the money now, it will make me happy to know that you can leave whenever you wish to, at a moment's notice.

I will do so if it pleases you, said Vargas.

It would please me enormously, Byron replied.

And so he had, the faithful Vargas, taking advice from one of his old colleagues who had made a tidy sum at the stock market, and now that Byron has been the one to leave Vargas can rely on this very adequate pot of money in addition to whatever his master may have bequeathed to him in his will.

He returns shortly from the kitchen with three small cups of espresso on a silver tray, his face betrays no anxiety, nor any deep grief, as he hands us each a cup, moving with agility around the various boxes still scattered around the drawing room, for we have dispersed to its different corners, Nikhilesh, Arjun, and I, like animals in the wild setting up their territories, I am near the window that looks towards Ela's old school, the same window where I had suddenly been hit many years ago by the implausible gravity of my attraction to her, Nikhilesh is standing by the piano absently fingering the keys, and Arjun has flung himself into the great leather chair beside his magnificent desk, from where Byron would preside over his friends and acolytes every evening when they gathered around him, once.

Nikhilesh asks if he may play some Tagore songs on Byron's music system, it is what he would want, he says, as if that matters. I am happy to agree and Arjun shrugs as though indifferent, and suddenly I wonder if he is of the rare species whose souls cannot be penetrated by music, but then a wet wind enters the room and blows the hair out of his dark eyes and I feel embarrassed for entertaining such a thought.

Nikhilesh selects a recently remastered recording by one of their favorite male artistes, Debabrata Biswas, his voice engloves the room in velvet and sandpaper, *where did the spring go, why was there no song?* still sharp within me in its import although I do not exactly follow the words, *on this last night of spring I have come empty-handed, no garland have I brought this time, I have nothing to give you at all,* my ear turns away from the music for I cannot connect it to Byron's death, or even Byron as he was in his various ways of being alive.

And Nikhilesh too, instead of finding an outlet for his dazed grief, is uncomfortably transported to a time in their childhood when Byron's mother would play this same song over and over again, rendered in a particularly shrill female voice, on a scratchy 45rpm record in the darkness of her shuttered sitting room, something in the words must have resonated deeply with whatever sorrow she was nurturing within her at the time, Nikhilesh recalls, more vividly than he cares to, how hopelessly inconvenient it was to both the boys who were trying to study for their college entrance exams in Byron's room.

I would rather be subjected to the endless wailing of a female phantom, Byron had said finally in exasperation.

And where would you have heard such a thing? Nikhilesh had demanded, for a day of relentless revision had left them in a combative mood.

And Byron had simply rolled over on his back and crushed a spider dangling from the mosquito net piled atop the four-poster bed where they had been memorizing Sanskrit passages all afternoon, and said: No, I have never heard a female phantom screech, but I imagine the voice of this woman is a good template.

You are a master of the circular argument, Nikhilesh had said.

Circles are such pleasing shapes, Byron had replied.

Vargas enters and announces that breakfast has been laid out on the dining room table but Nikhilesh regards the suggestion of eating at this moment as impossible, and Arjun seems not to have heard at all that food is on offer. So I make my way to the dining room alone, determined to sustain myself somehow, as my mother had always recommended in the face of disaster, we had certainly eaten well at her funeral, all arranged by my sister, who had felt it the occasion to celebrate her passion for cooking, a passion that was never accompanied—in my memory at least—with any sensual pleasure in eating. Yet, of the necessity of eating—particularly in times of trouble—she was assured.

For myself, I have always preferred to take comfort in poetry, not out of any highmindedness but simply because it connects me to another group of people who suffer as I do, those others who cling to desire as I have done as the only alternative to death—not a physical death, but the death of the senses—those who have endured, like me, its ecstasy and, far more frequently, its intolerable pain. How deep the varnish on this agony, how fearful its perfect proportions, I have gazed upon almost as an outsider in awe even as I have struggled to tolerate it. And here I am courting it again, asking Ela to return to my life in a capacity even less satisfactory than before, here I am asking for the lips of the wound to be parted again, those that have never quite closed over, not yet. For a while I was protected from this need, I believe, by the righteous energy expended in coming to terms with Byron's misdeeds, but only for a while, now I am tossed again like a ruined bark upon the wide ocean, my sails refuse to fill with just any wind as I make my way to another sea.

I go to wash my hands, pass by Ela's old room and cannot resist entering it and casting my eyes around the walls that are soon to be stripped of her images, for surely they will sell this place, Byron has left what remains of his vast wealth to Adrija, his various properties having shrunk to this flat in Calcutta and the house in Digha. In fact the financial advice that he receives will prevent Nikhilesh from disposing of it ever, and it will remain occupied only by a dwindling coterie of old servants for the next twenty years. And when she is older, Adrija will sometimes stop here and someone will let her in and give her some tea or a glass of water, and she will wander into this room, still etched with her mother's achievements, not in search of remembrance but repose.
I return to the dining room, serve myself some undersalted

scrambled eggs and fried potato slices, and sit down to eat them. The clouds break and a cheap sunlight shafts in, I notice that Kathleen Blechynden's *Calcutta: Past and Present* is still lying dismembered on the sideboard. I reach for it and open it to a random page where I read:

Dinner over, and the wine on the table, the hookabardars would file in, each to lay beside his master's chair a small square of carpet, on which the hookah stood in all its bravery of chased silver stand and cover, with graceful drooping silver chains, and a long bright silken snake which carried forward to the smoker's hand the handsome silver mouthpiece delicately scented with rose-water. Then would rise the fragrant smoke from the glowing discs of prepared charcoal, the soft gurgling of the water filled the pauses in the conversation, and Nicotine in its fairest form held soothing sway.

I recall, almost with anger, what great pleasure this would have given me once, that the peculiarities of its style would pluck a few sensible chords of amusement within me, the evocation of this surreal world would scent my immediate environment with an exact measure of amusement and edification, all in a time before my life found itself clenching around the sublime expectations of unqualified desire, before it found itself coated quite unawares in its immemorial sap.

Footsteps, and Arjun enters the room, is there any more coffee, he asks?

I am sure Vargas will be happy to make you some, I reply.

He surveys the scrambled eggs and the cocktail sausages and fried potatoes.

For some reason I feel I ought to be eating vegetarian food, he confesses to me, I feel I ought to be on a mourner's diet, and more than that—give up shaving and cutting my nails for eleven days, all those customs that a son would maintain after his father's death.

Was he like a father to you, then, Byron? I ask with some slight mockery in my voice.

No, he was not like a father to me, but he was to her, he replies.

Do you mean Ela?

Yes, that is who I mean, says her husband.

He serves himself some eggs and sausages, his desire to conform to Hindu ritual clearly having rapidly evaporated, and seats himself across from me.

And yet you had no qualms about bringing such a serious charge against him as the murder of her dearest cousin? I ask Arjun.

None whatsoever, he replies.

Did you ever consider that she might have wanted this to be dealt with in a different way?

I have always stood in the way of what she really wanted, he says without a trace of regret in his voice.

Like what, I ask him.

Like you, he says.

As harsh and sudden as a ball of salt rolling into my gut, his accusation hits me and I say nothing, for what can I say? He has known her at a different time in her life, shot her down several times with his plastic gun, poked at ant nests in his father's garden with her, and then rediscovered her when she was sixteen and in her first full moon, already giving performances that he found himself sneaking into, unbeknownst to his friends and parents. He had found ways to meet her, walk in the park with her, take her to the movies, and then—when she was removed to England by her parents—he had written long and beautiful letters to her and she had written back. For five long years their relationship had subsisted on these letters, and then she had returned and he had claimed her.

How well we would have coped, her without me, and me without her, if we had never met, how particularly well I would have coped, anyway, unaware that life held any bliss but the sharing of it with a good woman like Barbara and the children who would have followed and a few more exotic cultures to raise them in, until the time would come to put down roots in Washington DC or somewhere similar and watch them flower into adulthood. With art and morality to support we would surely have succeeded in this, would we not?

And her, what of her, her soul watered from an early age with the poetry of Tagore, daily reaching through her dance towards an ecstasy of union with either man or god, was she not already drenched with expectation when I found her, sandalwood paste dried in streaks upon her hair, was it not her longing that drew from within me a strain of desire I had never imagined might exist there, or was it that some divine pamphlet had already contained details of this precipitous encounter, that somewhere above us an angel laughed and laughed until his wings were sore.

You surely do not imagine that I do not know how much she cared for you, says Arjun.

I have not given it any thought, I reply.

No reason why you should, he says, sprinkling salt over his eggs.

It is of no consequence now, I reassure him.

It was never of any consequence to anybody but yourselves, he says.

I'd like to think so, also.

Nothing a stiff whisky couldn't cure, eh? says Arjun Mitra.

I remember my hands reaching deep into her upon the stairs of a dark house, borrowed for that weekend from a friend somewhere in the depths of Wales, a miner's cottage with only a cast-iron stove for heat, and lights so dim elsewhere that we could not bear to turn them on, I remember making love to her upon the steep stairs of that small house and wishing that the closeness between us could be sealed within a cruel and mathematical certainty, and yet even as I did so my mind shrank back from the dangers that all certainties contain, and as we sat afterwards in the small sitting room, her sweet head upon my shoulder, making the kind of conversation one does in these moments, I felt somehow a little bit of a fraud, as if some part of me were willing to get up and walk into the wild wet Welsh evening and never be seen by her again.

How easy and trivial the danger of remembering her and all the sorry ambiguities of our relationship, with her husband sitting so close by, accusations of infidelity falling like simple crust from his lips, how easy to be fruitfully immersed in contemplation of the smoothness of her thighs and the wetness between drawing me in, how easy when he is at such a distance from the knowledge of the anguish that followed, each time unanticipated, for why should the aftertaste of such pure honey be like an arrow driven through the tongue?

I did not think she would be able to bear it if Byron were sent to prison, says Arjun.

You underestimate her strength of mind, I tell him.

What would you know of that? he says.

Just this, I long to tell him, just this—that she bore the pain as well as me, and better, that she plucked my child from her womb without the knowledge of anybody but Byron Mallick, who can have offered but scant comfort, imagining it at the time to be Arjun's, that it is for me that she has reserved the highest seat in her heart, knowing that it will forever remain vacant. I am the blade from which her life falls, I long to tell him, I am the blade from which her life falls, and I am never really there.

She is not made of porcelain, I say instead.

That sounds to me like an admission of adultery, he says.

And if it is? I boldly ask.

And if it is, so what, all water under the bridge, he agrees wearily.

You have nothing to fear, I assure him, although I do

not have the faintest idea what I really mean, all I know is that I am not lying, at least not to myself.

I know that, he replies.

Vargas comes in with fresh coffee, this time in a pot, he is observing the same morning rituals as he did with Byron—first a strong espresso made on a stovetop Bialetti and then filter coffee by the gallons with breakfast.

Perhaps you would prefer tea? he asks me.

And suddenly, for the first time, I see him as a man with a past, and even a future, and most importantly as someone in the present, whose every muscle twitches with loss, whereas we—Arjun, Nikhilesh, and I—are still thoroughly dislocated in time. As if to acknowledge my recognition of him as a person of flesh and blood and certainly of some disgusting habits, he lets his free hand drift down and give a shake to his testicles, something I have never seen him do before.

Coffee is fine, I tell him, allowing him to pour some into my cup.

He turns to Arjun—And you, sir? he asks.

I will have some coffee, says Arjun.

Milk, sir?

Vargas, says Arjun, you do not have to call me sir.

You have told me so often, says Vargas.

But he is dead now, Vargas, there is no one out there anymore who wants you to call anybody "sir," says Arjun, gesturing to the wide world.

Vargas clears his throat and gives his testicles another quick shake.

You seem to forget that there is me, sir, I am still alive, sir, and sir is how I wish to address you until the end of my days, he says.

I have managed to get through to Ela, says Nikhilesh, as Arjun and I troop back into the drawing room.

How did she take it, asks Arjun anxiously.

I thought she took it well, replies Nikhilesh, almost as if she was expecting it.

She was expecting it, I tell them.

Not a thought she would be likely to confide in me, says Nikhilesh.

The doorbell rings and Nikhilesh heads off to see who it might be, has word already got around of Byron's demise, are the scavengers and wellwishers already crawling in our direction?

Why are you so worried about Ela? I ask Arjun.

Lately she has not been herself, he confesses. Of course, she has had to live through a lot—her mother's death, then Damini, the trial, the horror of it all—but perhaps it is not that, perhaps it is just you, he says.

Me? After all these years?

Perhaps you are still capable of making life curl gray at the edges for her, Max Gate.

Nikhilesh returns with a newspaper in his hands—it was only the paper boy, he tells us.

And then from one of the shelves he takes down a small bottle of gin, and three shot glasses.

I think we could all do with a drink, he says.

I see surprise on Arjun's face and realize that, like myself, he considers this somewhat out of his father-in-law's character.

Nikhilesh knocks back a shot, closes his eyes and says, The Royal Gin is a Lawful Spirit.

What? asks Arjun, fiddling with his own glass.

Just something Byron used to say, replies Nikhilesh.

He pours himself another glass, we need a picture of him for the funeral, he says suddenly.

We will find one, no doubt, says Arjun.

He used to keep one of himself in his desk drawer, says Nikhilesh.

Arjun, who is sitting by it, pushes his chair back so that he may open it, there are a lot of things in here, he remarks.

Nikhilesh walks over to the desk and examines the contents of the open drawer.

Here is an old photograph of him, I think he sent it to his mother from England, it is not suitable, of course, says Nikhilesh.

He passes it on to me for no obvious reason, and I am pierced once again by those eyes, darker in this black and white photograph than I ever remember them, but the gaze no less penetrating than that which had once drawn me so suddenly and swiftly towards a different sea, a wealth of questions and answers all atangle in its depths.

And suddenly I am standing there again before him, having just been introduced to him by the British High Commissioner. Thomas Maximilian Gate? he asked after I had given him my name in full, Thomas Maximilian Gate?

he queried, his eyebrows arching proud, and by that mere gesture thrown a knot into that long and otherwise immaculate thread of identity that extended from the moment of taking my first breath at the Massachusetts General Hospital, where my father was still in training at the time, through my childhood in New Jersey, my higher education, my choice of career, the elegance of spirit with which I had accepted the tragic fact that there was no novel within me, not even the one that apparently eventually takes residence in every person by virtue of their having lived at all.

Byron is just a nickname, he had confessed.

Just in case I might have categorized him as one of the fleeting crowd who granted their children polymorphous names, as if to indicate that their access to an international existence is their birthright.

Bankim is my real name, but it has been cast aside like a powdered wig for a very long time now, Byron explained.

I can hear his voice, his voice still so alive within me when he is not. I hand the photograph back to Nikhilesh who scrutinizes it again. It shows Byron in some sort of silken roll-neck shirt, very '60s, sitting in front of a typewriter, his hands are on the keys but his eyes are not on the page, he is smiling at the photographer.

He always looked so good in black, says Nikhilesh.

Bankim Chandra Mallick, his death certificate will say, when they assemble later to pick it up and take his cold body to the crematorium, where rapidly, with the appropriate anointings, he will be reduced to ash. Years ago, at Byron's request, I had accompanied Ela instead of himself to her uncle's funeral, an undetected colon cancer having squeezed the life out of him in a matter of weeks while she was on one of her tours in Britain. And so I had driven her to a crematorium upon an industrial estate in Birmingham, watched them place Anchor butter, still unwrapped, in place of holy ghee by his head and feet, I had stood with her in a crowd of his aging Bengali friends, watching him being taken away in a cheap coffin to be incinerated, the thought of it makes me shudder now. I would not like to go through the same thing with Byron, no, no, no.

My return flight is booked for this evening, I tell Arjun and Nikhilesh.

And do you intend to be on it? asks Nikhilesh.

I have no desire to stay for the funeral, I tell them.

Arjun says nothing, but the contempt in his eyes is intense.

Even though you loved him so? Nikhilesh asks.

What has that got to do with it? I reply.

Nothing at all, I suppose, concedes Nikhilesh.

Loyalty was never love's most natural bedfellow, says Arjun.

Of that I am living proof, I admit to them both.

Nikhilesh hits the pause button which has been barricading the music since his telephone call to his daughter was answered some fifteen minutes ago, and this time it is Rajeshwari Dutta, with whom Byron had had a great friendship, particularly in the years of her widowhood, when she was alone and bereft in London, and he had occasion to visit her, *both happiness and sadness are over now for us*, she sings, *ahead of us is only endless night where we are travelers together, ahead of us is only the wide ocean where we must let sail our small boat*, the words fall into eggcups already arranged in my brain for this was the only song—and a difficult one, too—that Byron had taken the trouble to get one of his musical friends to annotate for me in western symbols, for the anguish in her rendition of this song had sunk deep into me when I needed a new language for my despair, Rajeshwari Dutta's loss of her soulmate had reached out to me for I was about to lose something myself (why can I not call Ela my soulmate? because she was more than that? or less?) and to fulfill this need Byron had arranged for her song to be rendered in western notation, a document that I have preserved with excessive care but never accessed since.

I remember, after her uncle's funeral, wandering with Ela within the utter anonymity of a country fair near Coventry where she had unexpectedly asked to stop.

He would have liked me to do that, she had said, referring to the wishes of the dead man, as so many do in these circumstances.

We came upon a stall that specialized in the craft of teabag folding but could only clutch each other's hands rather than laugh, and jumped afterwards on a Ferris wheel where she had dared, insulated by height from the crowds, to briefly lay her head upon my shoulder, while our seats had swung forward and lurched down, furiously concentrating my bliss.

A few hours from now Nikhilesh and Arjun will find her, already at Byron's bedside, his body sewn back up, the examination of his insides having advanced our understanding of his death very little beyond the surmises of the physicians, they will find her holding his lifeless hand, her eyes dark from the many tears she has spilled upon his now inanimate flesh, she will raise her brave eyes to them, her husband and her father, and she will ask: where is Max?

You be brave now, her husband will reply, you be brave, he will say, fully aware that he is addressing a loss that contains both Byron Mallick and myself.

For the moment, however, Arjun is dispiritedly sifting through the contents of the drawer, he finds there a flute fashioned from a mango kernel of the kind that Byron might have tried to make music with when he was a boy—can it have survived from such a time, he wonders, or is it something Byron picked up more recently, had he placed it among his precious objects simply as a representative of a dying craft or because every hair of it bristled with his boyhood, what had been his reason to conserve it among his antique pocket compasses and betelnut scrapers, his spectrometers and nesting cup weights, his Victorian setsquares and pantographs, his snuff boxes and tortoiseshell-cased magnifying glasses.

He holds up a small brass object with twelve cylindrical holes punched out of it and during a pause in the music, asks us: What do you think this is?

I have no idea, I reply.

It is a suppository mold, says Nikhilesh.

Was it Byron who told you that? Arjun asks.

Indeed, says Nikhilesh, remembering how the scatological edges of that mirth had triggered within them a long-needed connection to their past, of the time when defecation was still an act of mystery, a mystery they had been able to share so much more easily than the transport of sexual desire, which they had each kept private, unlike myself and the friends of my youth for whom it was a currency of human achievement at that time in our lives.

Nikhilesh takes the absurd object from Arjun and weighs it in his palm as if it is all that remains now of his own life, a life once full. He does not like to think that his life has become tragic and yet no other word will attach to it more easily, and he knows of no route he can take to purge himself of it. The death of his wife first, after her brief and painful illness, he had been able to accept, he missed her, of course he missed her, but this was a shape of his last years he had dreaded so often that when it came it was familiar enough not to be completely debilitating. Forty years' worth of memories proved to be enough to sustain him in his routine of reading and writing and meeting with other retired intellectuals, a routine in which she had come to play less and less of an obvious role anyway. Possibly, it was a time spent in the passive imagination of her actually being present in some part of the house immersed in her own activities, or visiting her various relatives and still extremely robust network of friends from school and college. And then, Damini, her life ending so hideously, taking with her somehow the remains of the days when his existence was pleasantly full of all the right people, and now even Byron and all the dubious roles he played in it has gone.

You should throw yourself into something, he had advised him only a few days after his trial had come to an end, Byron—already confident that he would be able to pull his own life back together—had advised Nikhilesh to seek means other than simple medication.

Such as? Nikhilesh had asked.

I don't know—write a book.

I am already writing a book.

On precolonial urbanization in West Africa?

What else?

Write a different book, your memoirs perhaps…

I have led a dull life, Byron.

But what about our childhood? Why don't you write about our childhood—that would have so much value for me as well as for you, Byron had suggested.

And now by leaving this earth it is as if he has left no choice to Nikhilesh but to commit these memories to paper, precisely for whose benefit he does not know. Memories of shivering under a shared shawl while they stayed up late to watch the same strolling players who came to entertain them every year during the Pujas with their grossly overacted mythological dramas, memories of stealing mango slices put out to dry on a neighbor's veranda and hiding in the bamboo grove to eat them afterwards, burningly raw, memories of coercing a lactating goat to offer a teat to a stray puppy they had decided to adopt, and yet also of mercilessly pelting with stones a gang of frogs that had gathered by an old well, memories of playing hide and seek within a group of ruined huts and suddenly feeling a loneliness as never before upon finding that Byron had gone home without telling him. He had imagined he would write in Bengali, but it is English that will come, not naturally—more like an intruder, in fact—it is English that will flow from his pen when he sits down to write. Years later, when it is finished, he will wrap it up and send it, for some reason, to me, but I will not be able to bear to read it, I will put it away in a filing cabinet where I am confident that I will not easily come upon it again.

Acknowledgements

My thanks go first to Ritu Menon for the exceptionally rewarding experience of editing this book with her.

I am grateful also to Esmond Harmsworth—and others at ZSH—for their very valuable inputs into the editorial process, and also to Gina Pollinger for reading and rereading a succession of drafts and offering her excellent advice.

I would also like to thank Lucy Luck and Richard Ford for providing me with the impetus to finish this novel at a time when I very much needed such encouragement.

My thanks go to Howard Barker, Mark Haddon, Helen Cooper, Charlie Lee Potter, Caroline Collins, John Hennessy, Amit Chaudhuri, and Aamer Hussein for reading the manuscript in its final stages and for their generous intellectual and emotional support.

Finally, I would like to express my enormous gratitude to Pam Thompson for undertaking to bring this novel to readers in North America. Hilary Plum's careful attention to reformatting the book has been invaluable, and we pay tribute in its publication to Juliana Spear, who designed the cover just a few weeks before her tragic and untimely death.